Return to Heart Creek – The Series

A HEART CREEK CHRISTMAS

A HEART CREEK SECOND CHANCE

A HEART CREEK REUNION

A HEART CREEK WEDDING

LYNN GALE

WINDSONG PUBLISHING CANADA

Copyright © 2025 by Lynn Gale and Windsong Publishing Canada

Print ISBN: 978-1-998643-02-5

Cover design by P.S. Cover Design & Author Services

Contents

A Heart Creek Christmas

Book One - Return to Heart Creek Series

Lynn Gale

WINDSONG PUBLISHING CANADA

A Heart Creek Christmas

A Return to Heart Creek Novel

*Originally published as part of **A Cowboy This Christmas, A Sweet Romance Anthology**, ISBN 978-1-777-755-5-2 under my pen name Joanie Wilde.*

Digital ISBN: 978-1-0688010-1-3

Print ISBN: 978-1-998643-02-8

Cover design by P.S. Cover Design & Author Services

Edited by Victoria Curran

Copy edited by Ted Williams

Dedication:

To JP; Katie, David, and Norah; and Evan, Heather, and Jonah – with all my love now and forever.

To Anne, love always. To Jess and Jasmine, from my heart to yours.

To my CaRWA mentor Katie OH!, you're the best! To Mac and Carrie, with love and thanks.

Thank you to Victoria Curran and Ted Williams for their fabulous editing, and my beta readers Katie OH!, Jess, and Julie.

Contents

Chapter One

Mac McCoy stared at the face in the hand mirror. Hard edges, tired eyes, and weatherworn creases from time spent outside belied his age. Today was his birthday, the first since he took a career changing, death-defying ride on a bucking horse aptly named I Got Your Number.

Concussion. Five level fusion. Five fused vertebrae, held together by two steel rods running parallel to his spine and hooking to his rib cage. Multiple surgeries and long, excruciating hours of physical therapy laced his last several months together into a mess of pain, disillusionment, and regret. Prognosis: permanent loss of use of his legs.

He cursed under his breath and stowed the mirror in the hospital bed's tray table. A broken-down cowboy at thirty-four. Washed up and hung out to dry. Alone. Useless

Being alone was his own doing. One by one, he'd pushed away his friends and family until only his mother and his older brother visited him. He knew his attitude left a lot to be desired, but he simply didn't know what to do. He was afraid, maybe for the first time in his life. And he did not like it.

The charge nurse, Hannah, entered the room, interrupting his thoughts. The familiar smile danced on her face. "I hear you're leaving us today, Mac," she said. "I must say I'll miss your witty repartee." She pursed her lips.

Mac laughed, despite himself. Hannah was by far his favorite nurse. At five feet tall, with blond hair twisted into her signature braid and a habit of wearing funny cartoon character scrubs, she looked more like a twenty-year-old student than the capable charge nurse she was. Her wickedly funny sense of humor was one thing he had enjoyed even on his worst days when her tough love approach was able to coerce him into eating or moving.

"Thank you," he said. "I appreciate all you've done for me."

Hannah's face was serious as she took his hands in hers. He squeezed back and she gave him a quick hug. "Take care of yourself, cowboy. And enjoy your birthday."

Some cowboy. He contemplated his future...bleak and alone. He sighed as she left his hospital room.

"Pity party for one?"

Mac exhaled sharply. His brother. Surely, he could feel sorry for himself after what he'd been through. He tamped down an inexplicable surge of anger with an effort that sounded suspiciously like a grunt.

He could feel Ryker standing there, silent.

Another grunt was all he could give him. He knew it wasn't Ryker's fault but somehow it didn't matter. Bitterness rose like bile in his throat.

"Hey birthday boy, they tell me you can leave this place," Ryker said flatly. "Any idea where you'd like to go?" Mac barely bit back the expletive that leapt to his tongue. He had nowhere to go. No one cared. He didn't even care if he lived or died. His life was over. Had been for months. He shook his head sharply, leaned back while he pulled the sheet up, and turned over in the bed away from his brother.

Ryker exhaled, a deep sound that reverberated into Mac's body. Suddenly Mac's head hit the mattress as his pillow was yanked away. "What the --?" Mac turned and glared at Ryker. Ryker shrugged and shook the pillow before shoving it back under Mac's head. "Just fluffing your pillow, bro."

Mac couldn't bring himself to look his brother in the eye. He knew he was being childish and unreasonable, that his family cared for him. But he didn't have an answer. After a couple of moments, Ryker spoke. "I think you should come home."

"I don't have a home," Mac muttered.

Ryker yanked his sheet down. "Okay Macaroni, you stubborn donkey. You know I mean home to Heart Creek. To the ranch."

Mac didn't react to his use of his childhood nickname—a love of macaroni and cheese was the reason his family called him Mac, instead of his given name, Malcolm.

"I can't," he said softly. Ryker's wince said the words landed.

"Mac, that's all you have left. You can. We want you to. We're your family."

Mac's jaw clenched. On top of everything that happened, return to Heart Creek?

Not as a rodeo hero. Not as the National Rodeo champion.

Just a washed-up cowboy with useless legs, a twisted back, and a broken spirit. A failure.

Carrie Saunders parked her SUV and breathed in the cold crispness of the morning air. She was no stranger to the fall season but somehow here in Alberta near to the mountains, the air was exhilarating. Heart Creek was charming, boasting an idyllic creek meandering through town and breathtaking views of the foothills and mountains. Maybe the extra vibe was her own excitement at being at the Heart Creek Ranch and the realization of her childhood dream to work with horses.

Not just any horses, she reminded herself. Rodeo horses – former bucking and racing champions now retired. Her job as an equine osteopath – her passion – was to keep them pain free with the best quality of life she and the ranch could offer. An opportune meeting with Ryker McCoy in Houston this past spring just as her specialized training was ending and his subsequent job offer to work at Heart Creek Ranch was a huge step forward in her career. He'd been slightly skeptical but interested in what she did and the six-month contract he'd offered her gave her time to show him results.

"Morning, Carrie."

"Morning, Boss. It's a beautiful day in the mountains!" Carrie grinned at the big cowboy making his way across the gravel parking lot. Over six feet tall, broad-shouldered, and lean bodied, Ryker McCoy exuded confidence and strength. His weathered face and somber demeanor made him appear un-approachable at times, but he had always been respectful and kind towards her. She'd witnessed his gentle, compassionate side with the horses and knew there was a layer of softness in there somewhere.

Ryker smiled broadly as he replied, "That it is. Ready to meet our newest rodeo royalty?"

"Can't wait! Lead on."

Anticipation flowed through Carrie's body as she walked along the hard covered path to the second barn. In the months she'd been at Heart Creek Ranch, she'd become acquainted with several horses – all retired from the rodeo circuit, all needing love and attention.

She had yet to meet the most recent arrivals – a new crop of champions in the last years of their lives. Her goal was to ease their pain and help them transition from racing and competing to retirement smoothly, giving them a sense of peace and belonging after a hectic professional life on the road.

Her breath caught as she entered the spotlessly clean large facility. Roomy and comfortably lit, the size of the stalls highlighted the status of the horses housed within. Rodeo royalty indeed. These were horses bred and trained for specific events, and even past their prime they were magnificent.

"Meet Play Misty for Me. We call her Misty these days – come on over and introduce yourself. Misty, welcome Carrie. She's here to help you feel better." Misty snorted and tossed her golden head.

"Oh, you are so beautiful, Misty," Carrie crooned to the big mare. As Carrie crept slowly into the stall, Misty pulled away frantically, moving as far from the door opening as she could. Misty's trembling broke Carrie's heart and roused her anger. This is what she hated most about rodeos – the aftermath on the animals. In spite of all the organizers did to ensure animal safety, sometimes things went wrong. Not every animal suffered but those that did had it rough. "I'll see you again soon," she whispered to the quivering animal. "We'll be friends, I promise." As they closed the stall door, Carrie inhaled deeply, regaining her composure before they continued. God, she detested rodeos. Ever since witnessing the death of two horses at the Rangeland Derby during the Calgary Stampede when she was ten, she'd sought a way to help the animals. Working at Heart Creek Ranch – a ranch designed specifically for the treatment of retired rodeo horses, plus rescues – ticked every box on her wish list. She couldn't stop rodeos or racing, but she could help with the care of the horses after the fact. "Ryker," Carrie said. "I know we've talked about it briefly but what made your family change from a horse training facility to a rehab facility?"

Ryker scratched his chin before he answered. "When the doctors first diagnosed my dad with cancer, his heart went completely away from training horses. He wanted to do something different. At the time, and even now, I guess really, there weren't too many places for retired race or rodeo horses to go. Their owners didn't want to put them down and the idea of a place where they could go appealed to Dad. Sometimes, if the horses are young enough or well enough the owners take them back but most times, they stay with us until they pass. Kind of a giving back."

Carrie nodded. "That's amazing. Happy to be part of it. Sorry about your dad." Ryker smiled. "He was a great guy and his vision for this place spread to the rest of us. Well, most of us, anyway."

They moved down the row of stalls as Ryker introduced her to four more former champions. None of them were as uncertain or traumatized as Misty but they still needed comfort and gentle healing. Strong in body and spirit, they'd lived a hard active life. As they slowed down, or healed from injuries, they craved solace at a slower pace. Not easy for an animal bred for strength and speed to learn to relax. She led the first horse out of the barn into the covered arena and began her assessment.

"Okay, Carrie, time for lunch. Let's head to the house."

Carrie couldn't believe that more than three hours had flown by. Her stomach did though, it grumbled. Loudly. Ryker grinned. "Let's go before you faint from hunger."

"Don't think that's likely but don't want to take a chance," Carrie replied, slightly embarrassed but not so much so that she'd turn down lunch.

As they strode towards the big farmhouse located on the home quarter, she could see several vehicles including an oversized van in the curved front driveway. She glanced at Ryker. He grimaced. "Ah, our special package has arrived. I'll see you inside."

Special package? She shrugged. She'd learn what it was soon enough if it were any of her business. His long legs moved him quickly away from Carrie and she became lost in her thoughts. Misty was on her mind while she climbed the porch, went inside the large farmhouse, and washed up. As she came out of the washing up area to the left of the front door, she was creating a starting plan for Misty's treatment and collided with a wheelchair she hadn't even noticed.

The next thing she knew she was on her backside being glared at by a man with the most intense dark blue eyes she'd ever seen. The breath flew out of her, and she struggled to speak.

"Oh, I am so sor—"

"Don't!" the man snapped, yanking his wheelchair back a couple of feet.

She took a shaky deep breath, trying to regain her composure.

"Ah, I see you've met Mac," Ryker said dryly, stepping around the wheelchair. He extended his hand to Carrie.

"Mac, this is Carrie Saunders, the equine osteopath I mentioned to you a few months back."

The man in the wheelchair shook his head, as Ryker helped Carrie to her feet.

"You must have forgotten to share that little nugget of information," Mac drawled. His lips were so tightly drawn that Carrie was amazed that words could even escape his mouth.

"Hello, Mac, I'm Carrie." As she spoke, she took in the man in front of her.

A big man, although not as big as Ryker, a cowboy judging by his belt buckle and perfectly creased yet baggy jeans. Streaky blond hair long enough to curl over his collar. A handsome, tired face etched with pain and lifelines. Sun-touched but pale, his skin was almost gray. Startling eyes – deep smoky blue – burning with tension. Every morsel of his being was infused with anger, from the tight grip of his hands to the set jawline. This was a man of intense emotions, barely under control. Negativity rolled off him in waves. A small involuntary gasp whispered from her lips.

"If you are finished staring at me, maybe you could move out of the way so Ryker can take me to my room?"

Carrie flushed deeply and automatically moved out of the hallway into the nearest doorway.

Ryker spoke as he pushed the wheelchair down the hall. "Carrie, don't let my brother bother you with his rudeness. He was raised by wolves and adopted but obviously not in time to fix his manners."

Tears of embarrassment hovered on Carrie's lashes as she nodded. She had no idea what to do, what to think. She felt like she'd been body slammed. Mac's pain was tangible on every level, and she could feel its effects lingering over her.

As she slowly made her way to lunch, she wondered what had happened to Mac, why he was in a wheelchair, why he was so angry. Questions for later. Right now, she needed food and coffee. Lots of coffee. Mac was a discussion for another time.

Chapter Two

"You were danged rude." Ryker closed the bedroom door behind them. Mac didn't reply. All he could think of were the tears quivering on Carrie's beautiful lashes. Is this what he had become? A mean bitter man who terrorized women. It would seem so. His mother would be ashamed of him.

"What the heck does an equine osteopath do? And why does the ranch need her?" he ground out.

Ryker walked around the chair to face him. "She works with the horses, as you well know. She heals them. A massage therapist and holistic practitioner. Quit being such a jerk."

"Whatever." A massage therapist for horses was ridiculous.

"She's here on a contract. Until Christmas. I'm hoping she can improve the horses who don't seem to be responding to our normal treatments. Or any other animals who need it, for that matter." Ryker looked pointedly at Mac.

Mac grimaced at his brother. Ryker continued to unpack Mac's suitcase.

"She's having good success, Mac. We'll see how it goes. In other news, lunch is ready, want some?"

"Not hungry. I just want to sleep." Mac suppressed a wince as Ryker helped him onto the bed. His brother's silence was recriminating. Sweat poured down Mac's body with the physical effort despite his brother's help. Physio was helping but his upper body was still weak, especially when he was tired.

"See you later."

"Whatever."

Mac turned his head, not moving until he was sure Ryker had left the room. Carrie's shocked face stuck in his mind. He hated pity. He was more than capable of feeling sorry for himself.

Self-pity was the one thing he was still darn good at.

Carrie wasn't sure which stung more – her backside from landing on the floor or her embarrassment at literally running into Ryker's brother. In a wheelchair, no less. To be fair, she could see him being annoyed. But not rude.

"Still hungry?" Ryker's voice cut through Carrie's thoughts, and she realized she was standing in the dining room with an empty plate in her hand.

"Actually, I am," she admitted. "Just distracted. Thinking about Misty." Not the whole truth but close enough. She moved forward, making selections from the laden buffet, her hunger returning through the delectable smells. Once a week, the ranch hosted lunch for the ranch workers - something

Carrie appreciated immensely. One less lunch to put together for herself.

"Don't let him get to you."

Ryker was more perceptive than Carrie had given him credit for. She found herself a chair at a small table in the corner. Ryker joined her and they ate in silence. Inhaling the delicious coffee, she gazed out the window. The room was large, with floor to ceiling windows on two sides, and the view of the mountains was calming.

"I'd like to say that my brother's bark is worse than his bite, but sadly that is not the case."

"Can I ask what hap—?" Carrie's question was cut off as more people entered the dining room and jostling for place in line took precedence. Plus, she didn't want to seem like she was gossiping in front of the rest of the staff.

It didn't matter about Mac. She was there for the horses, not for a bitter cowboy with a bad attitude. At least that's what her mind said. Her heart whispered something different.

That evening, after a plate of stir-fried vegetables mixed in with leftovers from her fridge, Carrie started the electric fireplace in the tiny living room of her cottage and curled up on the recliner. This little house near the edge of town was a welcome surprise. Having envisioned living in an apartment during her limited stay, it exceeded her expectations. Plus, it was close enough to walk to Main Street but far enough to be private and less than ten minutes to the ranch. Her neighbor Ida was an elderly lady who owned the café in town. Ida's son Finn was the town's veterinarian, and her daughter Rosemary ran the café now that Ida was semi-retired.

With a small bedroom, compact kitchen, and small but cozy front room, her home's main calling card was the windows overlooking the mountains. The bathroom was small as was the back yard. It came furnished with older but well-taken care of furniture. It wasn't the home she longed for, with a husband, family, and several pets, but it worked for this job. Once she had Heart Creek Ranch's endorsement on her resume, she could move on to bigger and better things.

Pulling her mom's quilt over her legs, she reached for the laptop on the low table in front of her. It only took a moment to type "Mac McCoy" into the internet's search engine. Article after article about Malcolm "Mac" McCoy popped onto the screen and Carrie read about the former rodeo champion's nearly fatal last ride. The vivid explanation of the details felt like a physical blow.

Poor Mac. No wonder he was angry and bitter. She thought her life had been hard and all she'd had to deal with was her mom's ALS and her dad's abandonment when she was twelve.

She set the laptop aside and snuggled into the soft quilt and gazed at the fire. Her mind swirled with thoughts about Mac and his injury while the logical and practical side of her brain warned her that Mac would not welcome her sympathy or any efforts to help.

Loneliness washed over her. She needed a friend. Heart Creek was her temporary home, and she hadn't made many friends yet. She needed someone to listen and cuddle. Her dreams of husband and family were far in the future. The answer struck her like a bolt of lightning.

"I *could* get a dog."

Clapping her hands in delight, she ran the idea through her head from all angles and couldn't find a thing wrong with the idea. She could get a dog this very weekend and leave Mac to his family to deal with. She went to bed with that thought in mind and slept soundly.

The county shelter opened at ten on Saturday mornings. At ten minutes to, Carrie was impatiently waiting in her SUV. She leapt out as soon as the open sign turned on and went inside. She expected to have limited options but there was an astonishing array of dogs to choose from. The sheer number of them saddened her.

Originally, she was thinking of a puppy but realized that might not work well with her long days at the ranch. There was a whole row of wonderful dogs who were beyond those painful potty-training days. The hard part was choosing only one to take home. *This time just one of you, but when I get my own place, there will be more.* Her dream of having her own plot of land for a rescue center seemed far off but one day, it was going to happen. It just had to.

After disinfecting and donning gloves, she was debating between a happy mixed breed three-year-old mutt and a dainty retriever when she saw a pen she'd missed near the back.

"Those are the senior rescues." Danny Wells, who looked after the shelter, was young and earnest. His voice lowered as he confided to Carrie that few people wanted older dogs because sometimes, they needed extra care or had medical issues.

Carrie nodded, but she kept gazing over at a medium black dog curled in the corner. "Okay if I go in?" she asked Danny. Danny nodded and opened the gate. Carrie made her way over to the black dog and sat down.

"What's your name?" she cooed, gently rubbing the dog's ears.

"That's Winnie," Danny answered. "She's deaf. She was a rescue found wandering down the highway. She was a mess, and her ears were so crazy infected, she lost her hearing."

Carrie gazed into Winnie's soft eyes as the dog lifted her head. Carrie continued softly scratching and Winnie leaned into her hand. The dog's thin body shivered under Carrie's caress and her heart melted.

"I'll take this one."

Danny said, "Are you sure?" He went into a litany of Winnie's maladies.

"Yes, I'm sure."

Danny grinned. "All righty then. I'll get the paperwork together. The vet has already looked her over and her shots are up to date. We'll give her a bath and run our final checks. Can you come back in a few hours or on Monday?"

"I'd like to take her today if I can, but I need a few things. Is there a pet store in town?" Carrie asked.

Danny gave her directions and Carrie left the shelter on a mission, her heart as light as her step. Pawsitively Purrfect was two doors down from the Homegrown Café and across the street from Bellissimo Hair Salon on Main Street. Reminding herself that she needed a hair trim sooner than later, Carrie entered Pawsitively Purrfect.

She spent over an hour choosing a dog bed, toys, treats, and a blanket, while having a long discussion with Selina, the store's manager, and Ida's niece about the type of food to feed Winnie. Carrie chuckled. In Heart Creek, all paths seemed to lead either to or from Ida. The last purchase was a medium-large travel crate for the back of the SUV. A quick stock up of her personal needs completed the list of errands before returning to the shelter.

Danny beamed as he led Winnie slowly from the back room. Carrie knelt and cuddled her close to her chest. Winnie was fluffy and soft and smelled like sweet, clean dog. Carrie's heart pounded as she took the leash and gazed down at the dog. She lifted Winnie's face until she could see into the dog's eyes. "Hello, sweetheart," she whispered, even though she knew Winnie couldn't hear her. Danny helped her place Winnie on the soft blanket inside the crate. Winnie was shivering but Carrie knew it wasn't as much from the cold as it was from fear of what was going on. She took extra care making sure Winnie was cozy and secure, all the while telling her about where they were going. As she drove off, she could hear Winnie shuffling as she settled in the crate. She couldn't wait to get home with her dog.

Mac groaned at the mess he was making in his room, as if the action would somehow make it neat and tidy. The furniture had been moved to allow his wheelchair access but his finesse with moving around in the chair was not the best. Getting dressed was a challenge – not the hour it took him the first time he pulled on his own jeans and boots but still more time than he had patience for.

Patience was a God-given gift that currently eluded him.

Ryker's knock preceded him. "What's up?" A smile tugged at his mouth as he surveyed the scene before him. *He'd better not be laughing at me.*

"Nothing fits right," he grumbled.

"You've lost weight, Mac," Ryker said more gently. "Do we need to go shopping? Or order something online?"

"God, no! There must be something here that still fits. Besides the boots. Not that I need those anymore."

They stared at each other for a long moment. The raw sympathy in Ryker's eyes was almost unbearable. His tough big brother, feeling sorry for him. Mac swallowed hard.

"Let's see what's on the shelves." Ryker reached up and brought down a pile of neatly folded shirts and sweaters. Mac's first impulse was to tell him not to bother but he was beginning to realize he had to ask for help.

"You must have a pair or two of old jeans that might work. Do you want me to give you a hand?"

A vehement NO came to mind. "Please."

Half an hour of struggling later, Mac's limited patience snapped. "Enough," he said.

The man in the mirror looked wan and tired but he wore a clean chambray shirt tucked into faded jeans and polished boots. His face was shaven, and his hair combed.

Mac nodded at Ryker. "Thanks."

Still adjusting to the wheelchair, Mac awkwardly wheeled himself out into the large family room and settled by the picture window. He was grateful the house was a bungalow so that stairs weren't a big issue. He heard his brother's boots on the hardwood floor before he saw him.

"Nice out there today. Great fall colors."

Mac nodded.

Ryker sat himself down in the comfortable recliner that used to be Mac's favorite.

"So..."

Mac laughed a little harshly. "So?" he repeated. Why did people keep trying to engage him in conversation?

Ryker shook his head. "Mac, what would you think about working here on the ranch?"

Mac made a face and pointed to his wheelchair. "With this?" he spat.

"You still have use of your upper body," Ryker reminded him "It's just your legs—"

"Just my legs. Bah."

"And your mind is sharp. You could be a major help around here with managing the ranch. Save me time for other things." He crossed his arms and returned Mac's glare.

"Don't need your pity job!"

"You may not need my pity, but you do need something to do, Mac. You can't sit here day in and day out doing nothing. Firstly, it's not your way. Secondly, it's not healthy. And thirdly, little bro, you need to cowboy up."

Mac's eyes widened and a hot flush of anger and frustration flooded his face.

"Don't you talk to me about cowboying up! I did that for years. Now I get a break."

"Mac, it doesn't work that way. You've had a run of tough luck. Real tough. Now it's time to move forward."

"And what exactly is it you propose I do?"

"As I said, help me run the ranch. Help with the horses – their treatment plans. Work with Carrie – you could be a great asset to her. You know horses."

"What? Work with Carrie? I'm in a wheelchair, for God's sake. In what way could I possibly help her?"

"I don't know, Mac, but you need to figure it out. And soon. I don't have the time or energy to babysit you and your bad moods. You weren't here much when you rode the circuit, but at least when you were here, you always lent a hand."

Ryker stood and left the room, his boots again thumping on the hardwood floor.

Mac turned back towards the window.

What Ryker was asking was simply not possible. Mac had nothing left to give.

Chapter Three

Ryker had arranged for a physio team to come out to the ranch twice a week to meet with Mac and after hemming and hawing, Mac agreed. He was tired of the exercises even though he could feel the difference as muscle tone and strength slowly returned to his body. He ate meals in his room, preferring solitude. He might not want to admit it, but he was sleeping better and his appetite, at least for food, was improving.

He had no idea what he was going to do with his life. He got an instant headache whenever the thought appeared, so he avoided thinking as often as possible. Much easier not to care.

Less than a week later, there was a knock on his bedroom door. When he hollered to come in, Ryker poked his head around the door with a big grin. "Today's the day, bro. We're going to the barn."

"You've got to be kidding me," he said even though he'd known Ryker wouldn't let it go.

"Nope. Let's go. Carrie is waiting for us. Kick that wheelchair into high gear and let's mosey!" Ryker laughed at his own joke as Mac pulled on a zippered hoodie and an old ball cap.

By the time they reached the barn, Carrie was in the tack area with a medium-sized but short-legged dog on a leash. He could hear murmuring as they approached. Her back was towards them, and her waist-length medium brown hair swung as she moved.

"Good morning, Carrie," Ryker called. Carrie turned, her ready smile slowly fading into uncertainty as she saw Mac. "Good morning, Ryker, and uh, Mac. How are you both today?"

Mac managed a small grin, hoping it didn't look maniacal. "Good morning, Carrie. I'm here, so that means I'm good. Or at least I'm here. Ha-ha." Heat moved up from his neck at his inane words. Why did he feel awkward? Oh, yeah, maybe because he'd been snarky and rude towards her when they first met. That could be the ticket to her coolness. Mental facepalm.

Carrie nodded. "Ah, I see that." Her green eyes took him in.

"And who is this little one?" Ryker knelt beside Winnie and stroked her.

"Meet Winnie, the newest member of my family," Carrie announced. "She's a rescue and deaf."

Mac's first thought was of course she is. Carrie was a rescuer, which was the last thing he needed or wanted in his own life. His head shook of its own accord just as Carrie's eyes met his own. He could see that she thought the headshake was directed toward her from the pinkness that rose on her cheeks and her subsequent downcast gaze. Yep, most definitely starting out on the wrong foot today. Or the wrong wheel, in his case. Sweat trickled down his back. He needed a diversion. Rolling his wheelchair over, he reached down to pet the animal. Winnie sat patiently, her eyes fixed on his face, and accepted his pets. When he stopped, he glanced up to find Carrie watching him with a peculiar expression. Had she expected him to kick her dog or something? Had he fallen that far?

"I'm heading to the other barn," Ryker announced, breaking the tension. "Things to do. I'll be back."

Okay, they were really doing this. Mac looked over at Carrie and took a deep breath. *Focus, cowboy. You can do this*. "Where do we begin?"

For the next couple of weeks, Mac met Carrie in the barn four mornings a week and they worked with the different horses. Sometimes he stayed until supper, other times only until lunch. She knew he was still physically hurting - she could tell by his face and the stiffness of his smile. But he did occasionally smile, and she felt herself warming to him despite herself.

His rodeo career went completely against what she believed in. These horses were in this condition because of people like him. And even more to the point in this situation, he was in this condition because of the rodeo. She was having a tough time making sense of that.

She knew he was trying. He was listening attentively and asking engaged questions about her processes. He was able to hold the horses in place or nuzzle their heads while she massaged them. The love they shared for the horses was apparent and she found herself explaining more of what she hoped to accomplish with the horses than she'd expected to. It was wonderful to share her work with someone who was interested, not only in the horses but in what she was doing. It put him in a whole new light. Not too long ago, he'd been dismissive and rude- both to her and her profession. A complete one-eighty on to the Mac who sat beside her, assisting where he could. She was drawn to him against her better judgement.

This was not good. She was here on the ranch for two reasons and two reasons alone – to get more experience in her field and obtain a good reference from Ryker to continue her path to her dream of owning her own place. She was only here until Christmas. Why that thought suddenly made her sad was beyond her. She had a plan, darn it. Nothing was going to compromise that. Except for one teeny tiny little inconvenience. That niggling bothersome bug that wouldn't go away.

She was starting to have feelings for a certain blue-eyed cowboy.

Chapter Four

The second weekend of October was Thanksgiving. Carrie's only remaining family was in Thunder Bay and although she was fond of her cousin Amy, flying there for a long weekend didn't make financial sense. Besides, she was only in Heart Creek until the end of December, and although things were going well, she didn't need any distractions from her work at the ranch.

She'd spoken with Ryker and learned that their sister Avery would be home for Thanksgiving as well as their mother Elizabeth. Their sister Chelsea would also be there – she lived just outside Heart Creek. Ryker explained that their father had died when Mac was young, from colon cancer. Elizabeth had run the ranch for years until her older sister's dementia diagnosis. At that time, Ryker had taken over the management of the ranch and his mom had moved to Lethbridge to care for her sister Agathe. As they aged, neither sister liked to travel so the only time his mom came back to the ranch was at Thanksgiving. Roads were too unpredictable at Christmas, so the sisters spent that holiday with Agathe's son and his family. Agathe also went to her son's home for Thanksgiving, so this year, his mom headed north to the ranch on her own.

On the Friday before the holiday weekend, Carrie was working with Misty. Still skittish but slowly calming down, the mare was getting used to Carrie's treatments and her ears perked up each time Carrie stopped by. As Carrie left the stall, talking softly to the horse, she was startled to almost run into a body as she closed the stall door.

"Oh, sorry," a sweet voice said, a hand reaching out to steady Carrie. Carrie turned with a smile and apology only to be stopped short by a beautiful tall redheaded woman grinning at her.

"You must be Carrie. I've heard good things about you," the woman said. "I'm Avery, middle sister to the two reprobate cowboys you've already met."

Carrie couldn't quite hide her surprise. "You don't look anything like them," she said. "Great to meet you, Avery." She reached out a hand to shake Avery's then noticed she still wore her gloves from tending to Misty. She blushed.

Avery laughed. "Oh, you are adorable!" she announced.

Carrie frowned. Adorable wasn't the perception she wanted people to have of her – she preferred professional or competent. Catching sight of herself in the small mirror on the barn wall, she realized where Avery's comment was coming from. Her hair was messy with loose curls mixed with straw, her face smeared with goodness knew what, and she looked about fifteen years old. Good grief.

"My sister and I take after my mother," Avery confided. "Our brothers look like Dad."

"Oh, that's interesting," was all Carrie could think of saying. She turned to make sure Misty's stall door was secure, feeling awkward.

"Fill me in on what's happening. How is everything progressing?" For a second, Carrie was uncomfortable and worried. Could Ryker have sent his sister to check into what Carrie had been doing? Was he doubting her work or her methods? Her stomach clenched. This contract was so important to her – she couldn't mess it up. She must have looked unsure because Avery sent her a kind look.

"Not a test, honestly," Avery said lightly. "I am genuinely interested. That's why I wanted to meet you – I dabble in alternate therapies."

Carrie relaxed a little and started talking. "Well, that was Misty – Play Misty for Me – and ..." she gave Avery a rundown of Misty's treatment to date. To Avery's credit, she listened intently and like Mac, asked thoughtful questions. After they'd discussed the horses currently in the barn, Carrie realized she didn't know what Avery did for a living, so she asked her.

"I am a happy momma to two-year-old twin boys," Avery shared. "I teach horseback riding and make jewelry. My husband and I own a ranch near Cochrane, about two hours from here."

Carrie squealed. "Oh, I love babies!" She could have head-smacked herself. She'd squealed, actually squealed aloud.

Avery grinned again. "You really are a sweet one," she said. "See you later. Better get unpacked while I can, before my twin troubles wake up. By the way, arc you coming to Thanksgiving dinner? Ryker mentioned you didn't have family nearby."

Carrie nodded. "Yes, your brothers were kind enough to invite me." She waved goodbye to Avery and strolled to the stall next to Misty's. One more treatment for the day then home for a quiet Friday evening. Before she entered the stall, she looked outside, surprised to see light snow falling. There had been flurries in the forecast, but she'd thought that was for later in the weekend. Winter obviously came early near the mountains.

Saturday dawned gray and grim, matching Mac's early morning mood. Not sleeping the night before didn't help. He kept thinking about Carrie. Mac's heart leapt at the thought of seeing her, which made him feel even more miserable. He'd been avoiding the idea of working with her and now he couldn't wait for Sunday. He had doubted she would accept their invitation to Thanksgiving dinner, but she had. She confused him – she made him feel uncomfortable, frustrated, and excited.

Yup, excited. Helping her – heck, even though the helping he was able to do so far boiled down to discussions about the treatments and not a lot more – made him feel better. He wasn't doing much, but as he slowly started helping with holds, supporting the horses as she worked, and bringing her blankets or supplies made him feel needed. He knew she could do the work perfectly well alone, and faster. It grated on him that his brother had pressured him into working with Carrie, but for the first time in many months, he didn't feel gloomy or cranky. The physio was helping him, and as his upper body strength returned, he felt less like a shell of a man. Still broken, but less useless.

At breakfast, Avery, being the cheerful upbeat pain in the keester she always was, put his teeth on edge.

"What's the plan, little brother Mac? I met Carrie and it sounds like her treatments are helping the horses. And helping you?"

Mac stared at his sister. "I don't need Carrie's help, Avery," he growled, pushing himself away from the table. He wheeled his chair over to the window and stared out at the ranch. The dull day held that odd light that he knew from experience was a precursor to more snow. "It's going to snow some more," he murmured.

Avery laughed. "Well, it's October, Mac. It does that in Alberta."

With a start, Mac realized he'd missed a season or two while hospitalized. Of course, over the last ten months, he had missed everything. It was novel to sit and look outside instead of just at the four walls of his acute short term care hospital wall. He still felt trapped, but the four walls and living space here at the ranch were much larger than his former accommodation. His chest eased slightly, and he realized how tightly he'd been holding himself together. He shrugged. *It was good to be home. Surprisingly so.*

"Mac. Hel-lo?"

He glanced over at Avery. She made a face at him over her coffee cup.

"There has to be a bigger plan, Mac."

Mac didn't know what to say. His hands clenched. Before his last ride, there had been a plan. Two more years of competing, then starting up his own training ranch. Now there was only him in a wheelchair. Competing and rodeos were over forever. His plan blew up in his face and he had no idea what came next.

Actually, that wasn't quite true anymore. Recently a new idea had started growing in his mind. After working with Carrie and realizing how far he'd come with his own recovery thanks to rehab and all involved, he'd envisioned a rehab facility for injured cowboys. A one-stop place for physio and healing, immersed in nature and the ranch. Could it work? He wasn't sure but then he didn't feel sure about anything right now.

He abruptly wheeled himself to the far side of the room. He heard his sister sigh as she stood and the clatter of dishes as she cleared the table. He didn't turn around. He couldn't. There were no words. Closing his eyes, he rested his chin on his chest, and let his thoughts drift away to happier times. Blessed, peaceful silence.

"It's snowing!"

Mac's head jerked up and he looked out the window. The snow was falling in huge fluffy flakes, already creating a winter wonderland. His heart thumped in excitement. "Wanna go outside?"

Avery did a double take but recovered quickly. "Sure," she said, "hang on a sec."

Less than five minutes later, she wrapped him in a blanket. To his dismay, while he appreciated the warmth, he unexpectedly felt trapped. His hat plunked unceremoniously on his head completed the ensemble while his sister squealed and wheeled him out onto the veranda then into the yard.

"We aren't five, you know," he said dryly, pretending he wasn't as excited as she was.

"Oh, don't be such a downer. I love snow!" Avery sent his wheelchair spinning across the yard and danced away, twirling in the heavy snowfall. There was sure to be a fair amount of accumulation if it continued at this pace.

"The twins are going to love this!" She pranced around, tossing snow onto Mac.

Mac tilted his head and felt the snowflakes on his face. Sticking out his tongue, he caught a few, the cool sensation reminding him of being a kid, carefree and happy. He thought about Carrie and how much he enjoyed helping her and being in her company. Then cold reality hit him. Those carefree, happy days were long gone. There was no happiness. There was no him and Carrie working – once she left after her contract, Mac would have to find something else to do. The blanket suddenly felt like it was crushing his lungs and he struggled to breathe, his breath moving in short sharp bursts.

"Enough. Take me back in."

"Take yourself if you want to go, Macaroni. I'm having fun."

Mac growled at his sister, then grunted as he wheeled himself over the snow-covered grass and up the ramp to the house.

What was he going to do? Right now, he had to get through Thanksgiving weekend with his family. And Carrie. After that, he had absolutely no idea – his fledgling idea for a rehab center might work. Or it might crash and burn. After a short rest, he figured he'd better get the party started – the sooner it got going, the sooner it would end. With the extra people in the house, it took a while to locate his sister and her boys in the kitchen. To his surprise, his mom and younger sister Chelsea had already arrived. Mom was busy feeding one small child pieces of banana, while hugging the other one on her lap. She looked happy and her face was glowing. Mac figured the rosy glow was due both to the warmth of the room and the exertion of playing with her grandchildren.

"Hello, son." His mom's calm voice reached him across the mayhem of the room, and he wheeled closer.

"Hi, Mom," he replied, leaning over to kiss her cheek. For a moment, he wished he could sit on her lap and be fed goodies and cuddled like a little boy with no cares or worries.

"Hey, big bro," Chelsea, a mini version of their sister Avery with her red hair and sunny disposition, planted a kiss on his head as she swept by him. "How's things?"

"Going okay," he answered his sister. "And you? Anything new? Seeing anyone?"

Chelsea paused for a second and a sad look flashed across her face. "Nothing new," she replied. "And nope, same old same old." She headed out of the kitchen.

Mac turned back to his mother. "Still pining for Finn, I see," he commented.

"Yes, I expect that's true. She's had a hard go of it. And how are you, Malcolm"? his mom asked, taking a moment to look him over thoroughly. Mac could feel her eyes beaming into his soul.

"Mac, Mom," he corrected. She laughed.

"You'll always be my wee Malcolm, dear." Mac made a face, but he could feel the warmth of her love enveloping him. *Oh, Mom. So good to see you.*

"Tell me how you've been," Mac said, sliding his chair in beside her. Banana-covered hands grabbed his knees, as his mom released Nathan and Eric to their own devices. She turned to face him.

"I'm good, son. I am more interested in hearing about you." She rose and poured coffee into two cups, pressing one into his hand as she sat back down.

Mac caught her up on his medical progress and about working with Carrie. His mom listened to him intently. When he stopped, she spoke.

"And what comes next? Any thoughts? I know Ryker has offered you a position helping with running the ranch. Does that appeal to you?"

Mac paused then told his mom the idea about the rehab facility for injured cowboys. When he finished speaking, she gazed at him for what seemed like a long time. Long enough, in fact, that Mac was getting a bit edgy.

"Well, Malcolm, I may not always know everything, but I do know a few things. When your dad was sick, it took everything I had to support him through that. With Aunt Agathe, it's a different journey altogether. Illness, injury, and aging are tough. I've gained a great deal of insight into all three of those, and I can tell you that love, caring, and compassion go a long way towards building strength, not only of body but mind and soul. You know what being injured is like, so you can empathize with others in a similar situation. I am in full support of your idea. Your father would be so proud of you, just as I am." She leaned over to hug him.

You better follow through now, cowboy. You've got your mom's blessing. Don't let her down. Again.

Chapter Five

Over the next few weeks, winter blew in vigorously. By the beginning of November, it was as if the snow had been there for months. Carrie was grateful for her little SUV each time she drove to the ranch. In the evenings, Winnie greeted her happily. The little dog had taken to sleeping right behind the front door on a blanket, waiting for Carrie to get home from work. Then once supper was made and eaten, they would settle into the living room by the fire and Carrie would read while Winnie lay at her feet. She tried inviting the dog to sit beside her, but Winnie kept hopping down, preferring to settle on the floor. Someday, Carrie hoped, she would trust her enough to share the couch.

Early in November, Carrie met with both Ryker and Mac at the farm to review the remaining treatment plans for the horses on site and to discuss three new horses that were heading their way in December. As she was leaving after the meeting, Ryker suggested they head to Homegrown Café for lunch. Carrie had been meaning to try out her neighbor's café but hadn't had the opportunity. Mac looked like he was going to refuse but appeared to change his mind after Ryker sent him a look.

□"I'll meet you there," Carrie called as she drove away. The little café was only a few blocks from her cottage, and after lunch she could head into town to pick up groceries. The quaint main street was in the process of being decorated for Christmas and looked festive and jaunty with the old-fashioned Victorian streetlights surrounded by holly and the shop windows done up with Christmas décor. When she pulled into the café parking lot, the van from the ranch hadn't arrived yet so she popped into the pet store for pet treats for Winnie. By the time she was done, she spotted the van parked in front of the café in the reserved wheelchair spot.

□After admiring the café's festive storefront, she entered the quaint building, breathed in the amazing aroma of fresh baked bread, coffee, and unless her sense of smell was dreaming, roast beef. Ryker and Mac were at a table in the back, one of the chairs moved to accommodate the wheelchair. A young woman was describing the daily specials when Carrie sat down, overhearing the last few sentences.

"Ooh, shepherd's pie!" Carrie could almost taste the delicious meal – pure comfort food - that always reminded her of her mom.

The server, whose nametag bore the name Cleo in cursive script, smiled at her. "My favorite, too," Cleo confided. "Apple pie, anyone? Fresh baked today."

Carrie never could resist hot apple pie and she nodded enthusiastically. Ryker went for the Reuben sandwich and lemon meringue pie. Mac chose baked mac and cheese, and a chocolate chip cookie with ice cream, earning a grin from his brother.

"That's how the Macster got his nickname," Ryker told Carrie. "Always loved his mac and cheese ever since he was a little cowboy running around the ranch."

Carrie smiled over the table at Mac and their eyes met for a long second. Longing and desire slid through her as she got lost in his startling blue eyes. When she blinked and looked away, she struggled for air, suddenly breathless. Glancing back at Mac, he looked the same as she felt. *Wow. Just wow.*

The coffee was hot, delicious, and plentiful. Carrie's neighbor's daughter Rosemary, who ran the café popped out from the kitchen to talk to Ryker and Mac, cheerfully welcoming Carrie to town. She clapped Mac on the back and declared how wonderful he looked.

Carrie could have hugged her when Mac's face lit up. It changed his whole demeanor. He had gained a bit of weight and it was visible in his face - less drawn and gaunt. Such a different man these days than the one she'd literally run into that first day. Softer. Less angry. Calmer. *He was gorgeous. Oh, no, no, no. She didn't have time for a gorgeous cowboy. She had a plan. She had a plan, darn it, that didn't include cowboys of any kind. Even ones with blue eyes that she could drown in. Oh boy, she was in trouble. Big trouble.*

As they were leaving after lunch, they ran in to Finn, her neighbor's son, who was the local veterinarian. A bear of a young man with a full beard and a man bun. He didn't look like any vet that Carrie had ever met but she was impressed by his warmth and enthusiasm.

"Did you see Avery and Chelsea at Thanksgiving?" Ryker asked Finn.

Finn grimaced. "Sadly no, I was busy all weekend helping Mom fix a couple of issues with the house in town. Next time."

Ryker nodded. After Finn left, Mac confided to Carrie that Finn and Chelsea had been best friends in high school and college. "I think he's always had a sweet spot for our little sister," Mac said. "But then life happened, and they drifted apart." His face grew thoughtful.

"I really enjoyed meeting your mom and sisters at Thanksgiving," Carrie said. "And Nathan and Eric are adorable." She laughed, remembering the twins toddling around the kitchen while their mom tried to help with dinner. Mac's mom spent more time with the boys than Avery and Josh did. Elizabeth was an older gentler version of Avery and Chelsea and obviously in love with her grandchildren. While Carrie really enjoyed the meal, it made her remember how much she missed her mom.

Waving goodbye to Ryker and Mac as they loaded Mac and his wheelchair into the specialized van, she realized they felt more like old friends than boss and boss's brother to her. As she made her way to the grocery store before heading home, she replayed the lunchtime conversations in her mind.

Carrie, Carrie, Carrie. Don't let yourself get attached to these people or this place. You have a plan. Yes, today was amazing - if only every day could be like today. Except of course the gorgeous cowboy problem.

The following week, Mac and Carrie were leaving Misty's stall one morning when Carrie paused to look at him. It had been a good session and they were tired but revitalized. Suddenly, she reached over and hugged Mac tightly. "Thank you for your help today."

He tensed and froze, uncertain what to do.

She jerked backwards. "I am so sorry."

□Mac sat in his chair shell-shocked. When Carrie abruptly pulled away, he knew he'd hurt her feelings, but he didn't know what to say. No one except his sisters or his mom had hugged him for an exceptionally long time. *And this was Carrie. Carrie. He was in so deep with this woman. Like was too mild a word but love...love was out of his grasp, wasn't it? She deserved a whole man and that was something he could never be again. He had to stop this now. Before they both did something they would regret.* The thought brought a wave of pain, a different pain than he'd experienced before. Heart pain. But he knew what he had to do. For Carrie's sake.

□He rolled his wheelchair back a bit before he spoke.

□"Carrie, I don't think we can work together anymore."

"Wait, what? Hang on a minute, Mac, I'm so sorry. Did I hurt you? Oh, my god. That was completely unprofessional of me. I didn't mean..."

"What didn't you mean, Carrie? You didn't mean to be kind to me? Or you didn't mean to let me follow you around like some sort of puppy you feel sorry for and toss a treat to every now and then? Or you didn't mean to hug the poor, disabled man who had a terrible ride? What didn't you mean?"

Mac heard the harshness in his tone and knew he was hurting her. *For God's sake, it was killing him, too, but he had to do this. Now. Before his feelings grew any larger.*

Carrie flushed deep red. Her lips pursed and then she exploded.

"Is that what you think about yourself, Mac? Still? I feel sorry for you. You just aren't getting it. So, your legs don't work anymore – oh well. That's not what is keeping you broken. You have been feeling sorry for yourself for goodness knows how long. You are right, it is terrible what happened to you. But you knew the risks going in. I thought that horses being injured or killed at rodeos was bad enough but what happened to you is worse. And do you know what is even sadder than that? Your self-pitying 'I'm no good for anything' attitude. Yes, you're hurt. Get over it. Work with what you've got and quit sniveling. You are still the man you were. Maybe even better. Broken doesn't mean dead. Grow up and smell the coffee, cowboy."

Carrie stopped, suddenly winded. Her body shook to the core, but she stood her ground. They glared at each other, the energy crackling in the room.

Mac wanted to reach out and hug her and tell her he was sorry he was a donkey's behind and to please forgive him, but he couldn't make the words happen. He didn't want to make them happen. He couldn't let her get close. She was better off without him. What he didn't know was how he would be without her.

He backed his wheelchair far enough to reach the long table they used to house Carrie's equipment. He removed his gloves and moved the tools in his lap onto the table, then without looking back, he slowly wheeled himself out of the barn in silence.

He stopped on the veranda of the main house to give himself time to recover from his conversation with Carrie before he went in. Or rather, Carrie's conversation with him.

"Having a bad day?" Ryker asked, rousing Mac from his thoughts. Mac hadn't seen him approach.

"You don't know the half of it."

□"You're being mopey and miserable. What's going on? Have you given up again?"

Suddenly Mac's frustration boiled over, and he was furious. "Given up? How can you know about what I'm going through? You still have legs that work. You still get to do what you love. All I have is this crummy wheelchair and useless legs. Anyone can hug you and it doesn't matter. Ah, just forget it. Whatever."

Ryker shook his head. "You're being weird and self-centered again. It's not always about you. We've been through this, Mac. You have everything and everyone you need right here on the ranch. I thought that working with Carrie was helping. You enjoyed spending time with her. I thought your time together was making you feel better. What's going on?"

"I'm not a wounded horse for Carrie to fix," Mac retorted sharply. "Besides, I don't think we'll be working together anymore." He emphasized the *anymore*.

Ryker narrowed his eyes. "What the heck did you do?"

Mac opened his mouth to reply then closed it with a snap. Why did Ryker assume it was something he did? Of course, it was, but how did Ryker know that?

At that moment, a truck pulled into the parking space in front of the house. Mac looked over at his brother. They would continue this later.

"Howdy, Mac. Ryker." His old friend John Bonner got out of the driver's seat and headed towards Mac and Ryker. Two of Mac's old rodeo buddies joined him.

"John! This is unexpected – what brings you here today? Eric, Paul, how are you boys doing?" Mac's voice felt thick and not at all like his. His face was still flaming from his conversation with his brother.

The men responded one by one, clasping his hand firmly, and nodding their heads. He was used to seeing them on the rodeo circuit or at post-rodeo events, not here on his family's front veranda.

"We've brought you a check, Mac."

Mac was confused. "For what?"

John cleared his throat. "It's from the Benevolent Fund, Mac."

Then Mac knew. All the competitors contributed to a fund intended to help injured cowboys, or in the case of a tragedy, to help their families. He just never expected the person they were helping to be him.

"I can't..." he began as a flush moved up his neck to his face. Embarrassment and humiliation spread throughout his body. He should be grateful yet all he felt was shocked. The fund was for hurt cowboys and their families. Not him. Then he remembered. He was a hurt cowboy. In so many ways.

"Yes, you can, Mac," John replied quietly. "We are here for you, just let us know what you need. We had planned to see you sooner, but we wanted to wait to see what happened."

As in whether he died or not.

Stunned, Mac was unable to find any words. He couldn't have pushed them past the sudden lump in his throat anyway as the truth sank in. He had survived. Shame washed over him. He hadn't understood or appreciated the gift he'd already been given just by surviving.

"Coffee?" Ryker said from behind him. For once, he welcomed his brother's interference.

"Well, yo, cowboy, that's a big yes." The men all answered at the same time, causing a laugh, and breaking up the awkwardness of the moment. They found chairs on the deck and dragged them over to one of the tables. Once Ryker returned with the coffee, the conversation turned to general things. Mac tucked the envelope under his leg and forced himself to join in. *He'd been such a fool. What else was he being a fool about?*

Chapter Six

"Carrie?" Ryker poked his head around the side of the big barn door.

"Just finishing up with Misty," she said softly as she ran her hands over the horse's flank. Misty shuddered then relaxed with a long exhale. Carrie moved to rub her long neck, all the while cooing into Misty's ear. After a handful of seconds, she reached into her pocket and gave Misty an apple. "Such a good girl," she whispered, gently hugging the big animal.

Ryker whistled under his breath. "She's come a long way," he said.

Carrie smiled at him as she moved away from Misty and locked the door behind her. "Indeed, she has. Baby steps but she's trusting me more and that helps immensely."

"Do you have time for a break with the boss?"

Carrie brushed hay off her clothes. "Yes, I sure do."

"Let's go to the main house," Ryker suggested. Carrie blanched inside but agreed. She'd been avoiding the farmhouse for four days now. She couldn't exactly tell Ryker that she was wary of his brother and still embarrassed by what had happened, all that had been said on both sides. She'd told Mac off right to his face. She couldn't face him. Not yet. Hopefully, Mac was busy or out and she wouldn't even see him.

Twenty minutes later, they were sipping hot coffee and eating muffins while ensconced in big comfortable chairs in the front alcove.

"We haven't really talked for a bit," Ryker said. "How is it going?"

Carrie caught him up on her work, answering the questions he asked and going more deeply into her continuing therapy plan for each animal. She left out the argument with Mac. When she paused, he nodded.

"That's amazing, Carrie. I gotta say I am impressed by what you are achieving here. I'll refill our cups and then you can tell me how you like Heart Creek now that you've been here for a while. Different than Thunder Bay, I'll bet. And how are things working out with Mac?"

Carrie smiled as she handed him her cup. "Winnie and I are doing quite well."

His laugh rang through the room as she described Winnie's running around the house with squeaky toys the dog herself couldn't hear but that drove Carrie crazy. "Not sure what I was thinking when I bought those," she admitted, while chuckling to herself.

"Sounds like you two are having a good time."

Carrie almost dropped her newly refilled cup of coffee at the deep gruff voice behind her. Turning, she took in the tense cowboy in his wheelchair staring at her. Her cheeks flushed guiltily but she didn't know why. She'd spoken her truth that day. Just like he had. He just didn't like what she'd had to say. She didn't like what he'd said either. Not her fault – he'd started it.

"Hello, Mac," she managed to say.

"Hey, brother." Ryker got up and clapped Mac heartily on the back, earning himself a grimace. "Carrie was just updating me on the progress. Although I guess you've seen it? Since you've been helping her? Magnificent work with Misty. And the others, too, of course."

"Didn't realize the horses were a laughing matter."

Ryker cleared his throat and cast an apologetic look at Carrie.

"I was telling him about my dog," she started to explain to Mac.

"Not really important." Mac waved her off then turned to Ryker. "When you aren't so busy, I need to talk to you." He emphasized the word so.

Ryker nodded. "We're good here, I think. Carrie?"

Carrie drank the rest of her hot coffee in one big gulp and awkwardly stood up. "Yes, yes, we're finished. Thanks, Ryker. Thanks for the break. Bye, uh, Mac." She couldn't get out of there fast enough.

Outside she stood with her hot face against the cool door. What was that all about? How dare Mac be rude to her again? What an obnoxious man he was. Undeniably handsome but what a jerk! They'd gone from strangers to something resembling friends, and now he was back to being sullen and mean. Even accounting for his debilitating injury, he had no right. Carrie sobered. Why did she even care what Mac thought? He was nothing to her. You'd think she was sweet on him or something...or something. She couldn't pretend anymore.

After all the shifts they'd worked together, he'd still ended up being a rude unhappy man she barely knew – their last conversation confirmed that. And yet, somehow when she looked into his eyes, she did know him. Old souls connecting. Spine-tingling, all-encompassing, knowing. She was sweet on him. Head over heels sweet.

This job was becoming increasingly complicated. Carrie disliked complicated. Breathing deeply, she shook off the remaining vestiges of her emotions, moving calmly towards the stables. The horses. She was at the ranch for the horses. She needed Ryker's good reference to move forward. An annoying cowboy tugging at her compassion and pressing her buttons was the least of her concerns. She had the horses to keep her occupied for the next few weeks and they were top priority.

What about keeping your heart occupied? Her little inside voice nudged. *Oh boy.* That was going to be a little harder to uncomplicate – emotions always were. Avoidance would help and that she could easily do. No matter how much the annoying cowboy crept into her heart. No matter how much she wanted him there.

Chapter Seven

How was it halfway through December already? Full of the Christmas spirit, Carrie decided not to leave Winnie and home and took her beloved pet with her to the stables. She would check in on the horses then they could head to town to pick up pet food.

All was quiet when she pulled up at the ranch. The snow crunched under her boots. Inside the barn, she tied Winnie to a post and shed her coat. She wanted to check on one of the new arrivals – including a skittery mare with arthritic hips – as well as say hello to Misty and her other favorites. They all ended up being her favorite, even the cantankerous ones.

Like Mac. Cranky and cantankerous. And complicated.

"Hello, Betty," she whispered to the mare who was observing her warily from the other side of the stall. Bet on Me Honey had only been at the ranch for two days, and she still wasn't sure what to make of it all. She limped and even though the vet prescribed medication to help reduce her pain, it didn't seem to help. She pulled her lips back and reared her head as Carrie slowly entered the stall.

"Are you hurting, sweet one?" she cooed, reaching out to caress Betty's nose. All was going well until suddenly Betty backed up and rushed Carrie, knocking her over and pinning her against the wall. Then Betty's knee gave way and she swayed towards Carrie. The horse tried to stand up but couldn't, sliding onto the ground and trapping Carrie beneath her.

Searing agony sliced through Carrie's leg and the side of her body, stealing her breath. She pushed frantically at the horse to shift the large body off her leg but the awkward twist of her body as well as the several hundred pounds of horseflesh were more than her agonized body could manage. Betty tossed her head and snorted but couldn't move her body. They were both trapped.

Betty squealed and struggled, trying to roll over or get up. For a fraction of a second, her weight was lighter, and Carrie managed to roll away just before Betty gave up and fell again.

Carrie's head smashed against the side of the stall, and her body twisted but at least most of her body wasn't under the horse. Her leg and side were on fire. Carrie forced herself to breathe in deeply, despite the torturous pain in her chest. She closed her eyes, trying to make sense of what was happening. Her left leg skewed, pressed up against the wall, and she was sure the leg had broken. It throbbed in time to her elevated pulse and the pain was excruciating. Biting back screams that seemed never to end, she struggled to calm down so she could listen to Betty.

The horse's breathing was raspy and shallow. She wasn't moving. Carrie clucked at her repeatedly, willing her to move, to get up. Then words. "Betty, get up, sweet girl, you can do it." But the horse didn't move.

"Help?" Carrie called weakly. Her cell phone was in her coat, beside Winnie's bed. Winnie. Her dog was here in the barn. "Winnie?" Carrie's voice was barely a whisper, then she sheepishly realized that of course Winnie couldn't hear her. Besides, the dog was tied up so it wasn't like she could get assistance.

People were in and out of the barn all day; all she had to do was stay conscious until they arrived. She kept talking to Betty, in between tears and gasps for breath, trying to ignore the growing pain in her leg and the panic rising in her body. The stall faded into gray then came back into focus. In and out. In and out, the dark periods got longer as each minute passed.

In the far distance, a dog barked over and over.

Mac had taken to wheeling himself around the ranch as often as he could when the paths were clear. He knew he needed to continue to rebuild the strength in his upper body and arms and was reminded of how much he missed being outside in the cold and snow.

Was that a dog barking? He stopped the wheelchair so he could hear more clearly without the crunch of the snow beneath the wheels. Yes, it was a dog. Strange bark though. He frowned and started over to the barn where the sound was coming from. When he got there, he could hear frantic barking as he keyed in the door code. Ryker had refurbished a couple of the doors on the house to allow easy access for Mac. The barns were already installed with sliding doors with keypad access that someone had the foresight to install high enough to access on horseback but low enough for shorter people - or in Mac's case, a man in a wheelchair.

Before he went in, he quickly dialed Ryker's cell to alert him that something was going on.

"Wait for me," Ryker commanded.

"Yeah, no." Something was wrong. He was going in there. His brother could catch up. When he opened the door and rolled himself through, a small barking dog jumped up and down its leash that was tied to a ring on the wall. Looking around swiftly he spotted a coat on the chair in the tack room and recognized it as Carrie's. Rolling closer, he tugged on the leash and the dog startled and pulled back. He realized it was Carrie's dog and remembered she was deaf. What was her name? Cindy? Something like that. "Hey, girl," he said, reaching out to pet her. The dog crouched, growling. "Where's your mama?"

Where was Carrie?

The barn housed six large stalls. He wheeled down the center aisleway, grateful that Ryker had insisted on only the best for the horses, which included state-of-the-art lighting and extra-wide aisles. He called out Carrie's name then paused to listen. Nothing. The dog was silent, and Mac felt sick with premonition. This wasn't good.

"Carrie?" he called out repeatedly. "Carrie, where are you?"

Betty's breathing had slowed to a guttural rasp then faded to an occasional hiss. Carrie knew that sound wasn't good – the horse was dying. What had happened to her? Tears welled in her throat and fighting through the pain in her leg, she tried to pull herself onto Betty's side, struggling to maintain consciousness. Her head was thick as if it were full of cotton wool. She hugged Betty as tightly as she could, running her hand across the mare's side. Then she heard a different sound. Was that someone calling her name? The barking had stopped. Betty was silent. "Help me..." she whispered and weakly banged her head back against the stall wall." Help..."

"Carrie?"

Mac.

Carrie wept with relief. "Oh, Mac...I'm here. Betty's dying or dead, I don't know...I don't know what happened."

"Are you hurt?"

Carrie answered slowly. "Yes..."

"I'm coming in."

Carrie tried to stop crying, to gather her sense of calm. "Betty fell funny, and her leg twisted. So did mine."

"Is she on top of you?"

Carrie gasped as she struggled to speak. "Just a little, I think." She could see Mac now, his head barely high enough to see into the stall.

Mac reached through the bars on the gate, but he couldn't reach her. She was on the other side of the fallen animal.

What was he going to do?

"It'll be okay," he promised, as he gazed frantically around the stall. If he could open the gate, he could climb over the horse and get to Carrie. Unlike the keypad entry for the main barn doors, the stall doors slid open manually. Somehow the horse was lying in such a way that her body was pushing against the gate.

Opening the gate would not be easy.

But he could do it. He had to.

Eying the mechanism, he got himself into position and locked his wheelchair wheels. He pulled, pushed, grunted, and managed to get the door to move slightly to the left. Not enough space. He moved his chair over, reset the brakes, and kept at it. Sweat poured down his face and his back and arm muscles both welcomed and repelled the force he was using.

He had to get to Carrie. Now. He grunted and pushed as hard as he could.

The stall gate noisily and unwillingly moved a couple more inches. He paused and checked – yes, there was enough space for him to get through. Undoing the seat belt on his wheelchair, he used his arms to lift himself off the chair and onto the ground. Pushing the wheelchair away from him, he pulled himself to the gate opening. Little by little, he dragged himself through, grunting and groaning from the effort. He kept talking to Carrie as he went. She didn't reply but he kept going.

Hanging onto the horse's mane, he finally pulled himself on top of her and reached out his hand towards Carrie. He found her hand and clasped it with his own. Laying his head on the horse's side, he caught his breath and closed his eyes. He felt an answering light squeeze in the hand he held. "Thank God," he said, tears of relief flowing from his eyes. "Carrie, I'm here. It will be okay." He laid his head down gratefully, resting for a second. Deep breaths. "Carrie, let's see if I can move you towards me. Gently – I don't want to hurt you." Carrie didn't respond.

"What the...?" Ryker's deep voice boomed from the gate. "Mac, what's going on? I told you to wait."

"Carrie's hurt," Mac ground out, his energy completely spent. "The horse fell and died."

"Joe, Ralph, over here." Ryker's voice rang out. "Now!"

"Mac, let go of Carrie and we'll pull you out."

Mac released Carrie's limp hand and allowed himself to leave her. Once outside the stall, the men gently placed him in his wheelchair and one of them covered his shaking shoulders with a blanket. He watched wearily as they then re-entered the stall. After a brief discussion, they decided not to move Carrie until the EMTs arrived, but they placed a blanket around her while they waited for the ambulance. Someone pressed a drink into Mac's hand. People were speaking but all Mac could hear was the thump of his own heart still pounding in his ears.

The medics arrived and within minutes, they assessed Carrie and strapped her to a backboard. One of the medics gave Mac a once over and shook his hand. "Great job you did there, I hear. How are you feeling?" They had a quick discussion but other than being exhausted, Mac was in decent shape. "I used to follow you on the rodeo circuit," the young EMT said. "You were a great competitor. Sorry about your accident."

"Thanks," Mac managed to say. *I used to be great.*

Mac lifted his head as they lifted Carrie out of the stall over the horse's body. "Carrie..." but she must have been unconscious as she didn't reply. He looked around through bleary eyes.

"Ryker?"

"I'm here, Mac." Ryker dropped a gentle hand on his shoulder. "Are you okay?"

"Yeah, I'm fine. Carrie, is she okay?" Mac's voice cracked.

"They're going to airlift her to University Hospital in Edmonton. They're concerned about potential damage to her back. Could be a cracked rib or two as well. We don't want to take any chances. She's stable, though. They gave her something for the pain."

Mac's voice broke. "And the horse?"

Ryker shook his head. "Unfortunately, too late for her. The vet's on his way. I'll contact insurance and Finn will arrange for the necropsy and removal of the body. Obviously, Betty had some kind of underlying condition. Heartbreaking."

Ryker started pushing Mac out of the barn. "Whew, I need a drink. Care to join me?"

Mac didn't need a second invitation. "We deserve TWO drinks. But first..."

As they passed Winnie, Mac leaned over and picked up the small dog. Ryker unhooked her leash. "Your mom will be okay," Mac whispered. Winnie licked his face. "You can stay with me for a while."

"Heck, three drinks! It's been quite the day. Quite the gosh darned day." Ryker continued to talk as they made their way towards the house, but Mac barely heard him.

Carrie was stable. She was going to be okay. Thank God.

Chapter Eight

M ac settled into his now favorite spot by the window on the veranda. Close enough to the fireplace to keep him warm but out of the way of anyone walking in or out of the house. A place where he could think. Still worried about Carrie, his mind flowed with activity. His idea for a cowboy rehab center continued to grow. If it worked, and of course that was an excessively big IF, he might be able to find his purpose. Something that could make a difference to other cowboys like him.

A small rehab facility for broken cowboys. He grinned just thinking of it. A welcoming place for recovery and rest while finding new paths to follow. With access to therapy of every kind, and people who understood their way of life. And of course, being around horses would play a key part in the rehabilitation. A place of healing for people, in the same way the ranch was a haven for retired horses. A place run by cowboys like him, someone who knew firsthand what it was like to be injured.

Where he could continue to heal.

Mac smiled ruefully. Healing himself was the least of his worries. He wasn't looking for miracles.

The money from the benevolent fund would help get it started and he had saved as much of his winnings as he could. Now that his own ranch was out of the question, he could funnel those funds into helping others. On the circuit, he'd lived in a fifth wheel trailer. He could sell that unit. He'd keep his old truck – it could be modified for him to drive with just his hands.

Another source of income for the ranch. A way to contribute. A way to give back. He rubbed his chin, thinking about Carrie and her gentle way with the animals. He ached for healing, for love. She deserved more than a broken and bitter man. He would never be whole. *But I saved her.* His heart leapt a little. *Yes, I did save her. Can I be worthy of her love?*

He couldn't get her out of his thoughts.

His vision for his future had come from time spent with her. Helping cowboys recover from injury, using whatever means worked. Alternative therapies, healing touch, gentle recovery. In his mind's eye, he could see them working side by side, she with the animals, he with the cowboys. A perfect circle. She healed the animals; he and the animals could help heal the cowboys and the joy of helping those cowboys could heal Mac himself.

Could it work? Was there a future for them together?

They hadn't spoken since the day in the barn. Betty had suffered from an enlarged heart, which combined with her other issues, had caused her collapse and later death.

Carrie had a broken leg, bruises, two cracked ribs, and a concussion. She was okay and healing. At least that's what Ryker told him yesterday.

"Why don't you go and see Carrie?" Ryker had asked.

"Nah, just wondered how she was doing." Mac's reply was offhand.

Ryker had leaned over and placed his hands on the wheelchair arms, looking Mac straight in the eyes. "You did good, little brother. We are all proud of you."

"Thanks. I wanted to do more..." Mac had replied.

'Mac! You heard the dog barking. You got the door open by yourself. You got to Carrie in time. What more could you have done?" Ryker had shaken his head, his expression puzzled.

Mac had stared back at Ryker. "Yes, I really did those things, didn't I?" He'd smiled. Ryker had smiled back. Mac's heart bloomed with an unaccustomed sensation.

Maybe there was hope, after all. Could it be enough? Could he be enough?

Chapter Nine

TEN DAYS LATER, DEC. 24

Cozy in her chair, with her injured leg propped on the footstool, Carrie snuggled Winnie in her lap. Carrie smiled at her wonderful dog, so thankful that she had barked so Mac could come that awful day in the barn with Betty. With her lower left leg in a cast, she was learning to get around on crutches. Her ribs were wrapped and hurt less, except when she sneezed, laughed, or moved.

Thanks to the McCoy's wonderful family and neighbors, Carrie had enough casseroles and cookies to fill her fridge and freezer. Ryker had delivered many of them when he brought Winnie home. The doctor had kept Carrie in the hospital for a couple of days for numerous tests, but once those came back with satisfactory results, she was able to go back to Heart Creek. It surprised her how much this town and her cottage felt like home. Especially once Winnie returned.

She was trying to figure out how to thank Mac. He'd saved her life. She owed him everything. Or at least something yummy to eat.

"I could share some chocolate chip cookies with Mac. That could be my thanks."

Or a good reason to go to the farmhouse and see him. It was Christmas Eve. Ryker had invited her and Winnie to join the McCoy family. All she needed was a ride and a simple call had Ryker driving over to pick her up. She packed up a couple of boxes of treats to take and share.

"Merry Christmas Eve!" Ryker boomed from the hallway. "How are you feeling?"

"It gets a little easier every day," she replied. *"I feel so bad about Betty. Though I know it wasn't my fault."*

*Ryker nodded sympathetically while he too*k Winnie's leash off the hook.

Ryker's truck was cozy, and they chatted about other things on the way to the farmhouse. Ryker helped her inside, and into the living room where a fire blazed in the stone fireplace and the family was enjoying snacks and drinks.

Carrie gingerly placed her offerings on the side table. "Thank you for having me," she said. She kept the box of cookies in her arms.

"Hi, Carrie!" Suddenly she was hugged by two small bodies as Avery and her family crowded around her. She rocked back at the abrupt assault on her personal space but didn't fall. Avery laughed and peeled her boys off Carrie. Enchanted by her cast, they kept touching it then giggling.

The sound of someone clearing their throat came from behind her.

Mac.

"Hello, Mac," she said softly as she turned to face him, careful on her crutches. Her handsome wonderful grumpy not-so-broken cowboy. Her heart fluttered.

"Hello, Carrie," he replied.

She lost awareness of anything but Mac as they gazed into each other's eyes.

His face was less pale and wan than in the past and his eyes were clear, and he was smiling. At her.

"I never had the chance to thank you for saving me," she stammered, awkward and suddenly breathless. "I brought cookies." She thrust them toward him.

"I didn't do anything." He took the cookies from her and placed them on the table.

"Really, Mac? Would you like to hear what you did?"

He shut his mouth.

"Mac, if you hadn't opened that door, my situation would have gone from bad to really bad. Thank you for that. You held my hand, you whispered sweet nothings in my ear, you --"

He cleared his throat. "Ah, it wasn't sweet nothings. And it was the EMTs who —"

His breath caught. "You heard what I said," he said softly.

"I sure did. Not such a hard cowboy, are you?"

Carrie watched Mac's face as he processed her words.

You're welcome?" he croaked out, looking down at his hands in his lap.

Carrie stared at the big man in the wheelchair. He looked back up quickly, their eyes met, and her words died in her throat. Awareness spread through her body, and she knew without a doubt that she loved this man. This rude, brusque, bitter, broken-down cowboy that always hid his gentle, caring side - the side she'd seen with the horses. And the side she'd seen the day she'd been hurt. With her. Her broken cowboy was a soft-hearted hero.

"Carrie? Come over here?" He opened his arms and waited.

She limped over and awkwardly sat on his lap. Handing her crutches to Avery, she wrapped her arms around his neck. This time, he didn't freeze. He simply smiled. Leaning forward, she planted a soft kiss on his mouth. She sighed. "Took you long enough, cowboy."

She kissed him again, thrilling as his arms surrounded her in a massive hug. Twirling around in his chair, she almost took out a nearby lamp. Winnie's startled bark momentarily silenced the room.

"Carrie, you were right. Everything you said. I was, I am, a self-pitying jerk. I was terrified. But I love you. I love you so much. If you'll have me as I am, broken, I'm yours."

"Mac, everybody's broken in one way or another. I love you just as you are."

"Is this a Christmas miracle?" Mac whispered and hugged Carrie tighter. He smelled like home, love, and hope. She buried her head in his warm shoulder, her answering nod lost.

"All I need for Christmas is you," she said, when she could speak.

"About time, you two!" Ryker boomed. "Welcome home, Mac, and welcome home to you, too, Carrie. Guess you'll be staying on with us for a while."

Carrie lifted her head and smiled, looking deeply into the eyes of the cowboy she loved with all her heart, and Winnie barked again.

Bonus Chapter

ONE YEAR LATER...

M ac chuckled as he tucked the velvet jewelry box behind neat rows of folded socks in his dresser drawer. It had taken him several weeks to decide on a ring for Carrie, and he had almost given up hope until his sister Avery directed him to a vintage shop in Rocky Mountain House. There, the perfect antique ring was waiting, the whimsical 1930's setting holding a beautiful pair of blue diamonds on either side of a sparkling white diamond. Delicate but strong, just like the woman he loved and hoped to marry.

He wheeled himself out of his room and into the spacious living room. The large windows highlighted the snow falling lightly outside, the colored Christmas lights reflecting on the glass. The spruce tree towering in one corner held memories in the decorations from when he and his siblings were children, plus a touch of style thanks to Avery and Chelsea's influence. Soon the rest of the family would descend on Heart Creek Ranch, filling the main house with love and laughter.

"Deep in thought?" a sweet voice teased, and Mac turned to greet the woman he'd grown to love and cherish. He lifted his face for Carrie's kiss and marveled at how much his life had changed. Not from the rodeo incident – that was said and done. No, the biggest change was the hope and life that Carrie had given him and what that had done for his healing. His body might still be broken, but his heart and soul were full and complete.

"Just thinking about how far we've come," he answered. She sank into a cozy armchair, and he swung around to face her.

"Yes, we have. I came here for my dream job and a chance to move up in my career. Didn't realize I'd get myself a real live cowboy to love as well once he'd had a bit of an attitude adjustment."

Mac reached over to tweak her nose. "Good thing you got that sorted out, eh?"

Carrie's grin said it all. Reaching toward him, she took his hands in hers.

"Can you believe that Heart Creek Haven is going to be a reality?" Drawing a deep breath, she let it out slowly.

"All thanks to you," Mac said quietly.

Carrie shook her head. "It was your idea, Mac, all I did was support you."

"I would still be whining in my bedroom, shutting out everyone and everything if it weren't for you. And of course, Ryker. He wasn't letting me get away with a darn thing."

Resting their foreheads together, they sat in comfortable silence. Mac's heart leapt when he thought about Carrie opening her stocking later that day and finding the ring. Oh man, did that mean he needed to think about what to say when he

proposed? He stifled a groan then mentally slapped himself.
He could do this. He had to.

Carrie leaned into Mac's warmth, relishing the feel of him.
Goodness, she loved this big man! She couldn't imagine her
life without him. Her decision to accept Ryker's offer to work
at Heart Creek Ranch was the best one she'd ever made. Now
she had her dog Winnie, her job that she loved, and of course
Mac. Being enveloped in the embrace of the extended McCoy
family was a major bonus.

As if sensing her thoughts, Winnie padded over to them, her
nails clicking on the hardwood floor. Leaning her soft body
against Carrie's legs, she nudged Carrie's hand off Mac's knee,
looking for a scratch.

"We're here!" Voices carried into the room, followed by a
flurry of activity as Mac's nephews flung themselves into their
uncle's lap. Winnie scurried away, not quite used to the energy
of the two little boys.

Suddenly the room was full of people, all wishing each other
Merry Christmas, the smell of snow and crisp winter air min-
gling with warm hugs and peppermint.

Carrie grinned as she hugged the twin closest to her. "Did
you have candy canes for breakfast, Nathan?" she teased. His
blond head nodded vigorously.

"Yes, it's Christmas," he reminded her. "Santa time."

Avery and Elizabeth entered the room, laden with trays of
fresh coffee, warm muffins, and goodness knew what other
delicacies.

After everyone settled, Ryker distributed stockings. "Gramma first." The twins' faces fell but they didn't say a word. Elizabeth opened her stocking and admired every item before taking pity on the little boys.

"Twins, next," she announced, and the boys yelled "yay!" before digging into their booty.

Finally, it was Carrie's turn. She took her time examining the beautiful handmade stocking. Everyone in the family had a stocking made by Elizabeth and in keeping with tradition, Carrie received hers this year. Made of red felt, with a small dog and horse on the front, with gold bells on the harness, hers was a work of art. She smiled her thanks through tears – it was wonderful to be part of this amazing family, and she never failed to be astounded at the depths of their kindness.

"For the love of all that is holy, woman, quit dawdling!" Mac's husky voice cut through her musings. Her lovely impatient cowboy.

Reaching inside, her fingers closed around something square and soft. She caught Mac's eye, and she knew what was inside. Teasing him, she drew out everything else first then said "I guess that's it. Thank you, Santa!"

Mac's eyes widened. "Check again," he demanded. He looked so anguished that Carrie relented.

"Oh, there is this," she added, holding the velvet box in her hands and showing everyone. "I wonder what this might be?"

"Candy?" suggested Nathan. His brother nodded enthusiastically.

"I don't think so," Carrie answered. She opened the box then closed it quickly. "No, not candy."

Mac groaned deep in his throat and wheeled over to her.

"Carrie," he pleaded.

"Yes, Mac, my love?"

"Carrie, I have something to ask you."

Carrie nodded. "Go on."

Mac sighed. He moved himself forward on his chair and took her hand.

"Carrie, dearest. I love you. Please marry me. If I could, I would get on one knee."

Carrie gazed into the eyes of the man she loved, watched as the dark blue color changed and deepened. She couldn't imagine anything better than spending the rest of her life with this man.

"Yes, yes, a hundred times, yes. I will marry you. And the get on one knee part? I don't need that. I only need you."

Mac leaned over and captured her lips in a kiss. He removed the ring from the box and placed it on Carrie's ring finger. The diamonds gleamed in the lights from the tree decorations.

Carrie sighed in pleasure. "I love it, Mac," she said. "Of course, you could have given me a twist tie, and I would have loved that too."

Mac grinned at her. "Oh, in that case, give it back and I'll get a refund."

Carrie pulled her hand away. "No, it's okay. I'll keep it, thank you very much. I didn't mean it *literally*."

Everyone crowded around to see the ring and as Carrie accepted their congratulations alongside her fiancé, she thanked the stars for bringing her to this ranch, this family, this man.

It was the best Christmas ever.

The End *for now...*

Read more about the McCoy family in the rest of the Return to Heart Creek series.

About the author

LYNN GALE

Lynn Gale has dreamed about writing romance ever since she read *If This Is Love* by Anne Weale in 1972.

Years went by and she fell in love with romance all over again watching movies like *American Dreamer*, *Romancing the Stone*, *Pride and Prejudice*, and, of course, Hallmark movies. During this time, her dream existed as a spark but recently, it burst into flames like a phoenix. She is finally ready to share her romance and cozy mystery stories.

Being part of the *A Cowboy for Christmas: A Sweet Romance Collection* **anthology** through Calgary Association of Romance Writers of America (CaRWA) was the start of that dream coming true. Originally written under her pen name, Joanie Wilde, *A Heart Creek Christmas* has now become book one in the Return to Heart Creek series – four novellas about the McCoy family of Heart Creek Ranch.

Each Heart Creek book can be read as a stand alone title as well as part of the ongoing series *Return to Heart Creek.*

You can find me at:
Email: lynngalewriter@gmail.com
Website: https://www.lynngalewriter.com
Facebook: http://facebook.com/lynngalewriter
Instagram: http://www.instagram.com/lynngalewriter
Bookbub: https://www.bookbub.com/profile/lynn-gale

Acknowledgements

This book would not have been possible without the assistance and support of many people in my life.

My mentor romance author Katie O'Connor, who has been instrumental in guiding me through the process of honing my craft. She was my first reader and champion and I am truly grateful for her direction and support, and for introducing me to my writing software Atticus.

My editor Victoria Curran for her insights and excellent editing. I learned so much!

My cover designer Laura Heritage of P.S. Cover Design & Author Services for the gorgeous covers for the Return to Heart Creek series.

My family for their love and support. I love you all so much!

My super fan and dear friend Anne Marie!

My amazing island bestie Pat – miss you always.

And my readers – omg I LOVE having readers! What would I do without you? Thank you thank you thank you.

xxoo Lynn

A Heart Creek Second Chance

Book Two - Return to Heart Creek

Lynn Gale

WINDSONG PUBLISHING CANADA

A Heart Creek Second Chance

A Return to Heart Creek Novel

This book is a work of fiction. Names, characters, places, and incidents are either products of the author's imagination or used fictitiously. Any resemblance to actual events, locales, or persons, living or dead, is entirely coincidental.

Published in April 2024 (e-book), Nov 2024 (print)

Digital ISBN: 978-1-7390527-9-9

Print ISBN: 978-1-0688010-9-9

Cover design by P.S. Cover Design & Author Services

Editing by Terri St. Clair

For my husband JP and my family
for your support and love.

For Katie O'Connor
for her encouragement and feedback.

For my island bestie Pat Maloney
I miss you!

Contents

Chapter One

Chelsea McCoy turned off the engine and sat motionless in her truck. Was this visit a good idea? Her heart thumped in her chest as she wrestled with her thoughts. The face in the rear-view mirror was pale, her green eyes pensive. She flipped her long red hair over her shoulder with a sigh, knowing she looked older than her thirty-two years. Who was this woman? At one time, Chelsea would have dashed off a flippant retort laced with humor. Now, she didn't know herself at all.

"And I prefer it that way," she insisted to the woman in the mirror. Much less painful than remembering the woman she used to be. Before Chance died. Before everything changed.

Time to get this over with.

Opening the truck door, she stepped onto the crisp hard-packed snow. A tall dark-haired man was walking across the parking lot toward her. Broad-shouldered and solid, he looked vaguely familiar but it took her a moment to register that it was Finn.

Her Finn.

Correction. Not hers. Not anymore. Not ever again.

Finn Buchanan stopped walking and raised his eyebrows. "Chelsea?"

"In the flesh. Dr. Buchanan, I presume? I didn't recognize you with your hair short and no beard." *Gosh, he looked good.* She'd forgotten how his six-foot, two-inch frame had made her feel safe, how his kind eyes had made her feel loved. She could almost feel his strong arms wrapped around her. *Whoa, girl.*

"What can I do for you?"

"I need to talk to you."

His hazel eyes narrowed. "About?"

"The county animal shelter."

"Ah, yes, the shelter. Bit of a dilemma there. Hey, how about we chat inside where it's warm?" He rubbed his bare hands together briskly. They sounded like sandpaper. "A bit nippy this morning."

Chelsea drew in a sharp breath. "Yes, that would be great."

Finn turned, walking toward the garage. "I live upstairs."

Chelsea hesitated – *was she doing the right thing?* – then followed the man she used to love into his home.

Be calm. Be calm. She mentally reviewed the list she'd painstakingly cobbled together for this meeting, welcoming the feeling of quiet resolve settling around her. She could do this. Her passion was animals. If not for herself, she could certainly do this for them. McCoys didn't give up. They might get close sometimes, but they always made it through. Except Chance. Pushing that painful thought away, she focused instead on her brother Mac. He'd found an amazing woman who was about to become his wife. Surely, Chelsea could find, well...closure for herself, maybe, hope for the shelter, and whatever else evolved. This first step was the hardest. *Keep it strictly professional, Chels. Forget your past with Finn, forget about Chance, and concentrate on what is important right now – the future of the animal shelter.*

Taking a deep breath, she tucked in her shirt and squared her shoulders. The apartment was small but neat and tidy. The tables beside the oversized deep brown leather recliner and sofa were piled with books and the electric fireplace had an autumn-hued woven rug in front of it. Chelsea relaxed slightly as she took in the warmth and coziness of the space. So very Finn. Or at least like the Finn she used to know. Before...

"Coffee or tea?" Finn derailed her train of thought.

"Coffee, please." Finn filled two large mugs from the pot, adding cream to hers without asking before handing it to her. Her heart pinged.

"You remembered."

"I remember everything." Finn's tone was wry as he lifted his mug. "Table or living room?" He paused for her answer.

"Table, please," Chelsea replied. At least having the table between them would hide her shaking legs and provide a safe barrier of sorts. She drank deeply, sighing when the rich coffee blend hit her taste buds and exploded into a myriad of sensations – the headiness of the sweet, rich cream weaving around the delicious bitterness of the coffee beans.

Finn raised an eyebrow as he too took a large gulp. Then he settled into his chair and gazed across the table at Chelsea. He didn't speak and the silence thickened until it became the awkward third person in the room.

Chelsea cleared her throat. "Finn." Her voice was hoarse. Raising a hand, she took another calming sip and a few deep breaths. *Stay focused, Chels. You've got this.* Her sweaty palms belied her thoughts as she wiped her hands on her pants and spoke again, her voice stronger.

"Finn, have you heard the news about the county animal shelter closing?"

Finn nodded. "Yes, I heard a few days ago."

"Okay, then you know they don't plan to reopen anywhere local. They are going to use the shelter in Montague instead."

"No, I didn't realize that. Huh. Montague is more than a hundred miles away. That doesn't make sense." He sounded as confused as she felt.

"I have an idea." *You can do this. You can do this.* "What would you say to opening a shelter here?"

Finn leaned back in his chair, clasping his hands behind his head. Classic Finn. He always liked to relax while thinking. He looked calm and even peaceful. No sign of what was going on in his mind. It was a trait that had always driven her crazy with impatience.

"Here? You mean here at the clinic? "He paused. "Haven't ironed out all the plans with Doc Olson yet," he added eventually, tapping his fingers on the tabletop.

Oh dear. She'd heard that Finn was taking over the practice and buying the clinic and land. Obviously, assumptions had been made. Embarrassment flooded her body.

"I thought it was a done deal. What are your plans then?" Her face flamed, realizing she was crossing a line by asking about private plans from a man she hadn't talked to in almost six years. "I'm so sorry, Finn. I assumed you were taking over everything from the Doc.... You know what they say about assuming. Sorry to waste your time." She rose abruptly.

"Chelsea."

She stopped but didn't turn around. Being around him was bringing up old hurts.

"Chelsea," he repeated. "You aren't wasting my time. Tell me more about what you are thinking. Sit. Please."

What to do, what to do? What could it hurt to let him know what she was thinking? She was here after all.

"If you're sure," she said, a little stiffly. She resettled in her chair and took a few calming breaths. In for a penny and all that. Her mind whirled as she tried to tame her thoughts into some semblance of order.

"That's an interesting idea, having a shelter here," he said when she hadn't spoken for several moments. "As of now, I don't know who will own which parts of the property. I'm not sure my financial situation will accommodate purchasing it all on my own. I had hoped to have a partner...." His voice trailed away.

A partner. Tears welled unbidden in Chelsea's dry throat. A partner for the practice. A partner for his life. Chance. And her.

"I can't do this. I have to go. I'm sorry to waste your time." She rose unsteadily, put her cup in the sink, and left the apartment. She could hear Finn saying something but all she could hear was a roaring and the word *partner* buzzing like an angry bee.

This was a bad idea. Stupid even. Silly girl.

Chelsea sat in her truck for a few minutes, letting herself recover before driving. Ridiculously, she half hoped Finn might follow her, but he didn't. *And why should he? You've made it perfectly clear over the last several years where he stands in your life. Absolutely nowhere.* She jammed the truck into reverse and hit the gas.

As she drove away, their conversation played in her mind. The warm spring sunshine that melted the last of the snow and gently dappled the trees did nothing to calm her frantic mind or aching heart.

She'd done the research and there wasn't a suitable and accessible area of land big enough for an animal shelter available within a comfortable driving distance of Heart Creek.

Except for the land around the vet clinic.

It was a double whammy – the forced relocation of the shelter due to the new highway and the county's budget cuts. As an animal health technician, she was familiar with Doc Olson's veterinary clinic. She'd done her practicums here and worked with Doc Olson on issues with Heart Creek Ranch's horses. Somehow, she'd managed to avoid Finn for the past several years but now with the old doctor retiring, those days were coming to an end, shelter issue or no shelter issue.

Finn Buchanan. Dr. Finn Buchanan, DVM. Doctor of Veterinary Medicine. The boy she'd loved when they were kids and the man she loved when they grew up. Until her brother Chance's death when everything changed. As his twin, she'd felt Chance's death deeply. It had taken months to recover a small semblance of normal, and even now there were dark days. She coped by keeping busy with the ranch, working for the shelter, and not thinking about the past. Now the past was apparently ready for her to deal with it – but was she ready to move forward?

Her family's ranch could have worked for the shelter relocation, but her brother Mac got there first with his idea of building a rehab center for rodeo cowboys. Part of her was annoyed and frustrated, but she knew the cowboy clinic he and Carrie planned to build at Heart Creek Ranch would be a welcome and beneficial addition to the ranch, the community, and Mac's life. She couldn't begrudge him that. The problem was what to do next. She had been so sure that Finn would buy everything Doc was selling. It never occurred to her that there might be an issue, financial or otherwise. She'd forgotten that Doc's previous partner had retired early and that Finn would be on his own once Doc left.

Like she was on her own. It wasn't supposed to be this way.

They were supposed to be together. Finn and Chance running the clinic. She and Finn married, with kids and animals and love. A family.

Everything was a mess. Again.

Still.

Finn muttered a few choice words under his breath. Chelsea had burrowed under his skin, again, after years apart. The beginning of a headache crept along the back of his head, winding around his temples. Rinsing their used coffee cups, he opened a cupboard searching for ibuprofen just as Chelsea spun out of the parking lot. He watched through the window, her frustration obvious by the way the tires dug into the snow and gravel. He smiled ruefully, shaking his head as he downed a couple of tablets. She always did have a flair for the dramatic. He missed her and her fiery temper and blazing emerald eyes.

Hang on! Where did that come from? He'd tried, quite successfully he'd thought, to put her into the part of his mind that seldom saw daylight. Now she was sneaking through the cracks. That couldn't be good. This wasn't going to end well for either of them.

Things hadn't ended well for them, his memory taunted, opening the door to a slew of places he'd rather not go. His headache escalated as he shrugged into his coat and headed to the clinic. He didn't have the time or energy to delve into the past. It hurt too much.

He'd heard the news about the county shelter on the radio while driving home from a call. As a large animal veterinarian, his days were long, he was often away from the clinic, but he loved the work. Now that Doc Olson was finally retiring, Finn's workload was increasing. The closing of the county shelter came as a shock. They'd all known about the new highway plans but thought it was a few years off. With the priority changes that the government made, the shelter had three months to find a new home or close. If it closed permanently, the rescues would be taken to Montague, a hundred miles away – almost two hours of driving – to the large shelter they had there.

Finn spent the next few days pondering what he could do to help. He didn't book appointments on Sundays – anyone with a problem was directed to an emergency practice half an hour away. Following a leisurely breakfast of eggs, bacon and toast, along with a few bracing cups of coffee, he tackled laundry and his personal version of housecleaning. Living in the apartment above one of the garages on Doc's property was a godsend. It had all he needed and was close to the clinic.

The idea of a shelter being built near the vet clinic stayed with him. It wasn't that he hadn't thought of it before, it was how to make it work. As he'd explained to Chelsea, he wasn't financially able to purchase the practice, house, and property on his own. Although Doc hadn't come out and said so, Finn knew that Doc was under the impression that Finn was going to take over the entire property. They had been advertising for a second veterinarian for months, but the pickings were slim. The combination of large and small animals wasn't necessarily what the prospects were looking for. Vets typically tended to focus on one or the other, not a combined practice. It didn't help that the partnership entailed a lot of driving and time spent away from the clinic. As a result, there was a delay and backlog of the small animal work. Thank goodness their veterinary assistant was staying on. She'd been there for almost five years and was invaluable to the practice. The receptionist was newer but already fit in well. What he needed was a full partner in the practice, and someone to run the clinic and manage the front end. And another vet assistant on top of that would be ideal.

Running his hands through his hair, he groaned out loud. Bottom line, what he needed was unlimited time and money. The reality was a little different, especially now with the animal shelter closing. The county needed a shelter closer than the far end of the next county over.

Pouring himself another cup of coffee, he dug out his laptop. *First things first. Financials.* He logged into his bank account. He already had one plan in place, but he could redraw his five year business plan and see what made sense, now and in the future, including buying all the land available around the clinic. Then he could talk to Doc Olson and pump him for ideas.

As a relatively new veterinarian, Finn didn't have the means at his disposal to purchase everything, he needed a partner both financially and professionally. It was much too large a practice for one doctor alone. Truth be told, there was more than enough business for two or three doctors. Hopefully, a qualified vet would apply soon, and he'd have some helping hands. How Doc Olson had managed on his own since his partner retired more than two years ago was beyond Finn.

His thoughts swept to Chance and their plans for a partnership in a vet practice. And those thoughts led to Chelsea – their completely and utterly devastated relationship and ruined plans for their future together. All lost in an instant. So much anguish. So much pain. *Oh Chels.* Sorrow swept through him as if it were that day so many years ago. He'd tried so hard not to think about her, to forget the pain he'd caused her and her family.

The plans the three of them had made in university flashed across his mind. Chelsea, along with her twin and his best friend, Chance, and himself. They were going to finish vet school and then open their own practice including a large surgery, rescue and shelter, pet food business, as well as a small and large animal practice.

Chance's death killed that plan. And killed Finn's relationship with the only woman he'd ever loved.

Finn inhaled deeply, running a hand over his suddenly throbbing forehead. Chelsea. His one true love. Chels hated him and blamed him for her twin brother Chance's death.

Unfortunately, she wasn't completely wrong.

And now, here she was, right in the middle of the county shelter mess. He knew she wouldn't let the shelter idea go – one of her biggest strengths was her passion for what she believed in. *She used to believe in you.* Even while his headache continued to throb, his heart leapt. He still loved her and even though the odds were stacked against them, maybe this could be a bit of atonement for what had happened to Chance.

Doc Olson's clinic was perfectly situated on several hundred acres of land, with numerous outbuildings in good shape. Of course, county approval would be needed to convert those buildings into workable kennels and working areas but that was a mere blip on the dream's horizon.

It was worth a try. Wasn't it? For what was, and what could have been.

The next morning, Finn left the bank after meeting with the loans manager. With his current financial resources, he couldn't quite buy everything from Doc. He needed someone else to partner with. Vets willing to come out this far into the country and foot the bill for a partial buy-in were hard to come by. He needed a better idea, an alternate plan.

Chelsea had money. Or at least, her family did. The McCoy family owned Heart Creek Ranch which sprawled over several thousand acres. And she was qualified to run a rescue and shelter.

He stopped in his tracks in the middle of the street. Fortunately, Main Street wasn't busy at this time of day so being run over wasn't an issue. Continuing to his truck, he turned the idea over in his head, first this way, then that.

Chelsea was a certified animal health technician. She had planned on becoming a vet herself. She had access to money to help with the purchase – he knew the McCoy family would support her financially in that way. She was good with people and more importantly, good with animals.

She just wasn't good with him.

But maybe that didn't matter.

Once the idea crept into his mind, he couldn't get away from it. It kept popping up, taunting him, teasing him. Whispering hopeful thoughts to him. No matter what potential problem he came up with, a possible solution appeared.

He had to talk to Chelsea again.

Before that, though, he needed to organize his thoughts so that his proposal would be clear and concise. Simply a business arrangement. She could work part-time in-house at the clinic, handling the small animals and he could do the large animal practice and callouts. On the days the small animal clinic needed him for surgeries or what have you, she could take care of the shelter.

That evening, he sat down and wrote it all out. He built spreadsheets and different scheduling ideas, broke down what Chelsea's work requirements would be, and came up with a plan. He needed money but he also needed help. Chelsea could provide both. They just had to get beyond the agony of their past.

Easier said than done.

Chelsea was nothing like her fraternal twin. She was green-eyed and red-haired like their sister Avery, and fiery like their brother Mac, while Chance had been blond and blue-eyed like their dad, and even-tempered like their mom. Despite those striking differences, every time Finn looked at Chelsea, he saw Chance. His best friend. His university buddy. His non-blood brother. A good man cut down in his prime.

Could he and Chelsea do this?

They had to. Not only did the future of his veterinary practice depend on it but the area did too. The animal shelter that they could build together would mean a lot to the community.

First, he needed to talk to Doc Olson about the land and clinic deal. Hurdle number two and probably the simplest part of the whole venture.

Convincing hurdle number one – Chelsea – to work with him would be a whole different matter.

Chapter Two

C helsea pulled into the parking area in front of the main
ranch house. Gazing around, she was hit with a deep
appreciation of the ranch's beauty and how much she loved
this place where she'd grown up. The huge, sprawling ranch
ran for as far as the eye could see and fed her need for space and
breathing room. The fieldstone-fronted rustic ranch house,
with its tiled roof, garnet red exterior, and wraparound cedar
deck, emanated a warm, welcoming vibe, and felt like a hug
every time she visited. She had intended to talk to her brother
Ryker, but she realized she wasn't in the right headspace after
her visit with Finn.

Changing her mind, she left the ranch and drove to her
apartment in town. She needed to regroup her thoughts and
figure out what to do next.

For the next few days, she went with her Plan A: searching
again for any other local land on which to build the shelter. She
scoured the area, sending out feelers to realtors and everyone
she knew to get a lead on any land that was available to lease or

buy. While there was certainly good land to be had, nothing was the size she wanted, or was located conveniently enough to work for a new shelter.

Nope, Doc Olson's land was the perfect fit. Not as spacious as Heart Creek Ranch, it still covered several hundred acres. There were already outbuildings in good shape that could be revamped. Access for the local community was ideal.

She had to talk to Finn again and see what could be worked out. The fate of the animals was more important than anything in her past. She had to look beyond that to the big picture.

When Finn messaged her right before suppertime the following day, she didn't know how to approach the shelter conversation again. His message was brief – simply "Can we meet for a bite?" For a wild moment, she thought he was asking her for a date, then she realized that would hardly be the case. She paused, conflicted. Part of her ached for him and what they'd had – more often than she would admit to, and usually when it was least expected. When her phone dinged again showing the words "business purposes", she relaxed and replied 'yes'. Then her mind started spinning. What kind of business purposes?

By the time she reached Homegrown Café, her anxiety was in full bloom. Finn was already there. He stood and waved when he caught sight of her hovering near the door. Her heart caught for a moment at the sight of his large frame and warm, smiling face. Swallowing quickly, she tightened her resolve and made her way through the crowded restaurant to his table.

"Hey, Finn." She slid into the booth opposite him.

He handed her a menu. "Thanks for meeting me on short notice." She gave him a slight smile, perusing the menu. She decided on soup and a biscuit, mostly to keep her hands busy. Her mouth was dry, and her tummy churned.

Once their orders were placed, Finn dove in to the reason he'd messaged her. "Chelsea, I have an idea. Could I ask that you hear me out before you jump in?"

At his words, Chelsea bristled. He was so, so *Finn*. Of course, she could wait until he was done. It wasn't like she had a habit of interrupting. Not often anyway. "My lips are sealed."

"I have a proposition for you," Finn continued. His eyes caught Chelsea's, his face turning beet red.

She wasn't sure whether to laugh or cry. Finn was just as nervous as she was! "For lil' ol' me?" she drawled.

Finn laughed a little and visibly relaxed. Chelsea's chest unclenched a bit, and she could breathe more easily.

"Let me try that again," Finn said wryly. "I've come up with a way to help the shelter and maybe help the clinic too. I want to offer you a share in the veterinary clinic, and a part-time job. I'm one hundred percent in favor of building an animal shelter near the vet clinic, to be managed by you."

Chelsea's mouth dropped open.

Finn continued to explain his plan. Partway through, Chelsea remembered to close her mouth.

When he finished, as she was about to speak, their server arrived with their food.

"Eat first," she managed to say. It would buy her some time to find words.

Inside, her brain whirled like a tornado. His offer stunned her. It was exactly what she wanted! The shelter would stay in Heart Creek! It was oh-so-tempting on many levels except for one big BUT – that he wanted her to buy into the vet clinic AND be a working partner in order to build the shelter.

She would have to work side by side with Finn. That was a mountain of a BUT and one big hurdle.

On the pros side, financially she had savings she could use for the buy-in. She'd lived pretty frugally the last few years and her savings reflected that. She knew her brother Ryker would help her with the balance needed for the shelter. Money-wise, it could work. But the partnership idea and the working together? Ohhhh. That was a different kettle of fish.

Her mind ticked off the reasons against the idea. She'd spent years being angry at Finn. They had too much past to overlook. He was responsible for her brother's death. There was a murky grey mess of tangled emotions between them. She still loved him. *Whoa, what? Where did that last one come from?*

Was what he was offering even feasible? Could they make it work? Her head said yes, but her heart wasn't sure. She ached for Chance and his lost life. She ached for her family and their lost brother and son. But mostly, she ached for Finn and their lost love.

"Yes, okay."

Chelsea couldn't believe she had just spoken those words out loud and agreed to his plan. There were many reasons – or at least one big one – why she should walk away but somehow, she couldn't. Despite all the ways in which this plan could go wrong, if it went right – a very big IF – if it went right, it would be extraordinary.

An unfamiliar feeling that felt a little like hope warmed her heart.

"I'll talk to Mac and Ryker about the financial aspects," she continued, a smile forming of its own accord.

Finn's face beamed. "Fabulous. I brought you a copy of the financials, and my draft of how the partnership would look.

We can talk more about it later. If you need anything else, let me know."

While they'd been speaking, he'd paid their bill. At the door, he smiled, and Chelsea's heart skipped a beat. *Finn. I have missed that smile.* Heady excitement raced through her body about the venture, and she wanted to hug somebody. Finn? She almost reached over to him before she remembered about Chance and hardened her heart. Finn handed her the paperwork he'd mentioned and left.

The next morning, it took a while to track Ryker down, but Chelsea was determined to talk to both of her brothers while she was still feeling positive about Finn's plan. Their plan, she amended. If this was going to work, it had to be together. Finn needed her help and her money. She needed his land and his outbuildings. They had to work as a team.

That last part was going to be tough.

Ryker was in the back quarter, talking to the ranch foreman, who rode away with a wave and a grin as Chelsea parked near the fenced area. She easily pulled apart the wire fence and scooted through, heading for her brother.

"What brings you out here today?" he asked as he enveloped her in a massive Ryker-sized hug.

Chelsea grinned as she disentangled herself. "You'll never believe it. Time for a coffee?"

"You read my mind," he admitted. "Meet you at the office." Mounting his horse, he took off for the big barn that housed the business office for the ranch. Chelsea climbed back through the fence to her vehicle and headed for the barn, her mind racing.

By the time she'd arrived, Ryker had two big mugs of steaming coffee ready. They settled into the conference room.

Chelsea took a long bracing sip of caffeine before beginning. "I've got an idea to run past you," she started.

"Okay, let's hear it." Ryker's face was open and interested.

Encouraged, Chelsea began. "I've been talking to Finn…"

Ryker's coffee sputtered out of his nose. Chelsea couldn't hold back her laughter as she handed him several napkins to wipe his face and the front of his shirt.

"Sorry," she said, in between guffaws. "Perhaps I should have started a little more slowly."

"You just caught me off guard," Ryker said. "Ow, my nose is burning!"

While Ryker moaned and whined, Chelsea took the time to rinse and refill his cup. By the time she was settled, Ryker appeared to have somewhat recovered.

"I'm okay," he said, in response to her query. "Please go on. I'm all ears."

Chelsea cleared her throat and started again. "Finn and I have been talking," she paused to make sure Ryker didn't inhale his coffee into his lungs again, and once assured he was fine, continued. "He has a proposition that I think you might be interested in supporting."

Ryker's eyes widened when she said *proposition*, but he nodded for her to keep talking.

She shared about her original visit to Finn to talk about the animal shelter idea, then their meeting last night and his subsequent offer for her to buy into the vet clinic and become a working partner. She detailed how they could then build the animal shelter near the clinic. She went over the initial financials he'd given her last night, noting that she had savings she could use for the buy-in. *Now the awkward part. The money ask from the family.*

She paused. Ryker remained silent, watching her.

"Would you and the ranch be willing to provide the balance of the funds we need to build the shelter, outfit it, and provide contingency funds should something not go to plan?" she managed to say. She gave him the amount Finn had felt would be enough.

"It's not an exact calculation," she hastily explained. "Mostly I just need you to say aye or nay so we can then get a full financial analysis done to ensure we have captured everything."

Ryker was silent for so long that Chelsea began to worry he would say no. Of course, Mac would also have to be included in this venture, but if Ryker was on board, she knew Mac would be an easy win.

He began slowly. "Chels, you'd have to work with Finn. Almost every day. In the same clinic."

Chelsea sighed deeply. "Yes," she acknowledged.

"And you would be okay with that?" Ryker looked at her, a questioning look in his eyes.

It was Chelsea's turn to pause. "For the sake of the animal shelter, yes."

"What about for your own sake, Chels?"

She met his gaze straight on. "I don't honestly, know, Ryker. But I am willing to give it a chance." Her eyes filled when she realized she'd mentioned her twin's name accidentally. She wiped her eyes and steadily gazed at Ryker. "It's time to move on," was all she could manage to say.

He patted her hand and grasped it in his big ones.

"We'll have to talk to Mac to get his buy-in," he said. "But based on what you've told me, and barring any surprises coming up with the analysis, I think it's a grand idea. Good for you,

Chelsea. And Finn too. This is a win-win for the clinic and for the community. I'm proud of you."

Chelsea smiled, as her eyes filled again. This time, though, it was with relief and joy.

And hope. Actual hope, that unfamiliar long forgotten feeling, crept into her heart.

Finn's plan just might work.

Even with the financing potentially in place, and both Ryker and Mac onboard, Chelsea still wondered if she was making a big mistake. Trusting Finn, trusting herself around Finn, and making herself vulnerable was a big ask. Then she thought about the shelter and those animals they'd be helping, like Carrie's Winnie, an old deaf rescue dog who had captured everyone's heart. She was excited about working as a tech again and she knew that Chance wouldn't want her wasting her life.

It was time to take a giant step forward.

Even if it meant her heart could be broken again.

Finn was ecstatic when Chelsea called him with her news and promised to talk to Doc Olson as soon as he could. Later that evening, Finn called with his own news. Turned out Doc Olson was completely on board with selling the complete parcel and even offered to work reduced hours while they got the temporary shelter going, and the permanent one underway. A second vet was still needed as well as more help for the shelter, but they did have a bit of breathing room.

Chelsea met with the receptionist at the clinic and together with Finn, they went through the schedule, separating them into clients that Chelsea could deal with and those going to Finn and Doc Olson.

She and Finn met with the county office officials about the next steps for the new shelter development. They were given the forms and information needed to apply for the required permits. After the county meeting, they walked the property with Doc Olson, pointing out what could go where. Chelsea marveled at the extent of the land and the possibilities it offered. Stables and barns, plus an assortment of outbuildings, would provide all they needed for the temporary shelter. The future permanent shelter would be built on part of a vacant quarter section. There would also be an expansion for the clinic. It was mind-boggling and terrifying to know that even though financially they were covered, there was still a tight budget and careful pre-planning was necessary to ensure future solvency.

Chelsea's ideas kept coming. She read about a shelter on Vancouver Island that housed a rescue boutique where locals donated items to sell with the proceeds going to the shelter. She knew her sister Avery could design custom tags, as well as make natural shampoos for the animals to sell in the boutique. Finn loved the idea when she shared it.

On Doc Olson's property, soon to be their property, there was a second small building behind the clinic with office space and a furnished apartment. Finn offered it to Chelsea so that she could be on-site – part of their 24-hour service commitment to the community that Finn really wanted to maintain. Chelsea agreed and quickly made plans to move out of her apartment in town.

From her new living room, she could see Finn's place and the clinic. Convenient, cozy, and somehow comforting. Also terrifying to be so close to Finn.

Oh Chelsea. You still have it bad for that man. Despite every-thing. She might love him, but she wasn't letting him back into her heart. Ever.

The first few days working in the clinic were awkward, to say the least. Both Finn and Chelsea were in the office and couldn't avoid each other. It was unusually busy – word had gotten out of their plan and suddenly it seemed that everyone's pets needed a clinic visit. It had taken a few discussions but they managed to hammer out details and responsibilities to their mutual satisfaction. Doc Olson was happy to take care of the out-of-town calls initially so Finn could concentrate on the clinic while getting the new schedule up and running.

By the time evening came each day that first week, Chelsea was exhausted but happy. Working at the shelter had been great but being back in the clinic and fully using her animal vet tech skills was fabulous. And if she was truly being honest, she was starting to enjoy being around Finn. His amazing ability to be caring with both animals and owners touched her deeply. The ice around her heart began to thaw, day by day.

Avery was ecstatic about the rescue boutique idea – her sister was chomping at the bit about the potential and already had ideas. Chelsea giggled as she recalled the joy in Avery's voice. Everything was coming together.

Except for her and Finn, of course. That ship had sailed long ago.

Thoughts of Chance and what could have been came far less often than they used to, due mostly to the busyness of her days.

A few weeks after she moved into the apartment, she invited Mac and Carrie over to dinner to share their progress on Heart's Haven – the sanctuary for cowboys who needed a place to recuperate. They were hiring an equine therapist – a friend of Carrie's – as an added option for the cowboys – psychology mixed with horses. Not necessarily riding them but simply being with them. Horses were amazing animals and cowboys already knew that. It would be like mixing chocolate chips into cookie batter – just that little bit better.

She planned a simple supper of beef and chicken kebabs and salad, with her special bourbon pecan pie for dessert.

"Hello?" Carrie's voice rang from the front door. "Be right down," Chelsea answered. She ran lightly down the stairs. "We are going to eat in the covered area behind the clinic," she told Carrie. The apartment didn't have an elevator or a ramp – something Chelsea intended to remedy – so currently, getting Mac's wheelchair into the apartment was a no-go.

Hugging her brother tightly, Chelsea marveled at the changes in him the past few months had brought. His face was less gaunt, and his smile reached his eyes. He was recuperating from his rodeo accident quite nicely. Carrie had been so good for him.

She enveloped her future sister-in-law in a big hug, then knelt to pet Winnie, Carrie's deaf rescue dog. Winnie had been instrumental in alerting Mac and Ryker to Carrie's accident several months back. Without Winnie, Carrie might have died. "Hey, sweet girl," Chelsea cooed. They knew Winnie couldn't hear them, but they all spoke to her anyway.

The day was still warm and sunny so sitting outside would be comfortable. They were using the space hat Doc Olson had previously set up behind the clinic as a patio, complete with a propane barbecue and counter. Chelsea hadn't had any time to do anything to the area behind her apartment's building yet, but eventually she'd have her own little yard. Mac rolled himself to where he could look out over the back pastures, while Carrie helped Chelsea bring down the food and prep the table. Soon the tantalizing smell of grilled meat and vegetables filled the air.

"Where is the good doctor today?" Mac asked, lifting one eyebrow.

"I think Doc Olson is on a call in Ridgefield, "Chelsea answered, not looking at her brother.

Mac's sigh made her giggle.

"I mean the younger good doctor," he drawled.

Chelsea stiffened for a moment then realized it was a natural question now that she and Finn not only worked together but lived near each other.

"He's in town getting some supplies for the clinic," she replied smoothly. "He also planned on checking in at the animal shelter to see how things are going with the move happening soon."

"How is everything going with that?" Mac asked.

Chelsea spent the next few minutes bringing Mac and Carrie up to date on what they had achieved so far.

Mac whistled appreciably when she was done. "Great work in a short time," he said. "I'm impressed."

"The volunteers will have the temporary shelters in place within the next two weeks," Chelsea added. "The permanent facility will be built in stages, starting with the animal housing area and finishing with the offices. Okay, the food is ready, shall we dish up?"

The three ate in companionable silence.

At last, Mac sat back, rubbing his stomach. "Oh, that was good." He groaned.

Carrie laughed. "You certainly have your appetite back," she teased. In response, he threw his napkin at her.

Chelsea envied their ease with each other and the way they kept gazing over when they thought the other person wasn't looking. Ah, to be in love.

You were in love once, her heart reminded her. *Maybe you still are*, added a little voice deep inside.

Chelsea shook her head. Mac looked at her, his eyes narrowing.

"Just clearing my thoughts," Chelsea replied to his unspoken question.

"I'll dish up the pie and you can tell me all about Heart Creek Center for Cowboys. I'm so excited."

With that, both Mac and Carrie launched into the progress of the rehab facility they were creating for retired or hurt cowboys and rodeo riders. Chelsea loved how they took turns speaking, their thoughts definitely in sync.

"Can't wait to see it! When do you think you'll be ready for your first guests? Of the non-four-footed variety, I mean."

Mac chuckled. "We've hired a social media expert to help us get the word out. We've started a waiting list and so far, we've had inquiries but no takers. Once the building takes shape, and our website and brochures show our real vision, I think it will pick up. I have a few friends who I know would benefit."

Mac didn't sound worried about the future of the new rehab center. As a broken cowboy himself, he knew that the cowboys would be cautious and hesitant, at least at first. It was part of the therapy they needed – no pressure, no rushing. Just gentle love and caring while they healed and pondered what their next steps were.

"Hi there," Finn came around the corner by the house. "Smells amazing out here."

Chelsea hesitated for only a moment. "There are still warm kebabs," she offered.

"Yes, please join us," Carrie added, moving another chair to the table.

Finn's face broke out in a smile that wove through Chelsea's heart. "Yes, please! Thanks!"

He dished up a plate of food for himself and sank into the chair. Glancing around the table, he smiled.

"So how is everyone? Looking great, Mac, and Carrie, you are as beautiful as always."

Carrie blushed as she responded. "Thanks, you're looking pretty handsome yourself, big guy."

Finn laughed, looking down at his faded jeans and old work shirt. "Ah, you are into the casual type, I see."

Mac's voice broke in. "Hey there buddy, get your own girl. This one's mine!"

"I think I will do just that," Finn responded softly. Chelsea kept her eyes down, looking at the table, while she cut the pie. She could feel their gazes on her, and the back of her neck grew warm.

"Pie?" she asked, finally looking up.

"Yes!" all the voices answered together.

"I can't believe you inhaled that food already," she said to Finn.

"I'll have you know I'm a hard-working man, woman," Finn replied. "Yes, please, to pie."

His face was so open and sweet that Chelsea forgot herself. Gazing warmly into his eyes, she placed a hearty slice of pie on his plate.

"Hey, how come he gets the biggest one?" Mac retorted.

Chelsea's face flamed as an odd tension grew around the table. "Are you always this competitive?" she asked her brother pointedly.

"Heck, yeah!" both Carrie and Mac answered at the same time.

Everyone laughed and the jovial atmosphere was restored.

Chelsea, Chelsea, she grimaced to herself. *You have it bad for that man.*

Ba-a-a-d.

Chapter Three

For once, the county didn't take forever to approve the plans and issue the preliminary permits. The temporary structures arrived on a cold windy day. The rain and wind continued for a few days, pushing back the setup. Fortunately, they had built contingencies into their plan.

Finn marveled at how smoothly it was going despite the weather delay. Chelsea had shared her idea for the rescue boutique, and he agreed wholeheartedly, with the proviso that all profits benefitted only the rescue center. His chest tightened watching her face glow when she talked about it. The glimpses of the old Chelsea were bittersweet.

He couldn't believe how quickly his old feelings for Chelsea had returned. He felt like a smitten teen again every time he saw her face. He loved working with her in the clinic and admired her easy manner around both people and animals. If it hadn't been for that one night when Chance...*no point thinking about it now*, he admonished himself. *Can't change the past.*

Could he change what he thought would be his future though? Did he and Chelsea have a chance themselves? He wished he knew. Sometimes, he caught her staring at him, or smiling with that smile he loved so much, and deep in his gut, he knew she still loved him. But love wasn't what he needed. Forgiveness was the only thing that could change anything, and that didn't seem to be on Chelsea's agenda.

Not now, maybe not ever.

Still, a guy could hope. She crept into his dreams and his waking thoughts at the most inopportune moments. Maybe he could do something to move things forward. It's couldn't hurt to try, could it? He was already about as low as a man could get in her eyes. He had absolutely nothing to lose and everything to gain.

"Hey Chels," he asked, one day after an especially busy day at work. "Wanna grab a cold beer and some supper?"

Chelsea paused. *Yup, here comes the big no*, Finn thought.

"Love to," she replied. He almost choked at her words. *Glory be*!

"The café?

"Let's go to the new place – Mulberry Corner, right?"

"Yes, I've heard it was pretty good."

"Okay, give me a few minutes to shower and change, and I'll be good to go."

Finn smiled. "Go ahead. I'll lock up and meet you at the truck in forty-five minutes." He couldn't believe it had been that easy.

Chelsea stood under the hot water in the shower and groaned. What on earth was she thinking? Finn was a no-go zone. Danger, danger. Why had she agreed to go out with him? Because he mentioned beer and food, her tummy reminded her. Yup, two of her weaknesses, especially at the end of a busy workday. He knew her too well. She was just getting used to working with him. She hadn't considered socializing in her toolbox of 'how to deal with Finn feelings'. *Aargh.*

Forty-four minutes later, she locked her door and made her way down the stairs to the parking lot. Inside her nerves jangled and her breath caught when she saw Finn waiting at the truck.

Cowboy hat, face freshly shaved, faded jean jacket on top of a fitted black tee shirt and jeans – the man was drop-dead gorgeous. She wanted to step into his warm embrace and stay there, feeling his body heat and listening to his heartbeat. Forever.

She sighed. This was getting complicated. Way too complicated.

He smiled and came around to her side of the truck. "You clean up well," he said, eyes twinkling.

"So do you," she replied. He opened her door, and she stepped in. "Thanks."

"My pleasure, ma'am," he drawled, shutting the door gently.

As he strode around the truck to the driver's door, Chelsea drew a ragged breath. Running her suddenly clammy hands on her long jean skirt, she tried to stop the excitement building in her chest. *Remember Chance.* When a small voice inside asked *why*, she was shocked. *Why indeed? Because Chance dying was Finn's fault.* Then the soft question came back: *Was it though?* Totally confused, she paused her train of thought, just as Finn opened the driver's door.

Startled, she jumped, and Finn guffawed, his big laugh cascading through the truck.

"Sorry I scared you," he said softly.

Not you buddy, she thought. *I'm scaring myself.*

The restaurant was busy as they drove by, but Finn found a parking spot not too far away. Once again, he opened Chelsea's door, offering his hand as she stepped out. She shook her head, but when he held out his arm as they walked along the sidewalk, she accepted.

A small booth at the back had just been vacated. Gazing around, he nodded appreciably.

"Nice place."

"I love the old-timey feel to it and how warm the real wood feels."

Their server approached. "Welcome. Would you care for a beverage to start?"

"Beer, please, for both of us. Whatever is on tap is fine," Finn said, smiling at the young woman.

"You got it," she smiled back at him.

"Oh, and a glass of water, please," Chelsea added. "Tap water is fine."

"Make that two, please." Finn smiled again.

He glanced over at Chelsea. She had an odd look on her face.

"What's up?" he asked. "Did I miss a bit when I shaved?"

She looked thoughtful. "No," she said. "I'd forgotten how charming you can be."

Interesting, Finn thought. Interesting. He mugged and pulled a funny face. "Oh yes," he agreed. "Charming is my middle name."

Her grin made his heart jump. *Chelsea, I've missed you.*

They took their time with the menu, sipping their cold beers and chit-chatting about everything, but nothing in particular. Finn enjoyed watching Chelsea's face, her expressions changing as she discussed their latest four-legged visitors, and a few of the two-legged ones. He'd forgotten how wonderful it felt to be around her. He'd hidden it away when she broke up with him. Now, the feelings surged back, just as powerful as they always had been.

If only Chance's accident hadn't happened. If only Finn had been able to stop him. If only...

Chelsea's head cocked; her expression thoughtful as she gazed at him. He realized he'd drifted away with his thoughts. A flush rose on his cheeks as he brought his focus back to the beautiful woman at the table.

"Sorry, wool-gathering," he managed to say.

"About?"

Finn paused before he spoke. Was now the time?

"Chance."

It was out there. The name hung like a frosty cloud on the suddenly chilly air.

Chelsea's eyes filled with tears as she swallowed hard. *Not such a good idea then.*

"Finn..." she started to speak but Finn held up his hand to stop her.

"I'm sorry – not the time or the place," he apologized, suddenly desperate to salvage as much of this impromptu date as he could.

Chelsea bowed her head for a moment while Finn waited in awkward silence.

As she raised her head, the server approached the table.

"Are you ready to order?" she said pleasantly.

Chelsea nodded and they ordered nachos to share. Once the server left, they gazed at each other for a long moment. Finn could feel the pain in her heart right down to his toes. He reached across the table and took her cold slender hand in his. There were no words, he knew. Simply two souls who had lost someone dear to them, and in the resulting chaos, also lost each other.

Chelsea gently pulled her hand back.

"Avery is excited. She's already started trying different blends for shampoos," she said into the silence.

Finn accepted the change of topic for what it was, a small white flag. *Someday they were going to have to address the elephant in the room, but today was not the day. Would that day ever come?* Finn hoped so, otherwise there would never be hope for them which was not acceptable to him. Not one bit. Being around Chelsea added color to his life – color he needed as much as the air he breathed or the food he ate. There had been too much gray, too much dark, and too much emptiness, for far too long.

When their food arrived, they ate in comfortable silence, punctuated now and then with light conversation. Neither of them had room for dessert. The drive home was peaceful.

At Chelsea's stairs, he paused, about to say goodnight, when she leaned in and kissed him on the cheek.

"Thank you for a lovely evening," she said. She stepped forward and kissed him on the mouth before he could reply. Soft lips grazed his and for a slight moment she pressed in, a sweet promise wrapped in poignant memories of past kisses. Her hands grasped the back of his head. His breath quickened and his body reacted in muscle memory before she gently pulled away.

"Good night, Finn," she murmured, then walked up the stairs.

Holy farm cats on a tear. What the heck just happened? Finn waited until Chelsea closed her door and turned off her outside lights before he went into his own home, the feel of her lips still warm on his, and the feel of her hands lingering in his hair. *Wowzah.*

Maybe there was hope for them after all.

Chelsea leaned against the closed door, emotionally drained.

What was she thinking? Kissing Finn? Twice, no less! Good grief. She was so confused. It was easier when she'd hated him. When he was out of her life. *Was it though? Or was it cold and empty and lonely?*

She shuddered. It felt so good to kiss him. And right.

Oh my gosh. What was she going to do? She was falling for him despite her best intentions. And worse, she was betraying her brother Chance.

Exhausted, she craved sleep but once she got into bed, she lay there for a long time reliving the feel of Finn's lips, soft yet firm, drawing her in, making her want more. Memories flitted through her mind and her body. She missed him and what they had. Eventually, she slid into an uneasy slumber.

Amazingly, she woke up feeling rested several hours later. With two days off, she appreciated not waking up to an alarm. Glancing at her phone, she saw she'd missed several messages from her sister. She grinned. Avery hated waiting! Like most of the McCoy family, patience wasn't her sister's best trait. Even so, a long hot shower was appealing, and Chelsea took her time making her toast and coffee before settling in to give her sister a call.

"It's about time," Avery's tone bordered on annoyance.

"Slept in," Chelsea answered, between bites of her toast. "Whatcha got?"

The next half hour passed in a pleasant blur as Avery hit Chelsea with more ideas for the boutique. By the time they'd said their goodbyes, Chelsea's head was buzzing. She could already envision the shop, incorporating all things for pet lovers, with charming crafts on the walls, and stuffed animals tucked into hammocks around the room.

Thoughts of Finn tucked deeply away, she dressed for her day's adventures. First stop was the temporary shelter. Located a few hundred yards from the vet clinic, the barn they'd chosen to renovate was a great location. A temporary structure was being added on one end, providing more space for additional kennels. The barn originally housed an office used by previous farm managers – way before the vet clinic came to be – and there was a small but workable bathroom and large clean-up area already in place.

The warmth of the sun graced her face as she walked over, noticing the grass peeking through the barely remaining snow. Spring was well underway. She marveled at how quickly the contractors had made the barn into a usable space. Smiling at the two men working in the temporary area, she moved into the main barn area and gasped. The holes had been fixed and the area was clean and bright thanks to new lights running down the center of the barn and over what had once been stalls. The stalls had been renovated into kennels, small, medium, and large. Built-in cabinets were ready for supplies, and a large stainless-steel countertop shone in one area, flanked by animal washing bays, and more built-in cabinets.

The current county shelter had a capacity of three hundred animals. This temporary one would be able to house about two hundred fifty but the permanent one would be closer to five hundred. Her research had told her that shelters were usually built to accommodate about three percent of the human population of an area. With the county area population currently just under twelve thousand people, the ideal shelter capacity would be at least three hundred sixty. The population of Heart Creek had been in a holding pattern for the past few years, but she and Finn had determined they wanted to make sure that the permanent shelter would be able to handle any growth that might occur over the next twenty years.

Chelsea also wanted to make sure that no animal was ever turned away. Finn agreed. It was something they both felt strongly about, and she was grateful to have his support in that decision.

The area designated for the rescue boutique was part of the temporary structure she'd passed through on her way in. It was a large geodesic dome that would allow light in and provide a wonderful feeling of spaciousness to the little store. The permanent shelter would have a four-season area attached to the entranceway, offering the boutique, a check-out area for the animals who left for new homes, and a small office area for the admins.

It was already beautiful and Chelsea was thrilled that her idea had manifested into this space. Her idea and Finn's. Their shared vision.

Once again, tears blurred her eyes but this time, they didn't feel like acid burning her skin. They felt gentle, her pain being soothed by a sense of peace and gratitude. A new feeling for her, one she hesitantly welcomed, curious as to what had changed, what was changing.

Maybe she was learning to forgive Finn.

To forgive herself.

Was that even possible? Stranger things happened every day, all over the world.

She shrugged her shoulders and wiped her eyes. This was not the day to ponder the past. It was the time to embrace what was happening right now. And right now, she was going into town to load up on groceries and other supplies. She turned around abruptly.

Womppphh.

Her vision went dark and for a moment she thought she'd walked into a pole. Then she heard the muffled curse.

Nope. It was Finn.

"Oh my gosh, are you okay?" she cried. "I'm so sorry, Finn, I didn't know you were there." She stepped back and rubbed her face before peering at him through her fingers.

He was bent over, making odd noises. Oh no, had she hurt him?

He stood up, his face red and laughter mixed with strange noises gurgling out of his mouth.

"I'm okay, I'm okay," he managed to say, in between deep guffaws and moans.

Chelsea stood watching him, trying not to think about the warmth and breadth of this man that she'd run into.

"Finn, are you hurt?"

"Good morning to you too," he said. "I'm fine, really. You took me by surprise."

"Were you lurking behind me?" Her embarrassment came out as annoyance.

"God no," he said. "I was walking over here to see how things were going."

"Hmmmm."

"And I'm fine, really."

Chelsea still felt bad for walking into him head-on. "I'm planning to go to town shortly," she said. "Need anything?" She could have smacked herself for making the offer. She was trying to keep their personal and professional lives separate. *Professional only. No more kissy-kisses. Focus, girl!*

He smiled and his eyes sparkled. "Bananas?" he asked. "And maybe some of those little tomatoes if they have them? And chocolate, you know what I like."

Chelsea didn't know whether to laugh or cry. She did indeed know what he liked.

Darn it all anyway.

"Sure thing," she agreed. "See you later then. If you aren't home, I'll leave the bag on your porch." With that, she nodded her head and walked away.

The rest of the day passed at a comfortable pace. Chelsea picked up her and Finn's groceries, taking far too long to choose the nicest bananas and grape tomatoes. She stopped into Bellissimo Hair to see if Marina had time to trim her hair and agreed to head back in an hour for a cut. Getting herself an almond milk chai latte from Homegrown Café, she stuck her head into Pawsitively Purrfect to chat with Selina, the manager, about how the new shelter was taking shape. They had met earlier in the week so she could make sure that the new rescue boutique wasn't going to hurt Selina's sales in the pet store. Once Selina realized that the profits from the rescue boutique would be directly benefiting the shelter, she'd come on board with the idea. Chelsea planned to only carry donated items or items that the local pet store didn't sell.

Settling into the salon chair after having her hair washed and conditioned was amazingly decadent. Sipping the last of her chai, she relaxed, letting Marina's skilled hands clean up her curls.

Lost in her thoughts, it was a few minutes before she cottoned on that she was being talked about. Gazing in the mirror, Chelsea glanced around and took stock of the woman sitting across the room at another stylist's chair and talking on her phone while her highlights set.

"...those McCoys are into everything."

Chelsea's eyes caught Marina's, silently acknowledging they'd both heard the woman speak. Marina moved to say something, but Chelsea lightly shook her head. Marina nodded.

"Yeah, that new vet is a looker. I hear he grew up here? Figured Chelsea McCoy would be right in there. Always was the princess, that one, always getting every thing she wanted, not caring who it hurt. Remember her brother? No, not the crippled one, the other one. The one who died. I hear it was her fault...she never owned up to it though. See what I mean? Princess poor little ol' me...."

Chelsea's vision blurred, and she felt her stylist's hand on her shoulders.

"Never you mind," Marina said kindly, "That woman is a gossip and a backstabber. Don't take mind of anything she says."

Chelsea waved it off. "My fault, for eavesdropping," she managed to say. "You know what they say, eavesdroppers never hear good about themselves."

When Chelsea paid for her cut, she could tell the woman was watching her. Marina smiled as she gave Chelsea her receipt.

"See you next time, princess," Marina spoke loudly enough for the woman to hear.

Chelsea grinned, glancing over at the now red-faced woman still in her chair, before nodding at Marina. "Thanks, my friend," she said. "See you later."

She was still smiling when she got into her car, but her heart ached. The woman was being mean and gossipy, but she wasn't completely wrong. Not about the princess part or the McCoy bit. About Chance. Chance's death *was* partly her fault.

Hers and Finn's.

It was time. Time to get it all out in the open. Way past time. No more burying it.

No screaming, blaming, or crying.

Just talking calmly and rationally.

Time to have a conversation with Finn.

Chapter Four

Finn gazed out his kitchen window as Chelsea drove into the parking lot between their two places. A few minutes later, as she strode his way carrying grocery bags, he sensed that something had changed. Something in the way she walked and held her head high. He didn't know if the change was good or bad, but he had a feeling he was about to find out. Opening his apartment door in case she had planned to drop the bags and run, he saw her determined face and knew his intuition was right. Something had changed.

"Chels?" he asked.

"Do you have time right now? I'd like to talk."

"Sure, your place or mine?"

"Mine," she said. "Just give me a few minutes to put these groceries away and come on over."

She turned and left. The air felt heavy with emotion, and in his gut, he knew she wanted to talk about Chance and what had happened.

Time for the big-boy pants. They were going to have it out.

Ten minutes later, he stood at the bottom of her stairs, wondering if he'd given her enough time. When she opened her door and gazed questioningly down at him, he made his way up.

"Thanks for the chocolate," he said. "I brought some to share. Oh and here's what I owe you."

He placed money on her counter, but she didn't even reach for it. She handed him a mug filled with hot coffee and motioned him to the living room.

"So..." he smiled, hoping to lighten the mood.

It didn't work.

"We need to talk...about..." she paused.

His mind told him to give her space while his heart ached. He didn't want to go there either, but he knew they had to if they were to ever have a chance at love again. He waited calmly.

"We never really talked about this before," she continued slowly. "I mean, I guess we did but nothing was resolved."

"No," he agreed.

"We need to talk about Chance."

"Yes."

"You already guessed?" she wondered aloud.

"Yes."

She nodded and twisted her hands together. Then she looked up and caught him watching her. For a long moment, he tried to communicate with his eyes. She didn't change expression, so he wasn't sure it worked. Wasn't sure she could feel his love and compassion. He dropped his gaze.

"Chance died." Her voice was barely a choked whisper.

"Yes, he did."

"It was an accident..." It wasn't a statement yet not quite a question.

"It was an accident," he agreed.

"Was it though?" she asked slowly and distinctly.

Finn flinched at her tone despite trying to stay neutral, to stay calm.

"Yes, it was." His voice was firm and steady.

"Tell me about it."

"You know that I only know what you know."

"And why is that?" she asked, her eyes on his.

"Because I wasn't there."

"No, you weren't. And neither was I!"

"I know that, Chelsea."

"And why, Finn, why weren't we there?"

"Because we were making plans for our wedding."

"Exactly. We were making PLANS while my brother died."

Finn drew a deep breath. "Yes, we were. There is nothing wrong with that, Chelsea."

"Chance died because we weren't there to stop him. Or more to the point – YOU weren't there to stop him."

Finn's body trembled as the emotions of that night came flooding back, like a tsunami bearing down on him.

"Chelsea, your brother had a problem."

"Yes, he did! His best friend and his twin sister deserted him when he needed them most!"

Chelsea was crying now, wringing her hands and gasping.

"Chelsea. You know how stubborn he was. You know he would have driven that car that night no matter what."

"No, he wouldn't have. Not if we had been there." The words were so soft he almost didn't hear them.

"What?" Finn couldn't believe she thought that.

"He couldn't control his drinking, Chelsea. Us, or even just me, being there wouldn't have changed anything."

"We could have stopped him. You could have stopped him. Like you did before."

Finn's breath caught in his throat. *Like you did before.*

She knew. She knew that he had been the one to keep Chance in line when his drinking got the best of him.

"How long have you known?" Finn asked, his voice quiet.

"I only realized it recently," she admitted, in between hiccups. "But that doesn't change anything. It is OUR fault he died. Your fault for not stopping him. My fault for not realizing he had a problem back when it mattered. When I could have helped him."

Chelsea had accused him before tonight of being the reason Chance died. He hadn't had the heart to betray Chance's memories and set her straight on Chance's drinking habits. He'd let her believe what she chose to believe. She hadn't been in any state to listen.

"Chelsea, if it hadn't been that day, it would've happened another time. Chance was out of control. He'd been talking about quitting vet school. He was depressed."

"No, I don't believe you!" she screamed. "If you had been there, it would never have happened. If I had been there, I could have stopped him. We could have helped him."

Finn paused and drew a deep breath. His hands clenched as he remembered his own feelings of helplessness where Chance was concerned.

"Chels, he didn't want to stop drinking. He did not want to. I couldn't make him, and you wouldn't have been able to either. He couldn't stop it."

"He didn't want to die."

Finn didn't say anything.

"Finn, he didn't want to."

"Chelsea, I don't think he wanted to die. But I also don't think he wanted to live."

She stared at Finn, her mouth open, and her face unbelieving.

"You are lying." She insisted. "You just won't accept the blame."

Finn's heart cracked in his chest.

"Chelsea, if you think you are the only one who blamed me for not being there to save him, you are wrong. I blamed myself too! Yes, Chance died that night, and we weren't there to save him. But he would have died anyway! We were never going to be able to be there all the time to save him."

"You're wrong. You are wrong."

"Chelsea, that night a wonderful person died. Your beloved brother, your twin, my best friend. But you know what? He was broken. And now we're broken too. A big part of you died that night. And a big part of me. But I decided to live. To live fully and happily and completely. When are you going to stop blaming yourself – and blaming me – for being happy on the night he died? When we were making plans for our future. Before we knew he had died? Why are you continuing to punish us both? Isn't one death enough?"

Finn was silently crying, the tears thick in his throat and sliding down his face. He was tired. Tired of being blamed. Tired of blaming himself. Tired of being alone. So tired.

"Get out!" Chelsea said quietly.

Finn bowed his head, squeezing his eyes closed.

"Get. Out. Leave. Now." she repeated, a little more loudly.

Finn left and didn't look back.

Chelsea stayed in bed the next morning. She couldn't bring herself to get up, to face the day. Exhaustion racked her body after years of holding her feelings in and then releasing them. She felt no better than before the conversation with Finn; if anything, she felt worse. She was still conflicted about Chance's death. She'd realized in the past several months that Chance drank a lot back then. When she recalled different memories, she could see him there, nursing a drink, always with a bottle nearby. She knew he'd been depressed. She just hadn't seen how far gone he was, not in time to help him. Was Finn right? Was she using blame – blaming him, blaming them – as punishment for not being there to stop Chance's death? Was their relationship the scapegoat?

"At least he'd been alone in the car," she said out loud. "No one else died except the tree he hit when he missed the curve at high speed."

No one else died.

But that wasn't quite true, was it? She had died, deep inside and so had Finn. Their relationship had died. Their plans for their future together. Their love, their hopes, their dreams. Those had died when Chance died. How would Chance feel if he knew? Was that what he would have wanted for them?

If the situation were reversed, would she have wanted that for him?

Would she?

She didn't know the answer. What used to be clear was muddy and distorted.

With those thoughts on her mind, she drifted into an uneasy sleep once more.

Finn spent the next day watching Chelsea's apartment for signs of life. He knew she needed time to process, but he wanted to keep watch in case she needed him. In the meantime, he cleaned his apartment and caught up on laundry before settling down to read a book, one eye on the words, one eye on Chelsea's door.

When he saw the kitchen light go on later that evening, he breathed a sigh of relief. He had no idea what was going to happen next after yesterday's conversation, but at least she was okay. That was a good first step.

He wasn't clear on his feelings. Old fragments of guilt merged with missing his best friend, losing the love of his life, and holding himself responsible for Chance's death. For letting Chelsea pull away from him. For allowing them both to deal with the aftermath alone. In the years it had taken him to realize that what he'd said to Chelsea was indeed true – that even if he had managed to save Chance that fateful night, he might not have been able to another time. He wished he'd known to connect Chance with mental health therapists or addiction counselors, or even AA but he wasn't sure how open Chance would have been to any of those. Chance had his own path to follow. Even with his troubles, he was still responsible for himself.

Finn's emotions were raw and vulnerable, his body ached and his thoughts circled in an endless spiral. He and Chelsea were reliving Chance's death repeatedly. He'd tried to make his own humble and tentative peace with it. Could she? And if she could, would she take a risk on him? On what they'd had? On what he knew they still had?

He didn't know the answer to any of those questions.

He wondered if this would affect their professional relationship and business contract. It was the biggest fear he had – that everything would be irrevocably broken. It was more than he wanted to think about right now. All it did was make him feel worse.

He'd see how Chelsea was in the morning when they were back at the clinic. With the new schedule, it would only be one day working together then he was covering the fieldwork for a few weeks. A break from each other might be a good thing.

As it turned out, the next day started with a bang. First, they had a dog hit by a car, then two euthanasia cases in a row – old sick cats who had survived surgeries but were fading quickly. It was after lunch before he ran into Chelsea and even then, it was only in passing as she paused at the desk to see who was next in the waiting room.

Finn met with Doc Olson before the old doctor took a few days off then headed into town for errands. When he got back, the clinic was closed for the day. He gazed up at Chelsea's drawn curtains and dejectedly headed home. *Give her time. Be patient.*

His first callout came a few minutes later and shortly after, he was heading north to the Olineski farm.

Chapter Five

C helsea heard the truck pull away from the clinic and realized Finn had gone without saying goodbye. That stung a little. A lot, she admitted to herself. It had been a busy day in the clinic and none of them had taken a break. Tossing together a chicken veggie salad and a big cup of tea, she tried to settle in with a blanket and a book.

She picked at half her salad before succumbing to the fact that she wasn't hungry. Her eyes kept dancing off the pages of her book, and she couldn't seem to relax. Her cell phone vibrated, announcing a call. She glanced at the caller ID. It was her mom.

"Mom?" Chelsea said.

"Hello sweetie," Elizabeth McCoy's voice brought moisture to Chelsea's eyes. She missed her even though Elizabeth had visited at Christmas, not that many months ago. She'd spent the past few years living in Lethbridge, caring for her older sister Agathe.

"Some sad news, I'm afraid," Elizabeth continued. "Aunt Agathe has passed away."

Oh, her poor aunt. She had suffered many years with dementia and the past months had brought a litany of physical issues as well.

"I'm so sorry, Mom."

"Me too," Elizabeth went on. "I will miss her. Very much. Now tell me how you've been, my dear girl."

To her utter horror, Chelsea burst into tears.

"Chelsea?" her mom's voice cut through her anguish. "Are you okay, love?"

"Oh Mom," Chelsea wept. "I'm...so confused."

There was a pause on the phone.

"Is it the shelter? Ryker told me about your plan with Finn," Elizabeth said. "I think it's marvelous and I support you wholeheartedly."

"Thanks," Chelsea blubbered. "No, no, that part is fine."

"Are you not well?" Elizabeth asked next.

"I've been thinking a lot about Chance," Chelsea managed to squeeze out the words.

"Ah," Elizabeth said. "Our sweet Chance."

"Mom, can I ask you a question?"

"Of course."

"Did you blame Finn for Chance's death? Or me?"

"What? Why, of course not, Chelsea. Why ever would you think that?"

Chelsea paused to wipe her nose before answering.

"We weren't there to stop him. To save him."

Elizabeth's voice was firm. "Chelsea, my love, no one was going to be able to stop our Chance. That boy was strong-willed and stubborn. His drinking was out of control.

He knew it, I knew it, and Finn knew it. We tried to help him but he didn't want to listen. He refused to accept that he had a problem."

"I didn't know it until recently," Chelsea admitted in a small voice.

"You always thought Chance was perfect, lovely," Elizabeth reminded her, her tone gentle.

"Hmm. I guess I did," Chelsea agreed.

"He wasn't. No one is. And no one, not even me, was going to be able to stop him until he decided to do so himself. He didn't want to go to AA, he didn't want to stop drinking. He kept telling us that it was under control and we were overreacting."

"Okay," Chelsea said, her voice small.

"Chelsea, have you been blaming yourself all this time? And blaming Finn? Is that why you broke off your engagement?"

Chelsea swallowed hard.

"Yes, I think so."

Her mom's sigh flowed through the phone. "Honey, I wish I'd realized that sooner. Believe me when I say that there was nothing you – or Finn – or I – could have done. We all have our demons, Chelsea. Alcoholism is a terrible disease. I think, eventually, Chance would have come to terms with accepting help to fight it but at the time, it was stronger than he was. His death was a horrible, terrible accident."

"Really and truly?"

"Really and truly. Cross my heart."

"Oh Mom, I've wasted so much time."

"Well, then, do something about it, dear," Elizabeth said frankly. "In the meantime, my love, I have a service to plan.

Aunt Agathe left specific wishes that I intend to adhere to. I'll be in touch with more details."

"Mom – do you need help?"

Chelsea could hear Elizabeth's smile over the phone. "No, dear, but thank you. We've known this was coming for several weeks. I am fine and your cousin Braden is here to help as well. You take care of you. I love you!"

"Thanks, Mom! I love you too." Chelsea's voice was lighter.

"Oh, and Chelsea? Say hello to Finn for me. I've missed that young man."

Me too, thought Chelsea. *Me too.*

"Yes, I will," Chelsea promised and ended the call.

For the next week, Finn got home well after dark and left each morning before dawn, as he attended to calls. While he enjoyed seeing the people in the area, he was surprised to discover he missed the steady pace of the clinic and being home for supper every night. Of course, that had everything to do with Chelsea.

Driving around the county allowed him lots of time to think. He still loved Chelsea, that was a given. He would do anything for her, including removing himself from her life to make her happy. Even if it broke his heart. Again. He'd lost her once. He could handle losing her again if that's what it took.

After several false starts, he mapped out an option they both could work with. Even though he preferred the in-town clinic work, he would stick with doing the fieldwork and change the search for a vet to include only the in-town portion of the practice. Doc would be fine to help for another month or so, and it might make the position more appealing to applicants if they knew it was ninety-nine percent in-town.

With him away most of the time, Chelsea could continue working part-time at the clinic as well as run the shelter, without fear of running into him. He'd make sure any in-town time was opposite her work schedule so the likelihood of working with each other was lessened. Their business arrangement could stay what it was. That would give her time before the shelter moved permanently and she took over its management to come to terms with their re-broken relationship.

It wasn't a perfect plan, but it came close. He could live with it. His heart was telling him no, don't do this, but his mind was set.

Once everything was in place, he'd present the plan to Chelsea. If she knew he wouldn't be around the clinic, it would ease any worry she had about running into him. Both of them could continue in their roles with the clinic and the shelter. Nothing had to change professionally.

Of course, on a personal level, they were broken and this time, probably irreparably.

Chelsea couldn't wait until Finn was home for more than a night. Since the phone call with her mother, the weight of Chance's death had lifted, and she couldn't believe how light she felt. Finn was right – she had allowed part of herself to die. He was right about many things.

Oh Finn. She'd been so wrong, and she hoped he would forgive her. It took everything she had not to phone him.

She knew her revelation was better delivered in person, face-to-face. At least then he couldn't hang up on her.

When he pulled into the clinic parking lot a few days later just before lunchtime, she was beside herself with joy. She dashed outside to meet him by the truck.

"Welcome home," she said, when he stepped out of the vehicle.

He reached into the back for his duffle. "This is a surprise," he said easily.

Chelsea shrugged. "I was hoping we could talk."

"I'd love to but first I desperately need a shower. I have an interview. I spoke with a young vet from Calgary who is interested in joining us. I'm meeting him in town this afternoon."

Chelsea's face fell but she recovered.

"Oh, that's great," she responded. "Maybe later or tomorrow then?"

"Sounds good," Finn replied and walked towards his apartment.

Chelsea's good mood morphed into a funk as she walked back to the clinic.

"How's the boss?" Gloria, the vet assistant, asked.

"Good, good. I guess he's interviewing a possible new doctor this afternoon."

"Oh, that's right," Gloria answered. "Craig Willmont. He'd been interested in the job before but wasn't too keen on the field work side. Now that Finn has changed the position to be in-town only, Craig's back on board."

Chelsea frowned. "What do you mean changed the position?"

Gloria's smile shrunk a little. "You know – with Finn deciding to stay in the field permanently and not switch off with another vet."

Wait, what? That was news to Chelsea. Big news, in fact.

"You'd think he'd have told his business partner," she mumbled.

Gloria looked embarrassed and glanced over at their receptionist.

"I'm sorry, Chelsea. I had no idea you didn't know."

"Not your fault at all," Chelsea hastened to assure Gloria. "I probably did know but it slipped my mind. Let's go check on that sweet mamma cat in the back. How is she feeling?"

By five o'clock, Chelsea was fuming. How could Finn not tell her what he was planning? Him staying out in the field was a big deal. What would that do to any possible relationship they might have, if he was gone all the time?

Wait and talk to him. He'll have a reasonable explanation for this. He probably just hadn't had time to tell her in the excitement of finding someone interested in the job. Even though he'd had time to tell their vet assistant and receptionist. Arrrgh.

The next morning when she rose, Finn's field truck was gone. She sighed. *Rats and double rats.*

The clinic was abuzz when she walked in. The receptionist beamed at her.

"Good morning, Chelsea. Isn't that great news about Craig?"

"Oh yes, "she agreed woodenly.

"And he can start almost right away. I'm looking forward to working with him. He's got great credentials and from what Finn says, sounds like a good fit for us. He called Gloria and me last night to let us know."

"Great fit for us," Chelsea agreed. "Great, great."

She headed to the back to prepare for the day, her mind in a fog.

"Isn't that great news about Craig?" Gloria, the vet assistant, exclaimed, as Chelsea gave the gleaming back counter an unnecessary swipe with a cloth.

"Oh yes. Great, great."

Gloria looked at her oddly. "Are you okay, Chelsea?"

"Yes, yes," Chelsea said. "I'm just freaking great."

At the end of the day, exhausted from smiling, she locked the clinic doors. Finn's truck pulled up as she made her way to her apartment, but she didn't bother to stop. She thought she heard him call her name but ignored it.

He can wait.

She stood in the hot shower for a long time, thinking. Why didn't Finn tell her his plans? She heard knocking on her front door but didn't acknowledge it. She wasn't up to facing him or anyone else.

She was in her jammies, curled up on the couch when she heard knocking again.

Sighing, she realized he wasn't going to give up.

She opened the door, just as he was heading down the stairs.

"Finn."

He turned and headed back up.

"Sorry to disturb you," he said. "You wanted to talk? Sorry. I've been a bit preoccupied."

Anger, disappointment, and frustration warred with the need to share her epiphany about them, about him.

Gazing at his handsome face, Chelsea threw caution to the wind.

"Come in, please," she invited, smiling.

"Okay," he agreed but his face was uncertain.

"Drink?" she offered brightly.

"No, thank you."

She girded her loins and gathered her thoughts. "Finn, I've been thinking a lot..."

"Me too, Chels."

"Yes, well, I want you to know that I don't blame you anymore for Chance's death."

Finn's eyebrows went up, almost to his hairline. "Oh, that's nice," he replied, slowly, his voice quieter than usual.

Chelsea frowned. "Nice? Nice? I forgive you, Finn. That's not *nice*, it's *fabulous*!"

"Oh, sorry. Thank you for forgiving me. I appreciate that."

What was happening here? This wasn't going the way Chelsea had planned. She tried again.

"Finn, you were right. It wasn't your fault or my fault – it wasn't anybody's fault, It just was what it was. I forgive you. It's a huge thing."

Finn's mouth pursed and his eyebrows furrowed. "You forgive me for Chance's death?"

There, now he was getting it. However, from the look on his face, Chelsea didn't know what was going on in his mind.

"Yes, and I am incredibly sorry I wasted all these years being angry."

"Me too," Finn said slowly, biting out each word as if it physically hurt him to speak.

"Chelsea, I've decided that I am going to stay on field-work permanently. Today I hired a vet who will look after the in-town work. That way you and I can continue our business arrangement but not have to see each other."

"Yes, yes, I heard, "Chelsea impatiently said. "Craig Willmont. Starting in a few weeks."

"Oh the girls must have told you."

"Well, it sure didn't look like you were going to," Chelsea retorted, still hurt by the omission.

Finn looked askance at her. "Chelsea, I am completely confused. You told me to get out. I thought you didn't want to be anywhere near me. This plan will solve that."

Chelsea wanted to stamp her feet like a three-year-old. *Why was this infuriating man not understanding what she was saying to him? This had gone so off the rails!*

"Finn. I. Forgive. You." She repeated slowly. "I forgive you. Didn't you hear me say that just now. We don't need a plan."

"I get that but it doesn't change anything," Finn replied. "There is too much that we can't get past."

"Yes, we can! We have gotten past it. We can be us again. I realized I was wrong for blaming you for Chance dying. It wasn't your fault. Don't you still love me?" Chelsea demanded.

Finn paused for a long time, not saying anything.

Chelsea's fear and anguish threatened to choke her. Her heart pounded. *What was going on.? Oh god no. Unless the worst thing possible was happening. Maybe he didn't hear what she'd said.* "Finn...do you still love me?"

He shook his head. "No, Chelsea, I don't. I'm sorry."

Chelsea couldn't believe her ears. He didn't love her anymore. Her vision blurred and she gasped out loud.

Finn stood abruptly. "Bye Chelsea."

She didn't even try to stop him. She just sat there, numb and shaking.

She was too late. Too late. Too late for love.

Chapter Six

I t took Finn three tries to close Chelsea's door. He stood outside, shaking. He wasn't quite clear on what had just happened. He replayed their conversation in his mind, unreasonable anger and frustration warring with his confusion and causing his head to pound. Bit and pieces of her words drifted in and out of his mind. *So, she finally forgave him, well whoop-dee-doo. Wasn't he supposed to be the one to forgive her for blaming him in the first place? Where did she come off forgiving him?*

He just out and out lied to the love of his life. Was he nuts? She said she loved him but somehow those words weren't penetrating. His head hurt and his heart thumped. Maybe he was having a heart attack? His left arm felt fine, so no. But something was going on with his heart and it wasn't good. He kicked the railing with his toe and trudged down the steps. He'd said what he'd come to say and it didn't matter. *Aargh.* Creating space between them would be the best solution. He'd already offered his apartment to Craig and found himself a place in town to

rent, at least for the interim. It would be easy enough to head
to the clinic from town to stock the truck with the veterinary
supplies as he needed them. As for him and Chelsea – well, that
was done. Over. Finished. Now he had to pack and get away
from here, the sooner the better.

Chelsea was in shock. Finn didn't love her anymore. What a
fool she'd been. She should have kept her mouth shut and her
heart sealed. She loved the clinic, with or without Finn. She
wanted to run the shelter. Nothing had changed, except any
possibility of reconciliation. That was a done deal.

Finn was off his rocker. Wasn't an apology what he wanted?
Wasn't that enough to make him love her again? And what
about her declaration of love? He'd acted as if he hadn't even
heard her. Was was that all about?

"Focus on work, Chelsea. You don't need Finn."

She could do this. She would do this. With or without Finn's
love.

Diving into her work over the next few days, she spent time
catching up on the temporary shelter's progress and paying a
visit to the county shelter. She walked through the aisles saying
hello to the rescues, pausing for pets and hugs where she could.
Her heart ached for these sweet souls. She longed for a pet of
her own and promised herself she would get a dog sooner than
later. She was looking for comfort, but their loneliness echoed
her own.

She was in the back of the clinic checking on the
overnighters when the door chime indicated a client. Knowing

the receptionist was out for a few minutes she headed to the front door only to stop dead in her tracks.

"Hello," the tall, blond and gorgeous man standing there said cheerfully. "I'm Craig, the new partner. And you are?"

"Chelsea, I'm Chelsea, Finn's other business partner," she managed to say, her heart hammering in her throat. Holy heck. Craig looked just like Chance. *Oh no, oh no.*

Numbly, she showed him into Finn's office and left him to get settled. Watching him covertly from the receptionist's desk, she dimly realized the resemblance was superficial, but it was there in the blue eyes, the big toothy grin, and the mop of golden hair.

"He's kinda handsome," Sammy, the receptionist, whispered into her ear, nearly causing Chelsea to jump out of her skin.

"Don't sneak up on me like that!" Chelsea hissed. "You nearly gave me a heart attack."

Sammy grinned. "Sorry, Chels," she giggled. "I'm back at my desk. He sure brightens up the office."

A moving van carrying Craig's personal effects arrived that afternoon. Chelsea knew from the office girls that Finn had moved out of the apartment but kept her distance. Her heart was already broken. Again. Why add fuel to that fire? Or kick a dog when he's down. Or, well, really any other cliché that came to mind. Move on or move out. Then she got angry at Finn all over again.

With that in mind, she approached Craig when the moving van pulled away. "Can I interest you in a welcome to the practice supper?" she offered. "There're a few great eateries in town."

Craig agreed to meet her in front of the clinic after work to head to town. Chelsea took her time to change into dressier clothes. She needed to feel better about herself, and sometimes nice clothes helped. *And sometimes they didn't.*

As they pulled away from the clinic, Finn's truck pulled in. Drawing up beside her, he indicated for her to roll down her window. She sweetly smiled as she did what he asked.

"Hello there," Finn leaned over to gaze into her vehicle. He looked past her to the passenger seat and nodded at Craig then turned back to her. "I see you've met Craig." His eyes narrowed as his gaze met Chelsea's. She didn't back down – she forced herself to continue smiling at Finn.

"Sure did. We're heading to town for supper."

"Ahh," Finn replied. "Maybe I'll join you...."

Chelsea inwardly panicked and made a quick decision. "Oh, I'm sure you're tired," she replied smoothly. "Next time." She floored the gas and pulled away from Finn's truck. She watched him in the rearview mirror as they drove away.

Craig chuckled and said "Oh, that's the way it is, eh?"

Chelsea snuck a glance at him. "What's what way?" she said, innocently.

"How long have you guys been together?" Craig asked, instead of answering her question.

Chelsea's mouth dropped open.

"Oh no no no, "she retorted firmly, with a laugh that even to her ears sounded forced. "We are so not together. You've got it all wrong."

Craig looked at her and tilted his head. "Do I, though?" he said softly.

Chelsea swallowed emotions better left unsaid and nodded.

***

Finn glared at the departing truck. So that's how it was going to be, he fumed. The first time his back was turned, Chelsea turned to the new guy. He parked his truck, seething.

Ummm, you told her you didn't love her. What did you expect?

"Not for her to pick up with the first Tom, Dick, or Craig that showed up," he grumbled aloud. "What's that all about?"

She should just sit home and be alone then?

"Yes, darn it," Finn snapped. "No, heck – geez, I don't know."

You are jealous. "I am not jealous!" *Yes, you are. You still love her.*

Finn rested his head on the steering wheel. Dang it. *He still loved her. Keeping his distance was not going to protect his heart. Dang it.*

He banged his hand on the horn repeatedly, swearing. The horn stuck and wouldn't turn off. Drat and drat again. He jumped out of the truck after opening the hood lever, trying to quiet the horn. Finally successful, he closed the hood. Walking back to the driver's side of the truck, he paused to gaze at his reflection in the side mirror.

What on earth had he been thinking? His solution seemed perfect in theory. Now all he would think about was Craig and Chelsea together. How had it gotten so messed up?

Craig was delightful company at dinner, but it took everything Chelsea had to smile and maintain her side of the conversation.

Once coffee had been served and dessert declined, she glanced at her watch.

"Somewhere else you have to be?" Craig asked, noticing her glance.

"I do have some shelter paperwork to do."

Craig nodded and asked for the bill. "Oh no," Chelsea shook her head. "I invited you, it's on me."

"Thank you," Craig replied. "It's not often I am treated to a meal." Chelsea was glad he didn't argue with her. Finn certainly would have. *Oh Finn. I miss you so much. You idiot.*

The ride back to the clinic was quiet but not in an awkward way. Craig headed for his apartment and Chelsea to hers.

She fell asleep on the couch not long after.

Chapter Seven

Chelsea's phone buzzed but she let it go to voicemail and pressed her head more deeply into the pillow. A sharp knock on the door startled her and she stumbled off the couch to open it. After a restless night filled with dreams of Finn and an impossible happily ever after, she was barely functional.

"Finn?" It was still dark! Why was he beating down her door in the middle of the night?

"There's a fire at the old shelter. Some of the animals have escaped. They're going to bring the others here to the clinic. Get dressed. We need to help."

Wide awake, Chelsea threw on warm clothes and hastily laced her hiking boots before slipping into her coat. As an afterthought, she grabbed packaged snacks and snagged two bottles of water.

Finn pulled out the second she climbed into the truck.

"Not sure how the fire started but I guess it's bad. We called as many volunteers as we could to move the animals. The fire department is on the scene managing the blaze, but the animals are an issue. Peace officers are helping, but they need more help."

They could see the blaze well before they pulled up to the barricades set up around the perimeter, the orange glow brilliant against the dark sky.

"Evening, Chief," Finn addressed the soot-streaked fire chief.

"Finn. Fire's not under control yet so can't let you any closer. Most of the animals that escaped headed that way. We aren't sure how many." Pointing towards the foothills, the chief shook his head. "Not sure how they'll fare but at least they are momentarily safe from the fire."

"Thanks. Chelsea and I will head that way. Craig and the girls are coming to take some animals to our new place. I have my radio for updates."

Reaching into the back of the truck, Finn grabbed a couple of portable cages, several leashes, and two backpacks. Chelsea donned one pack and Finn the other before heading into the darkness.

"There are headlamps in my bag," Finn directed. She rummaged and found them each one, pausing to attach them before they set off.

A few hundred yards up the way, they spotted a small glow in the underbrush. Finn motioned Chelsea to stop, and he crept towards the site after lowering the brightness on his headlamp. A few moments later, he emerged with a large tabby cat in his arms.

Quickly setting up one of the cages, Chelsea wrangled the terrified feline into the cage, then slid the straps over her shoulder.

Continuing their trek, they walked in silence, wanting to hear any noises that would alert them to more animals. They followed shrill yaps into a hilled area where they found a small dog tangled in the bushes. The dog was frantic as they approached but Finn was able to free the dog and clip on a leash. The dog scratched at Finn's leg until Finn picked it up, receiving licks and small growls in return.

Finn radioed their finds and advised that they would continue their search a while longer before returning to base camp with their animals.

Chelsea gazed around in awe. The night was gorgeous, the dark sky lit with shimmering stars and no moon. The moon would have aided their search but may also have led predators to their unfound escapees.

After more than an hour, Finn stopped. "Let's take a short break and reassess."

Chelsea was relieved to set down her backpack and small kennel. The load wasn't heavy, but it was cumbersome. Digging into his backpack, Finn removed cans of pet food and portable dishes. After offering food and water to the escapees, he spread out a groundsheet and invited Chelsea to sit. She handed him a bottle of water and a snack. Tucking the kennel and dog close to them, they sat in a small circle.

"Hopefully we can find more," she said softly. "Or maybe some of the other searchers will."

Finn nodded. "They will be terrified. Poor things." Chelsea heard the love in his voice for these living creatures and it stirred her heart. Such a caring man. She shivered. He turned as she shifted position, his face mere inches from hers. His eyes sparkled in the night, sending a different kind of shiver down her spine. Her mouth parted of its own volition and then

Finn's mouth was locked on hers, his sweet taste and gentle lip pressure doing crazy things to her heart and to be honest, her libido. She closed her eyes, willing the sensation to continue.

Suddenly, Finn drew away, and she opened her eyes, startled. He put a finger on his lips and touched his ear with the other hand. She strained to listen over the pounding of her heart. A whimper. Faint but there.

Finn indicated for her to stay still as he stood up. Taking the second kennel and a leash, he adjusted his headlamp and then moved silently toward the sound, pausing every few steps to listen. As he disappeared into the darkness, Chelsea put her lamp on low and hugged the trembling dog closer. "What's your name?" she wondered, moving her fingers around the collar, searching for tags. Peering at the one she found, she made out a word. "Leo?" she whispered. A small wag of his tail acknowledged his name. She pulled the small dog closer to her chest and let her chin rest on his head, enjoying the peace and warmth.

A howl sliced the night sky, followed by another, snapping her from her doze. Was that Finn? Or something else...something worse? The silence that ensued was worse than the noises themselves. She cuddled Leo closer and strained to hear. When her light caught Finn's shape appearing from the darkness, she expelled the breath she'd been holding. As he drew closer, she could see the kennel moving as he carried it.

"Thank goodness you're back!" Placing Leo gently by her feet, she hugged Finn as tightly as she could.

His face looked grim as he lowered the kennel to the ground then removed his backpack. "Coyotes found a few of the animals before I did. I have two dogs in the kennel. One's got a damaged leg. I did what I could for the others, but it was too late, I'm afraid." He swallowed hard. "These poor fellows are exhausted."

"Oh no." Chelsea moved to the kennel. Inside a German Shepherd cross and a black lab cross were smooshed together. The lab's front leg was wrapped, and she could see dark spots on his nose that were sure to be blood. She opened the door and neither dog moved. Finn handed her two small bowls of water that she placed by each animal's mouth. They lapped at it slowly but steadily. When they were done, she lifted the German Shepherd out of the kennel, and re-latched the door after ensuring the lab was comfortable. Clipping a leash to the German Shepherd's collar, she looked over at Finn for guidance.

"Let's head back." Finn drank deeply from his own water bottle. Laden as they were with the kennels, it took much longer on the return trip. Exhausted dogs on leashes didn't help either. The glow in the sky over the county shelter had lessened but firefighters were still on scene. She wept at the devastation – most of the shelter was gone.

As they loaded the animals into the clinic truck, one of the deputy chiefs approached them. "Thanks for your help," he said. "The other animals have been transported to your clinic." His soot-covered face looked tired, but his smile was genuine.

Finn shook the deputy chief's hand. "We'll take these ones over there now," he advised. "Any losses?"

The deputy chief grimaced. "Sadly, some of the cats. The fire started in the cattery. No known cause at this point. We'll take a few days to investigate. Gotta go. Thanks, again, Doc."

Chelsea smiled. "The new Doc, eh," she said to Finn. Finn grinned as he got into the driver's seat.

Finn was exhausted and glancing over at Chelsea, realized that she was as well. The animals in the back had quieted finally. He breathed a sigh of relief.

"Holy cow! Animals on the road! Hang on!"

Finn slammed the brakes as hard as he could and turned the wheel to the left. The action threw Chelsea forward and then back as her seat belt tightened. When the vehicle stopped, they were facing the ditch, parked sideways on the road.

"Are they okay?" Chelsea asked, her voice shocked.

Finn backed up the vehicle until the headlights illuminated the road ahead of them. A deer had been hit by a vehicle and killed, the body stark in the high beams. Huddled near it was a fawn, big eyes reflecting the light.

"Finn?" Chelsea breathed. "Do you think the baby is hurt?"

Finn shook his head. "I don't know. I'll go look." He started out of the vehicle and Chelsea opened her door as well.

"I'm coming with you." She hopped out before Finn could say no. Together, they crept towards the fawn, all the while talking softly. As they approached, the fawn sensed them and scampered onto unsteady legs. Finn couldn't see any damage to the small body or any visible blood. Loud barking shattered the stillness, causing the fawn to flee into the trees on the opposite side of the road.

Finn looked over at Chelsea. "Another shelter animal?"

Chelsea shrugged. "I'll go check," she said. Returning to the truck, she gathered her headlamp as well as a leash and her heavy gloves. Finn moved the truck to safety while she ventured into the woods. She could hear him chatting with Animal Control about the dead deer. So sad. Vehicles and roaming wildlife were never a good mix.

Casting her gaze as far as she could see, she made her way slowly through the trees. The barking had stopped but she could hear panting– the dog or dogs had to be close. Reaching into her pocket, she grabbed a handful of dog treats, intending to coax the lost wanderer. The next thing she knew, she was lying on the ground, breath knocked out of her. A huge dog slobbered over her, teeth grazing her palm where the treats had been. Grimacing from white-hot pain in her shoulder, she tried to rise and grab the dog's collar but suddenly, it bared its teeth and growled ominously. She wasn't going to win with this guy!

"Finn!" she yelled, with all the breath she could muster, her voice laced with pain. "Help!"

She could hear him running through the brush towards her. As he approached, the dog moved back, still growling, eyes glowing in the light of their headlamps. Finn followed the animal, chatting in a calm voice and moving slowly now.

"Be careful!" Chelsea managed. "He's a mean one!" She hated saying that about any animal, but this one was either hurt or starving or both. Any of those scenarios would make a dog furious. Trying to get up, she realized she'd smacked her shoulder against a gnarly stump. Excruciating pain radiated down her arm and side . She'd surely broken something.

Several seconds – or minutes later – Chelsea wasn't sure, Finn returned with a muzzle and leash on the dog. He gazed at her as he went by and realized instantly she was hurt. "Let me park this fellow in the truck and I'll come right back," he promised.

Chelsea closed her eyes. What a night. Warm tears ran down her face as she struggled again to sit up. Wasn't happening. She tried not to think about the pain in her shoulder and arm, concentrating instead on the sweet animals they'd rescued, even sending a prayer for the last mean one. She sent good wishes after the poor fawn, which made her cry more.

"Chels, I'm here," Finn said. He crouched beside her. "What hurts?" he asked, softly, his eyes moving across her body.

"My shoulder, my arm, " she whispered, her words broken by grunts of pain.

Finn paused for a moment. "I'm going to carry you to the truck. I'll wrap you in a blanket to stabilize your shoulder in case it's dislocated. Okay? Then I'll take you to the hospital."

"Okay," she agreed, then closed her eyes once more.

On the way home from the hospital, all Finn could think about was Chelsea. Her arm was broken just below the shoulder and her shoulder dislocated. She'd stay in the hospital the rest of the night. Craig had met him in the hospital parking lot to trade trucks and take the rescued animals to the temporary shelter at the clinic. Ashamed of his earlier annoyance at his new partner, Finn thanked him profusely and repeatedly.

Craig merely smiled and clapped him on the back, a knowing look on his face. "She's special to you," Craig said. "Anyone can see that. My pleasure to help out."

Finn's face flamed. Did everyone know how he felt about Chelsea? Why was he having such a hard time admitting it to himself?

When had things gotten so screwed up? Maybe when she told you she forgave you and you brushed it off? I was mad. Yeah, she said she forgave me but it was me who needed to forgive her for blaming me in the first place.

And have you?

Had he? The fear in his heart he'd felt when he'd realized she was hurt in the woods eclipsed every other feeling in his body. He loved this woman with all the parts of his being. He couldn't imagine a life without her. With a blinding jolt, Finn realized he had forgiven her. He'd truly forgiven her a long time ago.

Is it yourself you need to forgive, then? Do you blame yourself too?

Crikey! Finn slammed his hand on the steering wheel. He indeed blamed himself. He'd thought he'd put it behind him but deep down, he believed what Chelsea had believed – that if he or they had been there that night, they could have stopped Chance from driving, therefore saving his life.

Blast it all anyway. I didn't need her forgiveness – I needed my own.

Yup, you got it. You needed your own. Ding! Ding! Give the man a prize!

He headed to his place in town. When he walked into the almost bare apartment, he felt nothing. It wasn't home, it wasn't anything. Just like him without Chelsea.

He needed her in his life. He'd been a fool to pull away. He thought he was protecting himself, protecting her. All he was doing was hurting them both.

He had to fix this. And soon. But how?

Sinking onto the couch in the living room, his head in his hands, he contemplated his next steps. Yes, he desperately needed a shower and some food but those became minor compared to the mountain of a mess he'd made with Chelsea. And his plan. The plan that had backfired big time. Hiring Craig would become an issue if Craig didn't want to do any out-of-town calls - Finn had hired him to do the in-town work only. *Seemed like a good idea at the time.* He'd have to approach Craig and see if they could work out a different deal – maybe half and half, at least to start. Or offer to break their contract. Finn couldn't bear the thought of being away from Chelsea for that many hours each week. Even if it meant losing Craig for the clinic.

Of course, *if* Chelsea wouldn't believe that he really did love her, it didn't matter either way. He still owed it to Craig to be transparent and professional. It was the least he could do.

Through his own foolhardiness, Chelsea thought he didn't love her anymore. Would she ever forgive him for lying to her? He needed support. Maybe her family could help. Searching through his phone, he found Ryker's cell number. Hands shaking, he pressed the numbers.

"Hey there, Ryker, Finn here," he said. "I screwed up big time and I wonder if you could help me figure out how to make it right?"

Finn could hear Ryker pause, then a loud guffaw. "Let me take a wild stab at it...Chelsea?"

Finn nodded before remembering he was on the phone.

"Yes. Chelsea. I need help fast... "

For the next several minutes, he listened to Ryker's suggestions. When they finally hung up, Finn smiled to himself. He had a new plan. Now he needed to convince Chelsea that he was the man for her.

Easier said than done.

Chapter Eight

The next few days brought clear skies and sunshine. Chelsea had to spend a few weeks sleeping on her recliner so as not to disturb her broken arm. She hadn't seen Finn since he'd taken her to the hospital – she needed to thank him and so much more. Bored after a week in the apartment, sleeping and healing, she walked over to the clinic. Finn's company truck was missing but she assumed he'd gone out on a call. She was too busy introducing Craig to local pet owners for the next while as they showed up for their appointments to think about Finn. She did learn that Finn and Craig had done emergency surgeries on the injured animals she and Finn had rescued, as well as the ones rescued by other members of the community. Their recovery area was full but it looked like all of them would survive.

The staff from the county shelter had taken care of the animals relocated from the fire. She was grateful for their help and happy that the new shelter was complete enough to accommodate all of the animals. While she was in her office, she worked out a schedule for 24/7 staffing for the shelter, made easier by the fact that most of the current shelter workers were willing to continue employment with Finn and Chelsea.

After a few hours, she asked for a ride to the McCoy ranch. She needed to go somewhere to clear her head, and home was always a good place to start. Sammy dropped her off out front and Chelsea breathed deeply of the air on the ranch. She headed into the kitchen, not passing anyone on the way. She glanced out the window, seeing Mac's wheelchair and a few of the ranch workers – and was that Finn? Why on earth would he be here? Unless there was a problem with one of the ranch horses? She stepped carefully into a pair of rubber boots from the back door cubbies before heading out. As she rounded the corner of the house, she saw Mac rolling her way, with Ryker at his side. No one else. She must be imagining things, she thought. Yikes.

"Hey broken-arm girl," yelled Mac. "What brings you to the ranch?"

Ignoring him, Chelsea stepped into a warm hug from Ryker, melting into his familiar embrace. Brothers may not always be good for much, but the hugs were a godsend.

"You doing okay?" Ryker asked, holding her face in his hands to examine it. "You look tired. How's the arm?"

Chelsea swallowed the tears that crept into her throat and shook her head. "No, I'm not okay," she admitted, swiping at the few tears that escaped her eyes. "My arm hurts and I..."

'Wanna sit and talk about it?" Mac offered. Ryker nodded. "We have time now if you like."

Chelsea leaned over carefully, enveloping Mac in a big one-armed hug. "I could really use some brotherly advice, thanks."

A while later, sitting in the front living room, after spilling her guts and ending with "So that's that," she felt better.

Her brothers looked at each other and then Ryker said, "And you are good with that?"

"No, but what else can I do? I really do love him. I've spent so many years blaming him for Chance's death. And now it's too late. He fell out of love with me." Tears streamed down her face again.

Ryker rose to get her a new box of tissues. "Hmm," he said. "That's unfortunate. What are your plans then?"

Chelsea stared at him. "Plans? I have no plans. I'm locked into a business agreement with a man who barely tolerates me and who I still love. Not really a win-win from where I'm sitting."

Mac nodded. "Yeah, I can see that. Would talking to him about it again work, do you think?"

Chelsea shook her head. "I wish it would but I seriously doubt it."

Mac persisted. "But if it could work, what would you say to him?"

Chelsea groaned. "I'd ask him to forgive me for blaming him in the first place, then ask if there was anything I could do to earn his love again."

Mac nodded. "Good start."

"But Mac, I doubt if he will even talk to me."

Ryker jumped in. "Chels, you never know what goes through a man's mind. All I can tell you is that love, once given, seldom disappears. Pride, hurt, fear – those things come into play to mask that love but the love is still there, deep down."

Chelsea stared at him. "That sounds like you know exactly what I'm going through. Something happening that I don't know about, Ryk?"

Ryker smiled. "We all have our secrets. All I meant was that sometimes love hides behind other emotions."

"Why don't you give him some space before you talk to him again? He probably needs time to process what's happening and realize the truth himself," Mac advised.

"Good plan. Thanks, guys. Tears aside, it feels good to share that with you. I appreciate your ears. And your lack of judgment." She glared pointedly at Mac, her biggest critic when they were younger. He just laughed.

"Time to go. Can you drive me home, Ryk?" As she rose, she caught movement outside the big south window. "Who was that?"

Ryker glanced outside. "I don't see anyone," he remarked. "Are you sure that you're all right?"

Chelsea slapped his arm with her good hand. "Yes, I think I am." He grinned and patted her head.

The next morning, as she walked to the clinic, she noticed a sign on the path to the temporary shelter structure. 'Path closed for maintenance.'

Craig was not in, so she and Gloria handled the morning clients. After lunch, Craig was handling two surgeries then a last-minute rabbit incident that resulted in them working late. It was dark by the time she locked the clinic doors.

Walking past the path to the rescue, she noticed the sign she'd seen earlier was down. She could see twinkling lights lining the pathway. Making sure her Maglite was in her pocket in case she needed more light, she walked along the path. A tarp had been thrown over the geometric dome, but she could see faint light from within. The doors to the temporary structure were locked, as were the ones to the permanent shelter.

That's so odd, what is going on?

"Good evening."

She squealed. Jeepers creepers! She almost jumped out of her skin.

"Finn?" she whispered to the dark shape in the shadows.

"Yes, it's me. Come on in, I want to show you something." He disappeared further into the darkness.

Chelsea crept forward, reaching with her good arm to move the tarp so she could go inside. She barely touched the tarp when it slid right out of her hand and completely off the dome. Her breath caught in her throat as she gazed inside. Fairy lights lit every part of the dome, twinkling in a myriad of colors. A portable fireplace was set up on one side, with a thick furry rug on the hearth and thick fluffy blankets. A glass table set for two – champagne with elegant crystal flutes, roses everywhere, a tray of charcuterie, and strawberries dipped in chocolate.

And Finn. Her heart trembled.

Finn wore pressed black jeans with a long-sleeved black sweater molded to his torso. He stepped forward and took her hand, leading her to a comfortable-looking chair beside the glass table.

"Welcome," his voice was just above a whisper.

"What is this?" Chelsea asked, confused.

"This, Chelsea, my love, is an apology, an affirmation, and a proposal rolled into one."

What? Was he joking with her? She lifted her eyes to his and saw nothing but shining love. For her.

Her heart beat wildly and her breath caught in her throat.

"I thought you didn't love me anymore. Remember?"

Finn shrugged as he leaned over to fill her champagne flute. "Hmm. About that..."

Chelsea held her breath and waited. One second turned into two, turned into ten, turned into an eternity.

Finn knelt on the ground beside her, close enough to touch. Her hand inched toward him and she pressed it into her thigh to keep it still. She didn't dare interrupt this moment.

"Chelsea, I love you. I loved you yesterday. I love you today and I will love you all the tomorrows that we are gifted. I have never stopped loving you."

Chelsea let out a ragged breath.

"Why did you say you didn't love me anymore then?" A tear slipped down her cheek.

Finn gently touched the tear with his fingers.

"I lied," he said simply. "I was hurting and frustrated, and I didn't know what to do. I thought it would be better to stay away. I thought that was what you wanted. So I lied."

Chelsea gazed into his eyes and something shifted deep inside as if their souls connected.

"And how did that work out for you?" she teased.

Finn chuckled and kissed her. "Not well," he admitted. And kissed her again.

He took her hands in his.

"Chelsea, darling Chelsea. I love you with all my heart. Will you please forgive me and marry me before I do something even more stupid?"

He opened his hand, a sparkling engagement ring on his palm. The one she'd thrown back at him after Chance died. The one she'd said she didn't want.

She paused, taking in every inch of his beautiful kind loving face. Her Finn.

"Yes, yes, I will."

He gazed at her swollen left hand for a moment, then without missing a beat, he reached for her right hand. "This one will do," he said, as he slid the ring onto the ring finger.

She stood, leaning into his embrace, soaking up his essence, his Finn-ness, his strength, his warmth, his love.

The fairy lights seemed to pause for a moment then sparkle more brightly, as if the universe, or maybe her departed twin, wholeheartedly approved.

Chelsea smiled at Finn with happy tears in her eyes.

"Chance sends his blessing," she whispered. "I love you, Finn."

"Thanks, Chance," Finn said seriously. They raised their flutes to the sky and gave a silent toast to the man they'd lost and the love they'd finally found again together, forever.

Chelsea paused. "Oh," she said, covering her mouth with one hand. "I forgot..."

Finn stepped back, a look of angst on his face. "Oh, please don't change your mind..."

"Oh no, I won't do that," she laughed. "But I do have to tell you about Leo."

Finn groaned. "Another man?"

Chelsea grinned. "Kind of," she concurred. "But I think you'll like this one. He's going to be part of our family."

She pressed her lips against his once again.

The End

About Lynn Gale

Lynn Gale has dreamed about writing romance ever since she read *If This Is Love* by Anne Weale in 1972. Years went by and she fell in love with romance all over again watching movies like *Romancing the Stone*, *American Dreamer*, and *Pride and Prejudice.*

Her first sweet romance novella *A Heart Creek Christmas* was published in 2023 as part of *A Cowboy This Christmas: A Sweet Romance Anthology* through the Calgary Association of Romance Writers of America (CaRWA) under the pen name Joanie Wilde. This novella will be released as a stand alone title in February 2025.

A Heart Creek Second Chance can be read as a stand alone title and also as part of the ongoing series *Return to Heart Creek*.

Acknowledgements

This book would not have been possible without the assistance and support of many people in my life.

My mentor romance author Katie O'Connor, who has been instrumental in guiding me through the process of learning to write. She is my first reader and I am truly grateful for her direction and support, and for introducing me to my editor and my writing software Atticus.

My editor Terri St. Clair, for her thoughtful comments and excellent editing.

My cover designer Laura Heritage of P.S. Cover Design & Author Services for the gorgeous covers for the Return to Heart Creek series.

My family for their love and support. I love you all so much!

My sister Anne – remember when we wanted to be authors? It's happening!

My super fan and dear friend Anne Marie – yes, there is a fine line between fan and stalker!

My amazing island bestie Pat – miss you always.

My readers – without you, these are just words on a page. Thank you for your support and for hanging in there with me while I develop my craft.

xxoo Lynn

A Heart Creek Reunion

BOOK THREE - RETURN TO HEART CREEK SERIES

LYNN GALE

WINDSONG PUBLISHING CANADA

In memory of my dear friends Tonette Hauck and Pat Wankiewicz.
Gone too soon, missed every day.

xoxo

· ❤ · ❤ · ❤ · ❤ · ❤ ·

Contents

Chapter One

Craig Willmott shrugged his shoulders, moving his neck from side to side. It had been a busy night at the veterinary clinic with back-to-back emergency calls. He desperately needed caffeine and sleep, preferably in that order. As he drove into the small town of Heart Creek, he pulled up to Homegrown Café, grateful that they opened at five-thirty a.m. The smell of fresh baked bread tantalized his nostrils as he entered the cozy warm interior and headed for the counter.

"Large, no make that an extra-large vanilla latte please, and a loaf of whatever is fresh... and a blueberry scone."

The café's owner Rosemary's pleasant face broke out in her usual big smile. "Rough night, Doc?" she asked as she expertly prepared his coffee, the hum of the machine breaking the cozy, relaxed ambiance the café instilled. She added a few sprinkles of cinnamon and lidded his cup, sliding it across the polished counter to him with a practiced hand. Seconds later, a still warm loaf of sourdough nestled in a brown paper bag and a smaller bag with a puffy scone joined the coffee. He reached for his wallet, and she waved him away, her blond ponytail bouncing with her movements.

"On the house. Your money's no good here, cowboy. We don't charge family and you're close enough." Rosemary was his partner Finn Buchanan's sister, and known to be more than generous to the local community.

"Oh Roe, you're the best I know," he sang as he gathered the bags and tipped his imaginary hat to the young woman. "Thank you," he added, more seriously. "Much appreciated."

She winked. "Get some sleep, Doc. You look like you need it."

"Yes, ma'am." He inhaled a deep gulp of sweet coffee. "You really are the best."

"Get on with you! And tell that brother of mine to stop by sometime. Haven't seen him in ages." She shook her tea towel at him. Laughing, he managed to get back in the truck with his latte intact before eating the scone in three bites. The sun wasn't up yet as the fall days were still growing shorter, but the soft glow over the mountains promised a glorious day.

Buzzing woke him six hours later. On his way to the shower, he passed the kitchen counter. Eyeing the loaf of fresh bread still in a brown paper bag, he envisioned gourmet sandwiches. In reality, he merely slathered locally made butter and raspberry jam on a hunk of bread. It was delicious and he debated a second slice before good sense took over. After showering, he gazed out the window that overlooked the clinic parking area, while his coffee brewed. There were a few cars, but nothing crazy. He breathed a sigh of relief. One of the perks of the job was this small apartment, located above one of two tall double garages. It was sparse but had everything he needed, with the added benefit of being right next door to the clinic. Chelsea and Finn currently lived in the other apartment, which was bigger than the one he was in. He didn't mind. He didn't need much.

Pouring the coffee into an insulated travel mug and adding a generous splash of milk, he gathered what he needed for the day and headed out. For the umpteenth time in the past three months, he thanked his lucky stars that Finn hadn't taken no for an answer after Craig had initially turned down the offer of a partnership in Finn's veterinary practice. Heart Creek felt like home, and he continued to be amazed by the warm welcome he received from the residents and surrounding area ranchers and farmers. Finn and his fiancée Chelsea, the third partner in the practice, were easy to work with. Most of all, Craig enjoyed helping animals. Loneliness crept in now and again, but having grown up as an only child, being lonely wasn't unfamiliar territory to him.

Locking the door and heading down the stairs, he continued musing. Did he want a family? Yes, and no. It was complicated but either way, at thirty-seven, he may have missed that boat. He had almost been engaged once but the relationship hadn't developed as he'd hoped. He enjoyed the company of women, but with the traveling he'd done across the country and in the States for several years, Heart Creek was the most settled he'd ever been. Even spending a year in Calgary had felt more like a pit stop than a home. Heart Creek was the real deal and the closest to home he'd found in years.

"Good day, Craig," Chelsea's sweet voice rang out behind him as he walked across the parking lot. "Did you manage to get some sleep?"

"Sure did," he indicated his travel mug. "Brought provisions to keep me awake.

"Finn's still sleeping. He got in about an hour after you. Sadly, the McPherson's cow didn't make it, but the heifer calf is healthy and there's another mama cow who will nurse her."

Craig reached over and gave Chelsea a small hug. They'd started off on an awkward footing when she tried to use him to make Finn jealous, but they'd become fast friends and good colleagues.

"I hate it when they die." Her voice was muffled against his chest. As an animal health tech, she knew only too well how hard it was to lose an animal of any kind.

"Me too, but it's part of what we do. We can only do our best, then the rest is up to God and the universe."

"I've seen you cry, too, big man! You aren't as tough as you think you are. Finn either."

"Too true that, but we can pretend, right? Otherwise, it's bad for my tough-guy image!"

"Is that you trying to steal my fiancée again, doctor?" Finn's deep voice boomed from the open window of the apartment over the garage. He made the 'I've got eyes on you' gesture while pointing at Craig.

"I can take you out, man," Finn growled.

Craig laughed. "Not in your jammies, you can't!" he mocked, then ran inside the clinic, fallen leaves swirling. Once inside, he regained his composure, smiling at Sammy the receptionist as he made his way to his office. The clinic was old but clean and bright, with large windows overlooking farmland and the front parking lot. He and Finn each had their own small office.

Starting up his computer, he looked over the schedule for the rest of the day and exhaled. Three appointments, but they were slightly difficult ones. It was going to be a busy one. He headed back to check in with the vet assistant to see how the animals recovering from surgery were faring.

Whistling a tune that was sure to drive the vet assistant crazy, he felt his body relax. Life was good in Heart Creek.

Avery McCoy-Dushane stood in front of the wall, mesmerized by the red circled day on the calendar. August 8th, Josh's funeral. That day had been an endless blur of people. Friends and family, folks she didn't know, and some she hadn't seen for years. Warm tears tickled her lips as she thought of her sweet boys with no dad and herself a widow at thirty-seven. A far cry from three months ago when her life had been stable, or at least as stable as a rocky marriage could be. She knew that after ten years together, it was natural for a couple to have some rough patches – they had before and always managed to work things out.

This time, it would be different. There was no coming back. "Ouch!"

As she ripped the August page off the calendar, blood welled on her thumb. A paper cut. Seriously? Giving the page a dirty look, she crumpled it into a ball and threw it into the garbage bin, shaking her head. It was September now and she needed to move forward. Running her hand under cold water, her mind replayed their last conversation on the morning of Josh's death. He'd been heading north to help with the forest fires. As a licensed pilot and certified Air Attack Officer, he was often called away from the ranch, happy to lend a hand. On that particular morning though, she was tired; the kids were sick with colds again, and she was less than enthusiastic about him leaving. Her last words to him were thrown out as he left the house. *"Family should come first. But do what you need to do. You care more about helping strangers than being with us."* He hadn't replied, merely got into his truck, and left for the airport. That was the last time she'd seen him alive. Later that evening, his Cessna 208B had crashed en route to gathering information on the massive wildfire in northern Alberta.

It was a freak accident, but she blamed herself for what she'd said to him that morning. Did those words contribute to his state of mind while he was doing his job? Maybe. Maybe not. Either way, she was here now, without him, with no idea what she was going to do.

Patting her hand dry, she reached into the drawer for a bandage. Her tummy rumbled, reminding her she needed to eat something.

Slicing a loaf of sourdough and popping a slice into the toaster, she opened the cupboard that held an assortment of teas. Frozen, she couldn't decide, and tears flowed again. Gripping the countertop, she wept, thoughts running wildly through her exhausted mind.

Financially, she knew they were fine. Life insurance ensured that she had a healthy bank account balance to see her and the boys through many years. More than healthy – she was a wealthy woman, which was ironic considering that money was one of the things they had argued about. Josh had wanted to expand the ranch, and she'd resisted. He wanted to renovate the riding stable and add more stalls so they could take in more boarding horses. He also wanted to move closer to his dream of a farm-to-plate eatery on site. While she loved teaching horseback riding and being near horses, she craved something different, something fresh.

Now she had enough money to do whatever she wanted.

Wiping her eyes and checking that the twins were still asleep; she reached into the cupboard and selected a random box. Turning the kettle on, she busied herself with getting a cup and buttering her toast. A steaming cup of chai in her hands, she sank into a chair and gazed out the window at their ranch.

Correction. Her ranch.

Her thoughts cascaded into tumbling blocks of questions. What was she going to do? She had a teaching degree and had taught for ten years before the boys were born, choosing to stay home with them after they were born rather than return to her job. She loved having her own classroom and found the upper elementary kids she'd taught fun and interesting. While they had tried for children from the start, she'd suffered two miscarriages before becoming pregnant with the twins and left her position when she was twenty weeks along because of health concerns for both herself and her babies. Fortunately, the boys had been born without incident at thirty-six weeks.

They were probably going to be her only children.

Wow, where did that come from? Avery knew she had much to be grateful for, but her heart and mind were grieving not only for the man she'd lost, but for the time they'd spent angry and arguing over the past few years. Looking after the boys didn't help, as they were often sick and one or the other usually needed undivided attention from at least one parent. Time alone to concentrate on only each other was rare and usually spent sleeping, as was typically the case with parents with small children.

Her phone vibrated, and she glanced at it to see a textmessage from her sister Chelsea.

How are you doing, Ave? Been thinking about you.

Chelsea and her fiancé Finn had recently reconciled after many years apart, and Avery couldn't be happier for her younger sister. It had been hard on all of them when Chelsea's twin Chance, had died, but especially on Chelsea. Now she and Finn were building a rescue center at their veterinary clinic and Avery was creating items to sell in the rescue shelter boutique. Or at least she had been before Josh's accident.

Avery's hand paused before she texted back, *I'm okay.*

That bad huh? read the quick reply. Avery managed a small smile. Her sister knew her well and that *okay* actually meant *not good*.

She picked up the phone and pressed her sister's number.

"Hey. What are you doing up so early?"

"Finn's out on an emergency call. Are the boys asleep?"

"Yes, thankfully. I'm drinking tea and thinking."

"Oh, sweetie, you need to stop blaming yourself. I know this is tough on you. What can I do to help?"

"Just hearing your voice is nice. Truly."

A sudden barking came over the line. "Hello Leo," she cooed into the phone. Chelsea's rescue pup, Leo, was a welcome addition to the family after a horrific fire incident at the old county shelter back home in Heart Creek. At one time, Avery had wanted to run a rescue shelter herself, or at least a kennel, but they'd decided to go with horses and the kennel had never materialized.

"Sorry! He wanted to talk to Auntie Avery. Such a brat!"

Avery sipped her tea as her sister regaled her with stories about Leo and other rescue pups in the new shelter. By the time the conversation ended fifteen minutes later, she felt a little more grounded.

"Mama!" Her sweet Eric was in the doorway, his blanket trailing behind him and teddy in his arms. "I'm not sleepy anymore."

Gathering his soft, warm body to her, she hugged him and gave him a big kiss. He wriggled in her arms. "I'm hungry."

Chapter Two

Loading the dishwasher after her financial advisor left, Avery paused. He'd reiterated that she and the boys were taken care of financially, then reminded her that she still had a list of places to contact about Josh's death. She'd forgotten, but thankfully the list was shorter than she'd feared.

Her three-year-old twins were with Josh's parents for the day. Bernie and Tasha were lovely people, and she was grateful to have them there for their grandsons. Unfortunately, being alone gave her more time to think.

What did she want to do? The ranch had been Josh's dream. Being there without him felt meaningless and empty. Her head ached at the thought of resuming her life on the ranch on her own with the boys. Without Josh, her heart just didn't want to do it. Despite their rocky relationship, she still loved him. She wasn't in love with him and hadn't been for a long time, but he was the father of her children, and she would always love him for that.

She could move. Standing up, gazing out the window at the ranch, her heart stirred. This was Josh's dream. Not hers. She could build a new life with her boys. A warm sensation flooded her body for the first time in ages. It felt a little bit like hope.

Maybe it was time to move back home. Most of her family lived in Heart Creek, where she'd grown up. Her sons didn't understand that daddy was never coming home yet. Everywhere Avery looked these days, there were reminders of Josh. It was almost more than she could bear.

She needed to reunite with her family. She needed a fresh place to start over, but where there were familiar people and good memories. And time for her and the boys to make new memories. Avery reached for the phone to call her ranch manager.

"Hello, Dan, how are you?" Arranging a meeting with Dan for the following day lit a fire inside her. Her last call was to a local realtor who didn't seem shocked to hear from her.

The ball was rolling. She and the boys were moving on.

Three weeks later, Avery smiled at her twins, safely secured in their car seats in the SUV. The back of the Expedition was loaded to the ceiling with clothes, toys, books, and the rooftop carrier was also bulging at the seams with more books and other paraphernalia. She went over everything in her mind one more time. The plan was to stay with Ryker at the family ranch house until her own ranch was sold. Then, and only then, she'd decide whether to stay in Heart Creek and buy her own place or move somewhere else. Ranches didn't move quickly in the current market, so she'd have several months to find her feet. The family ranch house was more than big enough for all of them. Mom had recently moved back from Lethbridge after the death of her sister, whom she'd cared for, over the past several years. Avery's brother Mac was there with his fiancée Carrie, establishing his Heart's Haven rehab project for former rodeo riders. Their dad had passed many years prior but most of the people she loved best were still there.

Breathing deeply, she turned to look at the ranch house bathed in October's autumn glow. After almost three weeks of preparation, she hoped she wasn't making a huge mistake relocating to Heart Creek, but she knew that staying here on the ranch was not an option. Not without Josh, and especially not with the memories of Josh lingering nearby.

"Mama!" Landon's plaintive wail permeated her thoughts.

She turned with a smile to her son. "Hey baby, what's up?"

He scrunched his face at her and mimed his hands on a steering wheel. "Go!"

Oh, her sweet impatient son–but he was right. It was time to go. She climbed into the driver's seat and fastened her seatbelt. As they pulled away, it took all she had not to look back.

"Wow, a welcoming party!" Avery drove up the curved front driveway to the ranch and parked in front of the main house with the covered wraparound deck. The first-floor picture windows reflected the snowcapped mountains to the west. Stretching, she gazed in the rearview mirror, noting that both boys were fast asleep as they had been for most of the drive. Quietly opening her door and unfastening her seat belt, she stepped out, breathing in the cool fresh air, layered with farm and country smells. The ranch was as beautiful as she remembered. She could see the barns in the distance, the dark shapes of horses in the fields, the trees alive with autumn yellows and oranges. Seconds later, she was caught in an enormous hug.

"Avery!"

She hugged Chelsea back. "Didn't expect to find you here, sis!"

"I wanted to help. Craig was nice enough to drive me over."

"Hi there. I'm Craig Willmott, the new vet." She stopped and turned toward the deep voice.

Oh my! Their brother Chance had risen from the dead and was standing right in front of her in the parking lot. Shaking her head, she peered again at the tall blond man. Definitely not Chance, but goodness gracious, the resemblance was astonishing and, at first glance, unnerving. On closer inspection though, the similarity was slight.

"You okay? You look like you've seen a ghost."

Avery swallowed and tried to speak. "Sorry, you just reminded me of someone. Someone who died a long time ago. I'm Avery, by the way."

"My condolences for your loss. I'm sure it's been rough on you."

Avery nodded, tears thickening her throat. "Thank you. We all miss our brother."

She looked into his eyes and a second shock resonated to her core. *Wowzers. Who was this handsome guy and what was going on with her? His voice tickled her spine in a way that made her toes curl. Definitely NOT her brother Chance.*

He paused too, holding her gaze for a long moment. The electricity between them was palpable, and she felt her knees going weak.

He cleared his throat. "I meant your husband. I understand he died a few months back?" Craig's face was confused.

"Yes, yes, my husband, Josh. Yes, he did. Uh, thank you. I thought you meant my brother." Her voice trembled. So, this is what love at first sight is like, she thought crazily, before her mind slammed rational thoughts right down on top of that feeling. What in heaven's name was happening? She took a few deep breaths and steadied herself.

Craig walked over to her SUV and opened the back hatch. "I'll start unloading," he offered.

At that moment, Landon woke up. "Mama?" he called. Avery and Chelsea opened the doors, and each one took a twin. Then they walked over to the deck where their brother Ryker now stood.

"Hey big brother." A second hug, this one massive, almost brought tears to her eyes.

"You look tired," Ryker said, peering at her face.

Avery sighed and shrugged. "You know how it is." She rested her cheek on his broad warm chest, the soft flannel of his plaid shirt comforting and familiar. Like the air, the scent of the farm lingered on his body and was the best welcome she could imagine.

Ryker hugged her tighter. "Welcome home," was all he said. Then he went to help Craig unload the overflowing vehicle.

Chapter Three

A week later, it was as if Avery and the boys had lived on the ranch forever. She was in the upstairs bedroom she'd shared with Chelsea as a girl, her twins next door, with a shared bathroom between them. Ryker had disassembled the bunk beds that the sisters had slept in as children, giving each boy a low bed with a side rail. Somehow, though, each morning, both boys ended up in the same bed. Avery didn't care, as long as they slept, it didn't matter to her where.

She was blessed with a big double bed, so she had plenty of room to stretch out while she slept or read – since sleep was still a fleeting friend. It was wonderful having help with the boys – between Ryker, her mother, and Moira, the housekeeper who was more like family than an employee – she'd barely had to do anything except play with her boys and cuddle for story times.

Today was special. She was going to tour the new animal rescue facilities with Chelsea and check out the boutique. Avery had plans for a line of herbal pet shampoos and lotions, as well as adding to her collection of jewelry for pets and their owners.

She loved creating with metal, stones, crystals, and hemp rope, but hadn't made any new jewelry for weeks. It was time to get back to life. Her life.

Grateful that her mother had encouraged her to sleep in, she sauntered down the oak stairs, savoring the delicious smells coming from the kitchen and the waves of nostalgia being back home brought. Below, she heard her sons' giggles.

"Moira, you are a godsend." Avery walked into the large kitchen, neatly sidestepping a pile of toys, and avoiding Ryker as he swung past her. He grinned and patted her head. Tall as she was, he was taller, and he never tired of reminding her of that fact.

"Good afternoon." His deep voice rumbled, laced with laughter.

"Hey, it's only 10," she retorted, before she realized he was teasing her. Snatching a piece of bacon from the plate on the table, she squatted down to hug her sons and steal sticky maple syrup kisses. In spite of their squeals, she grabbed a cloth and wiped their faces and hands.

"Coffee, Avery?"

She smiled yes at Moira and gave the older woman a grateful hug. Moira's round face blushed as she busied herself handing Avery a clean mug, pointing to the full pot on the counter. "Help yourself."

"Hey, okay if I take the boys to the barn?" Ryker paused in the doorway, his worn brown Stetson in one hand.

"Sure, take the Expedition," Avery replied, in between sips of glorious dark roast. "The keys are in the bowl in the front hall. Do you need a hand with the car seats?"

Ryker blew a raspberry as he walked away. "Been doing it all week," he muttered. "Think I can handle it."

Avery started. Of course, he had been, and she hadn't even acknowledged his help with keeping the boys occupied. "Thank you," she hollered after him.

Moira patted her shoulder. "It makes him happy," she said to Avery. "He hates feeling helpless. This is one way he can lend a hand." Moira's warm brown eyes were soft as she spoke.

Avery grinned, knowing Moira was right. Suddenly, a plate of pancakes, sausages and eggs appeared before her. "Oh, I don't…"

"Today you do." Moira smiled broadly and left Avery to eat. A few minutes later, Avery could hear her rustling in the spacious pantry. "Cookies, I think. Those babies could use some sweet stuff."

Family, Avery thought wryly, you gotta love them. A short time later, she looked down at her plate, amazed to see it was wiped clean. She hadn't realized how hungry she'd been. Placing her dishes in the dishwasher, she bid Moira so long and went back upstairs for a sweater.

Since Ryker had her SUV, she drove a ranch truck the few miles to the clinic. She was surprised to see the parking lot almost full. Exiting the truck, she slammed the door shut, then paused, unsure whether to go in. Was Craig working today? She wasn't sure whether she wanted to see him or not. That first meeting still had her rattled.

Texting Chelsea to see where she was, she slowly walked around the clinic, seeing the pathway to what she presumed was the new animal shelter.

"Good morning! Are you settled in now?" Craig's voice came out of nowhere, surprising her. Her spine tingled with awareness as he walked toward her.

"Yes, I think so. Umm, do you know where Chelsea is?" Avery's voice wobbled, and she fought to keep her composure. Wiping her sweaty palms on her pants, she tried to avoid looking at Craig but failed.

His deep gray eyes were as shellshocked as Avery felt. Judging by the look on his face, there was definitely chemistry happening between them and something else, something way more visceral.

"Right behind you, big sis. Just got here. Ready for the grand tour?"

"Can't wait to see everything."

"Enjoy the tour. Gotta run. Nice to see you again, Avery, and uh, Chels." He touched both of their arms and left.

Chelsea watched him go, then turned to Avery and narrowed her eyes. "That was kind of weird. Anything going on I should know about?"

Avery felt drained but so on fire and alive at the same time. "No, no, just chatting with your new partner."

Chelsea's doubtful face didn't seem to agree, but she didn't press the issue for which Avery was deeply grateful. Her insides were in turmoil and her heart was thumping so hard she was sure Chelsea could see her chest pulsing. How could she be this attracted to someone else when her husband had just died? What on earth was wrong with her?

Chapter Four

Craig paused inside his truck before he pulled away. His chest was heaving, and every nerve in his body tingled. What the heck was happening? What did he know about this woman?

Avery McCoy-Dushane. Widowed. Grieving. Stunning, with her deep red, long, wild curls and flashing green eyes, with an undertone of sadness. Tall, almost as tall as he was, so at least five ten? Creamy skin that he ached to touch. Freckles over her nose that hinted at her love of the outdoors. Mom to twin boys.

Being around her was like bathing in lightning and thunder, so bright and so loud that he could barely hold himself together. When their eyes met, he was a goner. He had never met anyone who had caused this kind of reaction in him, ever.

Can you fall in love with a stranger, just like that? It wasn't lust, although he was quite sure he could dig up some of that. The feeling he had was so much bigger. It was like an epiphany.

Holy smokes, he was in deep water with this recently widowed woman. What kind of man was he?

He snapped his head back at a knock on the side door window. Finn. Rolling it down, he perused his partner.

"You okay, bro?" Finn asked. "Saw you sitting out here, so figured I'd check."

"Yeah, yeah, I'm fine."

"You don't look all that fine to me."

Craig laughed, the raucous sound foreign and rough to his ears. "I just ran into Avery. Oh, and Chelsea, of course."

Finn chuckled and threw his head back, nodding. "Ah."

"And what does that mean?"

"I recognize the signs, bro. You fell deep into that woman's spell. She's got you now. Those McCoy sisters are like magnets. You can't help but be attracted to them."

Craig sputtered, hemmed, and hawed. "No, it's not like that. No way. For heaven's sake, Finn, she's just lost her husband. What kind of cad would rush in there?"

Finn laughed again. "Then what is it like, Craig?"

Craig shook his head. "I don't know. It was the strangest thing...anyway, I gotta go."

Finn laughed again and tapped the side of the truck. "Later, lover boy."

Craig started the truck and pushed the gear into reverse. He had to get out of here before his head exploded – or his heart. He wasn't quite sure which one and right now, he wasn't willing to find out. Work. He'd block thoughts of Avery out with work.

· ❤ · ❤ · ❤ · ❤ · ❤ ·

Avery tried to listen to what Chelsea was saying as they walked, but she was quite sure if there was a test, she'd fail. Her skin was still buzzing from the warmth of Craig's hand lingering on her arm.

"And here is the boutique."

Avery squealed in genuine delight as she gazed around the shop. It was quaint and whimsical, and fit the location perfectly. "It's fantastic, Chelsea."

Chelsea grinned. "I know, right? So much better than I'd even imagined."

The yurt had transparent walls and ceiling, with tiny lights everywhere on the wooden rafters. Wooden shelves and wrought metal stands were nestled in the space, combining whimsy with practicality. Everything was functional and extremely beautiful.

"Oh, the jewelry!" Avery bent to admire her own handiwork – handmade ID pet tags of all kinds, as well as bracelets and earrings for pet owners.

"This is the area over here where I'd like to showcase your natural products," Chelsea continued, drawing Avery's attention to a side bookcase. "Is that enough space?

"I love it! And yeah, I think so." Avery meant it. She could feel inspiration blossoming. Like hope, it had been a long time coming. "I can't wait to create a line just for you, a Heart Creek McCoy exclusive."

Chelsea paused. "You mean a Heart Creek McCoy-*Dushane* exclusive, right?"

Avery's tongue stuck to her palate. "Oh my gosh, yes, of course. McCoy-Dushane."

Chelsea continued to gaze at her for so long that Avery could feel every inch of the flush spreading over her neck and face. As a redhead, she flushed often and usually at the worst possible times.

"Let's go see the rescues," Chelsea said finally.

Avery nodded, relieved to step away from Chelsea's scrutiny. Cuddling time with sweet animals would restore her balance, lower her blood pressure, and provide a little grounding. Right now, her feet and heart were ten feet off the earth. It was going to take a lot of cuddles to bring those down to the ground.

Craig managed to keep his thoughts where they needed to be for the next several hours as he tended to animals in need. After the last call, exhaustion dragged at him as he headed home. He flicked on the radio to keep himself awake.

Need You Now came over the speakers. He changed stations with a click. *If Loving You is Wrong, I Don't Want to be Right* blared. Click. *Almost Persuaded.* Click. *Marry Me.* Oh are you kidding me, he thought wearily. Click.

He turned the radio off and looked out the window, peering into the dark sky. Was it a full moon or eclipse? Something peculiar was definitely going on and he didn't know what to make of it. Rubbing his hand over his eyes, he forced himself to focus his attention on the road.

The following morning, he still felt off. A hot shower and two cups of coffee restored his equilibrium somewhat, but Avery's beautiful green eyes popped into his consciousness at the oddest times such as while buttering his toast or rinsing his breakfast dishes. Times they had no business being there. In fact, they had no business being there at all.

It's not like you are fifteen, in love for the first time, he chided himself, only to catch himself replying that of course not, he was thirty-seven in love for the first time.

Oh brother. Now he was having conversations with himself. He needed to go to work.

Five minutes later, he walked out of his apartment, down the wooden stairs, and into the clinic, welcoming the familiar smells and feelings. Here he could breathe and forget those sad green eyes, if only for a couple of hours. But when Ryker stopped by and invited them all for a drink at the ranch after work, he jumped at the chance to see Avery again. He drove himself over in case Finn and Chelsea didn't go back to the clinic after the visit. He arrived before the others.

Avery was sitting in a big chair on the covered deck, wrapped in a thick plaid blanket, doing something with a long thin piece of metal wire. When Craig approached, she looked up. Her eyes held surprise mixed with irritation and something else that made her pupils widen.

"Am I interrupting?" he asked.

"This afternoon has been nothing but interruptions," she laughed and set aside what she was working on. "I wasn't expecting you though."

"Ryker invited us," he explained. "For a beer."

"And your beer is where?" she asked, pointedly looking at his empty hands.

He blushed. "Uh, I saw you sitting here and thought I'd come over..."

"Just teasing you, cowboy." She laughed, the sound wrapping itself around his heart, and at that moment, Finn and Chelsea pulled in, Ryker's truck not far behind. Finn came over and slapped Craig on the back, then followed Chelsea into the house. A few minutes later, Craig had his cold beer. The others went inside, but he stayed put, unable to walk away from Avery.

"What are you working on?" he asked, then took a big drink, letting the first sip of cold bubbly beer trickle down his warm throat.

"Trying to wrap crystals with wire, to fasten onto cat collars."

His first thought was *why,* but he squelched it. "Interesting."

"I like to think crystals have energies and healing properties," she explained. "For people and for animals. For example, rose quartz attracts love and can help a pet feel more connected with the love around him."

"Ah, do you think it really works?" he asked.

Avery ran her gaze over him before she spoke. "There are things in this universe bigger than you and me, and not easily scientifically explained. I think that if you believe it, then it will be so. Intention is everything."

Whoa! The rose quartz might not be giving off any energy, but Avery sure was.

Every nerve in his body quivered and tingled. Yesterday he would have said that it was due to simple biology, but now he wondered if it was something else. Something mystical.

"I can assure you my intentions are honorable," he said, then wanted to smack himself. Where did that come from?

Avery's green eyes widened, and her throat moved as she swallowed. "Are we still talking about the crystals?" she whispered, not taking her eyes off of his.

Holy cats! "I, uh, I think I drank my beer too fast, I'm a bit light-headed," he backtracked.

She laughed and looked away. "Maybe turquoise then to balance energies or hematite for grounding. Whatever you need, I've got it."

Craig was on fire. This woman dazzled him, and he didn't know what to make of it. "Did you love your husband?" he asked before he could stop himself. He had to know.

Avery looked startled, then sad. "Yes, I did, actually."

They gazed at each other for several moments. Craig stood abruptly, finishing his beer.

"Good night, Avery."

"Good night, Craig."

Chapter Five

The next morning, filled with inspiration, Avery left the boys with her mom and went in search of a place where she could create. When she woke in the night and couldn't get back to sleep, she'd spent some time sketching. She'd replayed her conversation with Craig, wondering what had gotten into her, and then reluctantly cast it aside to contemplate later. She needed to concentrate on what to do next. The sitting room at the front of the house was currently empty, so she set up her laptop and pulled up her design program. Laying out sample metals, she was soon deep in thought. A sudden crash from the kitchen, followed by a child crying, broke her concentration. Checking in with her mom to see that said child was still alive, she tried to think of where else she could go and not be disturbed.

It didn't take much for her to realize that staying at the ranch house wasn't going to work out long-term. As much as it was great having her mom and Moira taking care of her boys, she didn't have anywhere to work on her jewelry or her pet lotions.

With her mom, Ryker, and Mac living in the house, it was entirely too crowded and while she knew she and the boys were welcome, she didn't want to impose longer than necessary. She wasn't ready to buy a place until her ranch sold; that could take months, if not years.

A glance at her watch reminded her it was almost time to head out to meet her soon to be sister-in-law, Carrie. Carrie was engaged to Mac, who had been permanently incapacitated because of a rodeo accident, and together they were building Mac's dream on vacant McCoy family ranch land – a rehabilitation center for ex-rodeo and retired cowboys. Carrie and Mac would live at the center. For now, Carrie was renting a house in town.

Avery took along her twins and her mom for a tour of the cowboy rehabilitation center.

"Avery! It's wonderful to see you and look at these sweet boys!"

Carrie hugged Avery within an inch of her life and snuggled the boys until they laughed and fought to get down. Avery didn't know Carrie very well, but what she did know, she liked. Grabbing Carrie's hand, she admired the old-fashioned setting of her engagement ring, the cluster of blue diamonds sparkling in the morning sun.

"This is exquisite! I love it!"

Carrie blushed. "I do too. We were so happy to find it – it's exactly what I wanted. Understated but elegant."

"Just like you!" Avery hugged her again, feeling the warmth of Carrie's happiness washing over her.

"Looks like you've accomplished a lot."

"We've had an exceptional year for building and so far, fall has been warm. Mac and I will be able to move in next weekend. Our place is habitable and now fully accessible for Mac. After a slow start, interest has been increasing and our first four residents will be moving in on November first. It's amazing how quickly it's coming together."

"What's amazing is you and Mac. This cowboy rehab idea is unique and much needed. Just like the rescue horses and the small animal rescue over at the vet clinic. Heart Creek and Heart Creek Ranch are both growing into havens for souls of all kinds." From where they stood, the rehab center looked welcoming in the bright sunshine.

Carrie's face shone at Avery's words. "Thank you so much! Mac is beyond excited...well, you know, in his solemn Mac way." Carrie laughed.

"Mom, Mom!" exclaimed Eric as he ran up and threw his arms around Avery's legs. Landon followed, with Elizabeth, their grandmother hot on his heels.

"Hello, my children," Avery lifted Eric high and gave him a squeeze. "What's going on?"

"A dog, there's a dog!" Landon dropped to all fours and raced around, going '*woof, woof*' then lay panting across his mom's feet.

Eric nodded. "It's a girl dog," he told his mom. "Wwwin-nie."

"Oh, Winnie. That's Aunty Carrie's dog."

"She doesn't bark much," Eric added. "Can she come to our house? Oh, lookit..."

Mac rolled himself over the parking lot toward them. "Hello family." He had Winnie on a leash, which he handed to Carrie.

"Unca Mac!" The boys hollered and raced to his side, Eric almost jumping out of Avery's arms. They hugged Mac's knees and reached for the buttons that controlled the chair.

"Hop up," Mac said, and the twins wasted no time in settling themselves on his lap. As Mac backed up, they giggled, the sound continuing as Mac drove around the yard.

Avery kneeled to scratch the small dog's ears. She knew Winnie was deaf and also that she was a hero, having saved Carrie when a horse had fallen on her last winter. Winnie leaned into the scratches and Avery buried her face in the dog's fur. She took a few minutes before releasing Winnie, enjoying the dog's warmth and softness.

"About that tour," she smiled at Carrie, and looked around for her boys.

"I'll mind the twins while you wander," Elizabeth offered, her face hopeful and bright.

Gratefully Avery hugged her mom, then followed Carrie over to the new main building of Heart Creek Haven. Barndominium style, it was large but homey, and the ground level apartment add-on for Mac and Carrie was spacious, light, and inviting. Like Heart Creek Ranch's main house, it offered a roomy wrap around deck set with discreetly placed comfortable looking chairs and tables. A welcoming place for healing cowboys, with mountain vistas and only a short walk or golf cart ride on paved paths to the stables. She breathed in deeply and smiled.

"Hang on," Avery suddenly realized what Carrie had just said. "You're moving out of your house? Do you know if someone else is renting it after you?" A perfect solution to her rental problem!

Carrie laughed. "We haven't even let Ida know when we are moving yet. We weren't sure when all the approvals and inspections were going to be finalized."

"Maybe I could rent your place? Until the ranch sells and I decide what I want to do."

"That's a great idea. And it's furnished, so you won't need to move anything until you buy a place. Oh, maybe beds for the boys? Can you wait until we are completely moved in case there is a glitch? Then we can talk to Ida and get it all set up."

The women hugged and once more, Avery's heart loosened. Coming home to Heart Creek and family was manna for her soul. Coming home. The right thing to do.

"Let's go tell Mac!" Carrie was excitedly dancing around.

"And rescue Mom from my holy terrors," Avery added.

"That too! You know she loves every minute of it, right?" Carrie assured her.

They walked back to the parking area, Carrie pointing out the accessible riding corral and outside therapy area along the way, and Avery marveling at the difference a year could make. Last year, Carrie and Mac weren't even a couple and now they had a home, a plan, and were planning a life together.

She knew that to outside eyes, her and Josh's marriage had looked strong and healthy, while in reality, it was falling apart. It had needed something to keep them together, to keep them moving forward. Maybe you can find that something with Craig, she thought, then quickly stopped that thought from fully forming. She was broken inside and didn't need to drag Craig into her personal mess. What she needed to do was build a life for her and her boys. Anything else was too risky and right now, any risk was way above her comfort level.

***

Craig loved stopping to say goodnight to the animals resting overnight in the clinic. It gave him a chance to see how they were doing, and he adored their sweet faces, and being able to comfort them with a pat or a cuddle. Of course, there was always one who chose to be unfriendly, but he never let it bother him, figuring they needed comfort as much as or even more than the others. As with people, you didn't always know their whole backstory or how they were treated in the past.

After making sure all was well, he wiped down the tables in the examination rooms with disinfectant. He knew that the office staff or the vet assistants took care of that, but the repetition soothed him and gave him time to think.

He prided himself on being a man who knew what he was doing, a man with a vision. Lately, though, he felt more like a blind man, stumbling through his days, not really seeing.

Even though part of him longed for a relationship, he liked being able to pick up and move on when he wanted to, constrained only by opportunity and motivation. He knew that coming to Heart Creek was the closest he'd ever been to a stable environment, but he wasn't sure if subconsciously he was searching for a home, or if it was just too good a business opportunity to pass up.

Growing up, home wasn't always the safest place to be. His dad's temper often got the better of him and, from an early age, Craig became determined to stay single. What if he was like his dad, deep down? Watching his mother's deterioration over the years was almost more than he could bear just to remember, let alone inflict upon someone else. They were too poor to leave, but staying, well, staying killed his mom and almost killed him. His dad got physically abusive when he was drunk and there was no way Craig would wish that on anyone else.

When his dad passed away a few years after Craig graduated from vet school, he hadn't gone to the funeral. He'd felt nothing except gratitude that he didn't have younger siblings to worry about. It was just him, and he could handle himself. Now, he had a thriving career he loved, great business partners in Finn and Chelsea, and enough money in the bank to ensure he would never be in the position his mom had been in. He had it covered. He was happy alone.

So then, he wondered, why did meeting Avery affect him so deeply? He'd had girlfriends before, but no one had ever come close to stirring the emotions that now gnawed at his guts. Even Sarah, who he had contemplated asking to marry him, hadn't brought him to life like Avery did. He knew that technically Avery was available, but a grieving widow was not what he'd had in mind when he'd ever thought about settling down. Not that he had, he told himself, nor was he thinking about that now. But IF he did, it wouldn't be to prey on someone in such a vulnerable position. He hoped he was a better man than that. But was he?

The green eyes peering at him from within his nightly dreams would say no.

A final swipe and he was done. Locking the door, his shoes crunched on the fallen leaves on the way to his apartment. Noticing Finn's dark windows, he figured Finn was with Chelsea somewhere. He envied their loving relationship and ease with each other, knowing that for years, they'd been apart through choice and circumstances.

His almost empty fridge reminded him of his missed grocery trip. Settling for soup and crackers, he made himself comfortable on the sofa and clicked through the channels. An older movie he'd seen before came on, so he let it play while he ate. He wouldn't have described himself as a lonely man, at least not most of the time. But since he'd met Avery, he felt lonelier than he had for years. That woman touched every raw nerve, every feeling in his body – even inklings of feelings. He couldn't get his mind off her and her boys. Twin cherubs with blond hair and blue eyes. He never considered having kids, although he certainly had nothing against them. He'd just never really seen himself with them.

What if, deep down, he *was* like his dad? What if he wasn't the good guy? What if he became the one putting that sadness and resignation in Avery's eyes? The thought of her sharing the defeated look his mom had emanated terrified him to the core.

He had nothing to offer to anyone, let alone a woman with children who were already suffering and grieving.

Nothing to offer Avery at all.

Avery shut the door quietly, putting her hand to her lips as Elizabeth moved across the landing to her.

"Are they asleep?" Elizabeth whispered.

"Fingers crossed," Avery breathed the words as quietly as she could. They tiptoed downstairs to the kitchen.

"I made tea. Herbal." Elizabeth said as she poured them each a cup. Avery scouted the cupboards until she unearthed the tin of cookies.

"Aha!"

Elizabeth laughed at her daughter, reaching out a hand. "Hey, me too!"

Avery giggled, loving the bright camaraderie. Tea and cookies in hand, they wandered into the front room, settling into deep chairs in the alcove. Avery reached for a quilt and tossed one to her mom before turning on the television.

"Oh, I love this movie!" Avery squealed.

"Great choice."

Avery sipped her tea and sank a little deeper into the chair. Thinking she heard a sound; she cocked her head to listen, but it was nothing, merely something rustling outside the house. Her boys were worn out from the fresh air and running around with Winnie and wouldn't wake until morning.

Smiling at her mom, she let her attention be drawn by the movie. "It's good to be home," she said, smiling at Elizabeth.

"Yes, it truly is," the older woman agreed. "Are you feeling settled here?"

Avery swallowed her mouthful of cookies before answering. "No, but it's coming. I dream about Josh a lot and I know the boys miss him."

Avery sniffed back the tears that swam in her eyes. She still felt guilty over Josh's death, even though they hadn't been getting along. Rationally, she knew his death wasn't her fault, but emotionally, her heart reacted as if she were responsible. Glancing at her mom, she smiled through her tears, the loving sympathy in Elizabeth's eyes warming her heart.

"It wasn't your fault, you know," Elizabeth spoke softly.

Avery started. She hadn't told her mom about the fight she and Josh had the morning of his death – what did Elizabeth mean? What did she know?

"I am not sure why, but I can see that you are feeling guilty, my dear," Elizabeth continued, before Avery could speak. "Even as a little girl, you didn't hide your feelings well. They're written all over your face."

Ah. Mom intuition. Avery gave a tight grin then sputtered, almost spilling her tea. "I wasn't a very good wife."

Elizabeth held up her hand. "And sometimes, neither was I. Your dad and I had some tough times, as all couples do, but we got through it. You would have too. Or you wouldn't have. Can't make that call now. What's in the past is in the past. You have to move forward. Both you and Josh are and were, good people. You deserve to be happy."

Avery sniffled as her mom's words sank in. "Thanks, Mom. I needed to hear that."

Elizabeth finished her tea and slid farther under the quilt. "Just enjoy the movie and let life unfold as it will," she added.

Avery nodded and followed her mom's lead. The least she could do was try and let go of her guilt.

Chapter Six

Taking the twins to Heart Creek was going to be a hardship for Josh's parents, who were used to the kids being a short drive away. Avery had no intention of denying them access to their grandsons, or her sons to their grandparents, and she'd made it a habit to call them once a week, sending videos and photos of the boys often.

Almost three weeks after their arrival in Heart Creek, her phone rang, and she wasn't surprised to see their name come up on the caller display.

"Good morning!"

"Avery, how lovely to hear your voice! Bernie and I were just thinking about you and the boys and wondering if we could take them for a few days. We could come there and pick them up, or you could bring them here." Tasha's voice was breathless with excitement. One good thing Josh had ensured was that his parents had the proper car seats installed in one of their vehicles in order to transport the boys if they needed to.

Avery swallowed before answering. Not having her boys for a few days was a new idea. Was she ready for that? She wasn't sure.

"I can bring them to you, Tasha, then maybe you could bring them back? That way, you can visit with everyone here. We postponed our Thanksgiving dinner until Ryker returns from Houston."

"That sounds wonderful, Avery! We're looking forward to seeing you and the boys."

They continued to work out dates and details and by the end of the conversation had agreed that the boys would stay in Cochrane for a week, with Tasha and Bernie returning them to Heart Creek the first weekend in November, just in time for a late Thanksgiving with the McCoy's.

Avery's hand shook as she hung up the phone. It was one thing having Moira or her mom watching the boys in the same house, but having the boys be a couple of hours away for an entire week was scary and new. The twins had always been comfortable with their grandparents, and she had no qualms on that front. It was herself she was worried about. Could she cope without them?

Possibilities danced through her mind. She could go somewhere and relax. No, she decided almost immediately; she needed to keep busy. As much as she loved the idea of a week away somewhere hot and beachy, she knew that was taking it a step further than she was comfortable with. Maybe sourcing out fresh ideas for her pet jewelry and lotions (potions, as Josh used to say) would give her the best of both – rest and inspiration.

Toronto? Calgary? Oooh, Edmonton.... She could book into the Fantasyland Hotel for part of that week and peruse the mall for ideas, as well as find and reach out to local sources that she could use for her business needs. The more she thought about it, the more it worked. She could do this.

"Mom? Guess what?" She headed to find Elizabeth and share the news.

A few hours later, Avery bundled the twins into her Expedition and headed to town to visit Carrie and Winnie. She'd been at Carrie's place before, but this time she'd be checking out a potential new home. Carrie met them in the driveway. Carrie's neighbor Ida put down the broom she'd been sweeping her own front porch with and trundled over. The twins gave Carrie hugs but were hesitant with Ida until she promised to bring over cookies. Then smiles wreathed their small faces.

Avery shrugged. "What can I say? They love their sweets."

"Just like their mama and auntie," Carrie added, giggling. "Come on in."

At the door, Winnie trotted over to say hello, sniffing the boys' legs, making them giggle. She tolerated their squishes, then trotted off to her cozy bed near the front door, settling in while still keeping her eyes on the twins. They sat down to play with the dog's toys, so Avery took the moment to do a quick tour. She gazed around the cottage in delight.

The living room was small but had an electric fireplace and a lovely big picture window overlooking the mountains. She knew it was close enough to walk to Main Street but far enough to be private and less than ten minutes' drive to the McCoy ranch. Though the kitchen was compact, a quick glance told her it held everything she would need, with the added advantage of a window overlooking the fenced backyard and outside door access – great for both boys and small animals. The bathroom had a tub/shower which was perfect for the twins. The only bedroom was small with a queen-sized bed, long dresser, and just enough room to add two small toddler beds for her boys. It also faced the street with a wonderful view of the mountains from the two windows. The garage was small, yet large enough to park her Expedition inside. That would be handy once the snow came. The basement was low, with just enough clearance for Avery to walk without bending over, and held a freezer, washer and dryer, a deep utility sink, a tiny cold room, and lots of shelves for storage. It would be a perfect place for her home studio.

"What do you think? Will it work?" Carrie asked.

"It's perfect!" Avery hugged Carrie hard. "All I'll need is a gate at the top of the basement stairs for now and we should be good. Thank you so much!"

Carrie smiled. "I love it when things work out," she said, her eyes shining.

"Hello?" Ida called from the back door.

"Cookies!" hollered the boys, jumping up and down. Their movement startled Winnie, who decided it was safer to stay in her bed than follow the small children. Carrie plugged the kettle in for tea, and the three adults gathered around the small round table in the kitchen to visit.

"Finn and I were going to wait to tell you, Ida," Carrie said, "but now is as good a time as any. Our apartment at the Haven is almost ready for us to move in – probably as soon as a week.

Ida shrieked. "That is wonderful news!"

"And, I am interested in renting this cottage," Avery added. "If you permit small children?"

Ida leaped up and hugged Avery. "I would be delighted to have these wee ones next door."

The tension slipped from Avery's shoulders. It was definite – they had a place to move to. She raised her teacup.

"Here's to new friends and new beginnings," she toasted. "Cheers!"

Chapter Seven

One sunny morning, after cuddles with her boys, it occurred to Avery that it had been ages since they'd visited the barns.

"Want to ride horses?" she asked the twins.

"Yes!" They hollered and jumped off the bed to grab their small Stetsons.

Their excitement was catching and, for once, they wasted no time getting dressed and brushing their teeth. While Avery ate a piece of toast and filled a travel mug with coffee, the boys drank milk and munched a cereal bar. Avery filled a cooler bag with fruit, snacks, and juice boxes.

Cowboy boots took a moment to find, with only one fight over whose were whose before they stepped out the back door of the ranch house. The barn with the family horses was only a few hundred yards away, and the boys skipped and ran, pausing here and there to pick up rocks and other treasures. Avery's heart lifted at their obvious joy, letting the fresh clean air and beautiful sunshine ease the heaviness she'd been carrying of late.

Once in the barn, the boys waited while Paul, one of the ranch workers, brought out two small horses and proceeded to saddle them. Avery wandered over to greet the other horses. Leading Lady out of her stall, she called the boys over to help her saddle the mare while Paul finished with their horses.

"Good morning." Craig entered the barn, a smile on his face. He had his vet bag, obviously working.

"Do you remember Dr. Craig?" she asked the boys. "He works with Uncle Finn and Auntie Chelsea."

They nodded but hung back, unsure.

Craig dropped to one knee and extended a hand. "You must be Landon," he said to Eric.

The boys giggled. "No, I'm Eric. He's Landon! My hat is red."

Craig's face looked serious as he considered both hats. "Right, right. Red hat Landon and blue hat Eric. Got it."

The boys shook their heads and pointed to each other. "Landon hat is blue," said Eric. "MINE is red." The boys showed Craig their hats and he nodded solemnly and gave them a thumbs up. "Got it," he said.

"We're going for a ride," Avery said, then blushed, realizing it was probably clear why they were there in the barn, saddling horses.

"I haven't ridden for, well, I don't even remember the last time," Craig admitted.

"Maybe you can come too," Eric pointed out, now quite comfortable talking to Craig.

Craig and Avery spoke at the same time, then laughed.

"Ladies first."

"Dr. Craig is working. See his bag? He's off to help a sick horse."

Craig cleared his throat. "I was just finishing up," he stated.

Paul walked over, reins in his hand. "The horses are ready, Avery," he said. "I'll finish Lady for you. Maybe Lancelot for Dr. Craig?" he added, with a wicked grin.

Avery was about to protest that Craig was too busy, then she caught the hopeful look on both boys' faces. If Craig was too busy, he could say so himself.

"The more the merrier," she declared, lifting her hands in the air.

Craig couldn't believe he'd let himself be coerced into riding a horse. Two pairs of brilliant blue eyes sure could melt your defenses pretty quickly, not to mention Avery's emerald gaze.

Lancelot seemed huge, even to Craig's six-foot-one-inch height. He had ridden and, in fact, loved riding, but it really had been years. Was it like riding a bike, he wondered. Would muscle memory kick in? God, he hoped so.

They led the horses outside and once the boys were safely mounted, Avery deftly lifted herself onto Lady's back. Paul held Lancelot's head while Craig mounted and got settled, then handed him the reins.

"He's a follower," Paul said. "Easy-going guy. You'll be fine, Doc."

Craig wasn't overly optimistic, but so far so good. Avery took the lead, followed by Eric, then Landon. Lancelot automatically fell into place behind Sheba, Landon's horse. They walked for a few hundred yards, then Avery moved Lady into a trot, and the other horses followed suit.

Avery looked back over her shoulder often, calling out encouragement to her sons. Craig was impressed with how they rode. He knew they were almost four years old, but of course they had the confidence that children tend to have. Avery was a natural. She looked made for the saddle. Her long red hair blew in the breeze, and her face, even from where Craig was sitting, glowed.

Eventually, the trail they were on crossed a sparkling creek, wide, rocky, and about knee deep. Avery stopped and waited for the boys and Craig to catch up.

"Heart Creek?" Craig wondered, leaning forward to pat Lancelot.

"Yep, it runs through the ranch then cuts off to the southeast."

One at a time, she led the boys and their horses through the creek.

"You okay on your own?" she yelled to Craig from the other side.

"Sure." Craig's confident tone belied his apprehension. Apparently, riding a horse was not quite the same as riding a bike and his leg muscles, strong though they were, already felt sore from gripping Lancelot's massive back.

Gingerly, he led the big horse forward. Halfway across, Lancelot picked up the pace and Craig, not prepared, loosened his leg grip. He could feel himself sliding slowly, ever so slowly, and the next thing he knew, he was sitting on his butt in the creek and Lancelot was grinning at him from the far bank.

Craig tried to stand, but the rocks were slippery, and he tumbled forward onto his chest, face first. Now quite wet, and freezing from the icy water, fully humiliated and ticked right off, he shook his head, water droplets flying. He could hear the sounds of the creek flowing by him, and another sound that took a few seconds to identify.

Laughter. Out and out laughter from not only Avery, but the boys too.

"Oh Dr. Craig, you are wet!" Landon howled.

"You fell off!" Eric pointed out, quite unnecessarily Craig thought.

Avery dismounted and came over to the side of the creek. "Do you need a hand?" Her voice was steady, although he could see the laughter still causing her shoulders to shake.

"I may," Craig admitted. "Not quite sure what happened there."

Avery strode into the creek. "Okay, take my hand and I'll pull you up."

Craig reached for her hand and as she pulled, he hoisted himself into a standing position. Gazing into her eyes, he forgot to let go, even though she had loosened her grip. Pulling her toward him, they both tumbled into the water.

Oh, for the love of Mike.

Avery sputtered and flailed, before getting herself back up. Craig sat where he was, hearing the boys laugh louder this time.

"Mama! You fell in too!"

"It's fine, I'm okay, we'll be right there," Avery called to her sons, then turned to Craig with a deep glare.

"Doctor. Shall we try that again?" Her eyes flashed, and Craig's heart melted, warmth spreading through his body despite the cold water.

"Right. Yes, let's try that again," he agreed, teeth chattering.

"Perhaps let go once you are up," Avery added, sweetly. "Unless for some reason of which I am currently unaware, you like cold dunkings?"

"Yes, let go, okay." Craig nodded, shivering.

Avery braced herself and pulled, and this time, Craig remembered to let go. Avery wrapped her arm around his back.

"We need to go home and get warmed up," Avery commented, as he managed to stay standing this time. "I'll get the boys and horses and be right back." She led Craig back to the first bank and sat him down in the sun. Then she ran lightly through the creek and led the boys across. This time, Lancelot followed after the second horse.

Avery dug into her saddlebag and drew out two blankets, one of which she wrapped around Craig's shoulders, the other around her own. "Okay to ride by yourself?"

No, no. "Yes, I think so," Craig said. He was frozen through and through, although the blanket helped.

It seemed to take no time at all to get back to the barn. Avery helped Craig dismount, then the boys. Once the boys were brushing down their horses, Avery brought her thermal cup over to Craig and offered it to him. "Hot coffee, drink up."

Craig drank deeply, the warmth shocking his system on its way down.

"Thank you," he said. "I'm so sorry..."

"No apology necessary. It happens to the best of us." Avery shook her head. "You need a hot shower and dry clothes. You okay to drive yourself home? Eric, try the other leg. Thatta boy."

In spite of the hot coffee and the relative warmth of the barn, Craig's teeth still chattered.

"Yes, I'm okay. Wet, but okay."

"All right then," Avery said. "Take the blanket with you. I have a vest under my coat, I'll be okay. I'll walk you to your car. Oh, Paul, can you please watch the boys for two secs?" she asked, seeing Paul farther down the stalls.

"You bet." Paul trotted over and perused the boys' brushing work. "Nice job, guys."

Once again, Avery's arm surrounded Craig's back as they walked to the car. He couldn't feel her warmth, but the pressure was comforting, and he marveled at what a kind woman she was. He'd ruined her family outing, yet she wasn't giving him a hard time about it.

Waving as he drove away, Craig found himself thinking about this amazing red-haired woman he was getting to know and, yes, falling for more and more each time. She was special. And those twins – they were something else. He didn't have much experience with children, but they were easy to be around. A chill moved through him, and he turned his thoughts to a hot shower and more coffee.

Avery watched him drive away, concern and laughter bubbling inside. He was so embarrassed, and she felt bad for him, but it was funny when he fell off the horse and even funnier to see his reactions.

On the way home, the boys didn't stop talking about the doctor falling in the creek. When they got back to the ranch, they wanted to make cookies to take to Doctor Craig. Moira happily let them loose in the kitchen and a short time later there were three dozen, less tasters, of slightly grimy but delicious looking chocolate chip cookies cooling.

The blinds were down in the apartment when they drove over with the cookies, so Avery left the bag with a note 'Not to be immersed in anything but coffee.' She chuckled as she walked down the stairs, enjoying having someone to tease.

He was a good man. A kind, good man. Her spine still tingled whenever she was near him, but the feeling had spread into a delicious warmth, laced with laughter as she was getting to know him better. *Oh Avery, you are falling for this man. What would Josh say?*

Sighing, she pushed that thought out of her mind. One day at a time. That's all she could do.

Chapter Eight

C raig hadn't realized how busy he'd been until he noticed the Hallowe'en decorations around the clinic. Surprisingly, there wasn't any snow, which was unusual for their part of Alberta. The days were crisp in the mornings and most trees had lost their leaves, but the sunny days still held warmth in the late afternoon.

"Is there any chocolate?" He leaned over Sammy's desk hopefully.

"Well," Sammy drawled. "It IS technically for the kids, but since you are really a big kid in man's clothing, I will give you one."

"Only one?" Craig put on his best pleading face and was rewarded with a handful of small chocolate bars.

"Twix! My favorite!"

"Are there any you don't like? Sammy wondered, laughing.

"No," Craig admitted. "But I do like some better than others."

Wandering into his office, sweet tooth satisfied, he tossed the wrappers into his wastebasket. Sitting, he gazed at the computer screen before turning his attention to the window. A few leaves floated carelessly to the ground through light that was already paling to a thin pre-winter incandescence rather than the brighter glow of autumn.

"How're things?

Craig turned to Finn with a grin. "Good, good. You?"

Finn nodded. "The same. Can't believe how busy it's been. Definitely glad we brought you on board. Can't imagine handling this on my own. In fact, we may have to look at finding someone else, at least part time, next year."

"I've been thinking about that too, to be honest. At the very least, we'll need another two pairs of hands when you and Chelsea are on your honeymoon. We'll be down both of you."

Finn grimaced. "Still trying to figure out when the wedding will be, let alone plan a vacation." He dragged his hands through his hair.

"Yeah, lots to take into consideration, especially with the rescue center here now. Mind you, it pretty much runs itself most of the time. And Avery can look after the shop, I'm sure." Craig felt his face flush as he mentioned Avery's name. Dag nab it, him and his cursed fair skin.

"Ah, yes, Avery." Finn looked thoughtfully at his partner. He sat down on the corner of the desk. "What's the story there?"

"What? Wait, no, no, there's no story there. I did spend time with them riding. That was an adventure. And the twins made me cookies."

Finn laughed. "Yeah, heard about that, cowboy. Don't really believe nothing is going on, but if you say so. Change of topic

– there's a veterinary supply conference in November. It's just a couple of days. Care to go?"

"Sure, if we can spare me." Craig was so relieved at the change of topic; he would have pretty much agreed to anything.

"Okay, here are the dates. It's at the Edmonton Expo Centre. I'd say stay at the hotel in West Edmonton Mall – that way you can experience the big mall on your downtime. Here's the information. Sammy can book you in. You and I can touch base before you go and establish which suppliers I want you to talk to." Finn tossed a thick packet on Craig's desk.

Craig picked it up and leafed through. "Looks great. I'll get right on that. Nice to see a bit more of this province." And get away from Avery's green eyes haunting his every moment.

"Great! Oh, there's Chelsea. I need to talk to her about something. Later, buddy."

"Later." His stomach rumbled. Good thing he'd brought lunch. It was in the fridge in the staff room. As he munched, he ruminated. Edmonton. It sure would be nice to have a couple of days away. The conference would be busy, but it would be an enjoyable break from the constant go-go-go of work.

It was a great idea. He was already looking forward to the break.

***

Almost before she knew it, it was the day before the boys were going to Cochrane. Avery packed their clothes into a suitcase for each of them, remembering to include favorite toys and books. Then she packed a suitcase for herself as she planned to head directly from Cochrane to Edmonton. She still had a few niggles of worry but tried to keep those at bay. This would be a wonderful adventure for all of them. She hoped. She knew Bernie and Tasha were missing their son and having their grandsons around might alleviate a bit of that.

Even though her usual tires were rated all-weather, she had Nokian heavy duty winter tires installed on her SUV before she left. Snow was coming any day, and she didn't want to risk the roads without great tires. That was one thing her dad had always insisted on and something she had continued.

The boys were excited as she loaded them into the vehicle, waving goodbye to Moira, Grandma Elizabeth, and Uncle Mac before Avery drove away. It hadn't taken long for her childhood home to feel like a real home to the kids. The trip south was uneventful and the transfer to Bernie and Tasha took no time at all. The boys were as excited as their grandparents, and her heart was light as she drove away. Her plan was to spend the night in Red Deer with an old friend, then head north up the highway the following day to Edmonton. She hadn't seen Sherry since the funeral and looked forward to catching up with her.

As luck would have it, it snowed overnight while she was at Sherry's. Avery was fairly sure it hadn't been in the weather forecast, but this was Alberta, after all, and the weather could change in an instant.

Fortunately, the snowfall was relatively light and the traffic flow on the highway was good. The fluffy layer of snow brightened the overcast day and before she knew it, she was navigating from the highway into Edmonton and heading to West Edmonton Mall. She found the hotel side of the complex easily and parked in the covered parking lot. She checked in and took the mirrored elevator to the eighth floor and her room. It took all of five minutes to hang what needed hanging and she was free.

"Food, I need food." She surprised herself by speaking out loud. Her stomach growled as if it had heard the words. She picked up the mall brochure and looked through it, amazed at the multitude of food possibilities. She finally decided to head down and walk around, hoping to be tempted by one of the many food court or restaurant options the mall offered. Changing into her running shoes, she drew a brush through her curls, then tamed them into a ponytail.

As she stepped off the elevator and made her way to the main mall area, she stopped in amazement. It was huge! To her left was a coffee shop beside a large bookstore.

"Oooh!" Great place to start. There was a line in the coffee shop which gave her time to decide which decadent drink she wanted. Then, coffee in hand, she entered the bookstore and lost herself for a while before heading out into the mall.

Almost three hours later, her feet sore and hunger satiated, she went back to her room. Drawing a hot bath, she sunk under the water and thought about how long it had been since she'd done anything on her own. It was exhilarating. Unnerving and a bit scary but also amazing and fun.

Wrapping herself in a thick hotel robe, she settled on the king size bed and called to see how her boys were doing. Assured that they were well, safe, and actually sleeping, she let herself relax into the luxurious duvet and snooze. Her last conscious thought was that there would be plenty of room for Craig on this enormous bed.

Craig pulled into the hotel parking lot a little after eight p.m. His day had been busy at the clinic, but he wanted to get settled in and have the next morning free before the conference started at noon. Traffic had been heavier than he'd expected, but despite the new snow that had fallen, the highway was clear.

He barely registered the hotel's grand foyer as he checked in. Ninth floor. He leaned against the elevator walls and once in his room, didn't even unpack before falling onto the plush bed. He was almost asleep when Avery's green eyes pierced his sleep fog. Sighing, he rolled over and pulled the thick, soft quilt over himself. His last conscious thought before sleeping was that even here, she continued to haunt him.

Groaning, he rolled over and glanced at the alarm clock. Nine a.m. He stretched and dragged himself out of bed. Stripping off, he headed for the shower.

Once clean and refreshed, he realized he hadn't pre-ordered room service for breakfast. He could make himself a coffee in his room's coffeemaker, but he was hungry, and coffee would not cut it. Grabbing the mall brochure, he glanced through it, finding a restaurant name he knew.

Twenty minutes later, he was enjoying bacon and eggs, watching the mall come to life around him. He'd seen plenty of malls before, but this one rivaled the one in Minnesota for size and scope. Motion caught his eye. He inhaled sharply, almost choking on his piece of bacon. *Was that Avery?* He sat back, watching the back of a tall woman with a long, bouncing red ponytail as she walked down the concourse on the opposite side of the mall.

Squeezing his eyes tightly shut, he sat for a moment, then reopened his eyes. Nada. Whoever it was – Avery or not – they were gone. Oh buddy, he thought. You've got it bad. Avery's in Heart Creek, miles from here. Taking a big gulp of his coffee, he pulled out the information on the veterinary supplies event and mapped the address on his phone. Might as well head out early as he wasn't familiar with the city or the traffic patterns. Today's vendor showcase didn't start until noon, so he had plenty of time to get lost.

After finding her way around Edmonton and finding three ethical wholesalers who carried the ingredients she wanted for her shampoos, Avery craved a cold glass of wine and a hot bath. Thanks to her artist friend Deirdre, she had an amazing lunch on Whyte Avenue at a charming retro café, so supper was not an immediate concern. Loaded with bags, she lucked into a parking spot close to the hotel entrance and made her way to the elevator. When it dinged, she moved to the back before realizing she hadn't pressed her floor button.

"Eighth floor, please," she mumbled around her armload of parcels.

"No problem," rumbled a deep voice that was somehow familiar.

Peeking around her bags, she caught sight of a blond head in front of her.

"Craig?"

"Avery?" Craig turned, and his shoulder hit Avery's bags, knocking one to the floor.

"So sorry!" As he bent to retrieve the bag, Avery leaned over, her hair falling over her face and brushing against Craig's cheek.

"No worries, thanks. What are you doing here?" Hoping he didn't hear the tremor in her voice, she commanded herself to get a grip. All Craig had to do was to be near to her and her blood pressure rose and her neck broke out in a sweat. Talk about your animal magnetism, she thought, then silently giggled. Of course, he had animal magnetism – he was a vet, after all.

"Vet conference. And you? Shopping weekend?"

"I know it looks that way, but I've been sourcing local material suppliers for my pet jewelry and lotions. And yeah, maybe a bit of shopping, too."

Ding.

Avery looked away from Craig's smiling face to see that the elevator was on her floor.

"Bye." She scooted past Craig, inhaling his intoxicating scent as she brushed past him.

"Ah, Avery," he called as she walked away. "Care for a drink?"

Oh, good god no no no no no. "I'd love that," she replied, her words contrary to her thoughts.

"Downstairs in half an hour, okay?"

"Sure."

The elevator doors closed, and Avery sank into a chair in the elevator foyer. What was she doing? Playing with fire, that's what. This was not going to end well. Uh, uh, no way, no how.

Chapter Nine

C raig still felt the softness of Avery's hair against his cheek as he exited onto the next floor. *What was he thinking, inviting her for a drink? Bad, bad idea.* And yet, somewhere down deep, it felt absolutely right.

Thirty minutes later, he was downstairs, freshly shaven and in a clean shirt. Part of him didn't think she'd show, the other part was afraid she would. A few seconds later, she stood beside him, looking fresh yet uncertain.

"Bourbon Street?" she suggested. "I'm sure we can find a quiet place there. I mean, a place with drinks." Her face flushed, and she scrunched her nose, then spoke. "Not sure why I feel like I'm in high school on a first date," she admitted, laughing.

Craig joined in and his awkwardness slid down a notch. They were both unsure of what was happening. Interesting.

"Great idea," he agreed and offered his arm. They walked down the concourse, pausing now and again for Avery to look in store windows. When they arrived at Bourbon Street, they stopped in front of a small Italian place named La Trattoria Bella.

"This looks nice."

"After you, signora."

Once they were settled in a small booth near the walkway, where they could watch the comings and goings of the mall patrons but still be private, Avery sighed.

"Is everything okay?"

Avery nodded. "This place is charming. It's been a long time..."

Oh nuts. She was probably thinking about her husband, Craig realized. Probably not a good idea to come somewhere this intimate. What a doofus he was.

"We can go somewhere else," he offered quietly. "We haven't ordered yet."

Avery shook her head, and the tears in her eyes gleamed under the soft trattoria lights. "It's really okay," she sniffed. "I..."

At that moment, their server approached the table, bringing glasses of water and snowy white napkins. Avery decided on a glass of white wine, an appetizer plate of focaccia col Formaggio and a side of Caprese salad.

"White wine for me," Craig decided. "Hey, do you like artichokes?"

When Avery nodded yes, Craig added a plate of grilled artichokes with lemony herb aioli to their order. Once the server had left, he turned back to Avery.

"Want to tell me about it?" While he didn't really want to hear about her marriage to another man, he did want to know what was bothering her. Or maybe it was too soon after her husband's death, maybe he needed to back off.

Avery gazed at him for a long moment until he thought she was going to say no.

"Yes, I think I would, actually. If you really want to listen."

Craig's mind was going in circles. Fortunately, their wine arrived, and he took a sustaining gulp before answering. "All ears."

Avery smiled and took a sip of her own wine. Picking up the napkin, she started twisting it one way, then the other.

"Josh and I met in college. He was interested in farming and eventually getting into a pasture to plate operation. I had almost finished my teaching degree, so we didn't really run in the same circles, but we had some mutual friends and both loved horses. I was a barrel racer when I was younger and thought about raising horses. Horses and farming always remind me of home, Heart Creek home, I mean. Josh had an opportunity to buy a small ranch down near his parents' place in the Cochrane area. By that time, we'd been going out for a few years and when he asked me to marry him, I thought sure, why not? Not exactly a ringing endorsement to marry someone, is it? But he was a nice man, a good man, and I loved him. We waited almost ten years to have kids so we could get the ranch up and running. I taught school during the week and horseback riding lessons on weekends, and we had a good life. The twins came along, and I quit teaching. Josh took flying lessons, got certified. We bought our own little plane."

Avery paused as the server placed their appetizers on the table. "Shall we eat? Maybe tell me some funny stories about animals you've treated."

Craig nodded and reached for a piece of focaccia. As it melted in his mouth, he let Avery's words settle. By the time all the plates were empty except for a few crumbs, he'd managed to make her giggle a few times. When the server approached, asking about dessert, the strain in her face had lessened.

"Oh, I'm full, but a cup of tea and something chocolate would be divine," she said.

Craig agreed, and they placed their orders.

"Back to your story. You had your own plane now and the boys."

Avery sighed. "Yes. Josh took more lessons to become a flight instructor and started volunteering for the wildfire service." She paused and swallowed deeply before continuing.

"We fought a lot. I didn't like how much time the flying was taking away from the ranch and me and the boys. He wanted to continue making as much money as possible so we could expand the ranch. I thought we were fine as we were. In fact, the day he died, we'd had a big fight that morning. Sometimes I wonder if that's why…"

Avery broke down again, wiping her eyes ineffectively with her used table napkin. "Oh my god! I can't believe I just told you that. I shouldn't drink, I really shouldn't."

Craig reached across the table with a clean napkin. "It's okay, thank you for trusting me," he said.

"I don't know if it's trust or the wine talking," Avery retorted.

"Avery, I'm sure the crash wasn't your fault. Is there an official report? Or…." Craig spoke softly.

"Yes, there was. They said it was 'pilot error.' What does that mean, anyway?" Avery's voice was sharp. "I'm the one who has to live with it and know that I may have caused the death of my sons' father. No matter what you or anyone else says to the contrary."

Craig's words dried in his mouth. There was nothing he could offer to make her feel better.

Avery dabbed at her eyes a bit longer then raised her hand to signal the server. "Check please," she smiled at the young woman.

"I've got it," Craig reminded her, reaching for his wallet. "I invited you."

Avery looked like she was about to argue, then stopped herself. "Fine."

"Thank you." He rose and so did she, but instead of waiting for him, she strode out of the restaurant.

Avery couldn't believe she'd shared all those things with Craig. What the heck was wrong with her? She didn't even know him! Embarrassment and guilt raged through her body. She'd sounded like a whiny privileged homemaker. Her husband deserved to be treated better than that. Better than she'd treated him, in fact.

By the time Craig had caught up with her, she had calmed down a little.

"How are you?" Craig asked, two steps behind her.

"Confused. Embarrassed." She threw out the words, then realized she was almost running. Slowing down, she belatedly added, "Thank you for dinner."

"My pleasure. Especially now that you've slowed down to a walk I can keep up with. Gad, my aching knees."

Avery reluctantly allowed herself to grin as she gazed over at Craig. His cheeks were rosy, and he was puffing.

"Really, Doctor? You might be a bit out of shape."

Craig huffed and puffed. "You move at a surprisingly good clip for a woman in high heels."

Avery laughed and relented, bringing her pace to a gentle walk.

"That better, grampa?" she teased.

Craig nodded. "Much."

Craig got off the elevator at her floor, much to Avery's surprise. He reached out his hand and took Avery's in his.

"I wanted to say thank you for sharing. Wine or no wine. That must have been hard on you, and I appreciate it. And don't worry, your story is safe with me. I'm not a blabber."

Avery didn't know what to say. Craig's face was open and honest and in spite of her earlier embarrassment, it felt cleansing to have shared her story with someone. It was as if a tremendous weight had been lifted from her shoulders.

Before she could stop herself, she leaned forward and kissed him on the cheek. Their eyes met, and she moved her lips to his, startled at her body's instant reaction and her desire for more. It had been a long time since she'd felt loved, wanted.

Gently, she pulled her head back, breaking their caress.

"Good night, Craig."

Shaking, she didn't look back. She could barely open her room door. Thank goodness for swipe cards. She had no idea what she was feeling – a heady combination of love, guilt, warmth, regret, and, yes, even lust.

Not only had she been a terrible wife, but she was also a terrible widow.

Chapter Ten

C raig stood, flabbergasted. What just happened? He felt Avery's kiss right down to his toes. No one had ever kissed him like that before. *Whoa, whoa, and whoa*!

"Excuse me."

"Oh, sorry." Craig moved to allow the guest to exit the elevator, then he got on. Pressing the button for the ninth floor, he was barely aware when the doors opened. Once in his room, he washed his face with cool water and took a long drink from the tap.

Sitting on the bed, looking at the list of suppliers he needed to see tomorrow, he realized his brain wasn't thinking of vet supplies but of a red-haired woman with the softest lips he'd ever felt.

Lying down, he thought about what to do. Avery had confided in him and let her guard down enough to let him in, just for a moment. Was he taking advantage of a vulnerable woman, still grieving her dead husband? Or was she grieving him? He knew that grief looked different for many people.

This was all unfamiliar territory to him. He had no idea where to step, what to say, or what to do next. All he knew was that he had genuine feelings for her, unlike any he had ever felt before.

Avery looked at herself in the mirror in the hotel bathroom. Her face was flushed, with wine, with joy, and guilt. Plenty of guilt.

She had kissed Craig! What was she thinking? She wasn't thinking at all, that was one thing for certain. How could she face him again after that?

Sinking on to the bed, face in hands, she wept. She wept for Josh and for herself and for her boys, and for things she didn't even know she was crying about. And then, spent, she slept.

When she woke up the following morning, she realized she hadn't called to check in on her boys the previous night. After speaking with each of them, and being assured by Tasha that all was well, she allowed herself another half hour of lounging in her bed before she showered. Then she unpacked everything she had bought and laid it out on the bed, organizing personal from business, then determining what she still wanted to do while in the city. There were two more suppliers she wanted to meet with, but they weren't available until the following day, so today was a free day. Maybe a beach day at the water-park? She had packed a bathing suit and the more she thought about it, the better the idea seemed. And maybe a haircut. She booked an appointment for a pedicure and haircut at one of the spas on the second floor of the mall for later in the day.

An hour later, she was sitting by the wave pool on a lounge chair, coffee in hand. She'd stopped at the coffee shop for a large coffee and sandwich for her lunch later, as well as a sweet treat, then found a romance beach read in the bookstore to entertain herself while she lounged. Partway through the morning, she made herself go up the stairs to different water slides and splash in the pool afterwards. Napping on the lounger while she dried off felt like heaven, the noise of the waterpark a distant rumble.

After her lunch, she showered and roamed a few stores before her spa appointment. It was fun picking out polish for her toes – something she rarely indulged in – and the nail tech had filed and cleaned up her fingernails. She smiled at the hairdresser gushing over her hair as she settled into the chair.

"And what were you thinking of?" the hairdresser queried.

Avery looked at herself in the mirror and made a spur-of-the-moment decision. "Cut it off," she said. The hairdresser's eyes widened as he lifted her waist length, deep red curls.

"Are you sure?" he asked doubtfully. "It's healthy and you could get by with a trim."

Avery thought about it for a moment. "I want a change. Maybe a bob," she said. "Long enough for me to still put it in a ponytail. Maybe this length?" She held her hand at her collarbone and watched as the hairdresser pondered.

"Yes, yes," he agreed. "That will look nice. See?" He rolled her hair into his hands to show her the length she'd indicated. She nodded.

An hour later, she hardly recognized herself in the mirror. Her hair flowed smoothly down to her collarbones and swung gently when she moved her head. The length highlighted her cheekbones and accentuated her green eyes.

"I feel like a new woman," she smiled at the young man who'd created magic with her hair.

"You look fabulous," he said.

Avery contemplated her reflection, and, with a toss of her head, she agreed. She felt fabulous! The last time she'd felt this good was her wedding day, she remembered, then stopped, stricken. She was a grieving widow. She wasn't supposed to feel this good. What would people think of her out having a good time, spending a ridiculous amount of money on herself when she was in mourning? Kissing random men. Feeling things that weren't in line with grieving.

Paying her bill, she struggled not to cry. Again. It seemed she was turning into a weeping willow every time she turned around. She didn't know what to feel and every emotion dragged a suitcase full of angst. *Maybe I'm having a nervous breakdown? What if they take my kids away?*

By the time she returned to her hotel room, she'd wound herself into a state of self-loathing and self-judgment, placing herself somewhere between Lizzie Borden and Judas. *I don't deserve to be a mom. I am betraying Josh by loving, liking whatever I'm doing with Craig. I should be sad and lonely, not relieved, and indifferent. I should...*

The ringing hotel phone snapped her out of her pity party. Oh no, what if something happened to the boys, was her first thought. Then she realized Tasha would call on the cell. Unless Tasha herself was hurt... Swallowing, she answered.

"Hello?"

"Avery, it's Craig. My afternoon finished a bit early, and I wondered if you'd like to meet me for supper. Unless you've eaten?"

Avery glanced in the mirror above the side table before answering. Her eyes gazed back at her, reddened and huge in her pale face. Her hair was magnificent though, she thought, reaching a hand to touch its silkiness. Oh my god, what's wrong with me, she wondered, not for the first time that day.

"No, I haven't eaten since lunch. But no wine, okay?"

Craig's chuckle rumbled over the line. "Deal. Downstairs in twenty minutes?"

"Sure, see you then." Avery hung up the phone and twisted her hands together. Her spirits had risen as soon as she'd heard Craig's voice. How could something that felt so lovely be wrong? Closing her eyes, she remembered talking to her mom when she was younger. Tallest in her class, with a fiery temper, she hadn't fit in well with the kids at school. Elizabeth's words came back to her. "Be yourself, my love. Be kind and do what feels right to you. And don't worry about the other kids. You can't control what they think or do. You can only be you."

You can only be you.

Squaring her shoulders, she marched to the bathroom to press cool facecloths against her eyes. Then she brushed her teeth and found a sweater in case the mall was chilly. Her hands smoothed her hair, and she marveled as it flowed gently from side to side, happy now to be relieved of some length and weight. She needed to shed some emotional weight too.

Leaving the room with a bounce in her step, she couldn't wait to see Craig.

Craig was tired. Traffic had been tied up on the way to the Expo Centre because of a tractor-trailer accident, and the conference center was busy. He managed to get to the suppliers he'd wanted to connect with, and he knew there was at least one change Finn would want to make once they'd talked. For now, though, he needed to deal with his feelings for Avery.

When she stepped out of the elevator, he lost his breath. Her beautiful hair was smooth and shiny, brushing against her shoulders as she moved, a glorious mass of red brilliance. Somehow her green eyes held more glimmer and overall, she was stunning. When she gave him a tentative hug, he couldn't push her away, his need to hold her warring with his rational thoughts to respect boundaries and current vulnerability.

Tucking her arm into his, he began telling her about his day as they walked. When they arrived at Bourbon Street, he led her to Hudson's Pub.

"There's one of these in Toronto," he said. "Haven't been there for years. Does this work for you?"

"Absolutely! I love pub food!" Avery smiled at him. Almost the same height, it was unnerving to have her mouth so close to his.

Once they were settled, they ordered, deciding to share a pan of nachos and both choosing soda and glasses of water over beer.

"Craig," Avery started to speak but Craig held a finger to his mouth.

"May I speak first?" he asked intently. He had to do this before he chickened out.

She nodded and sat back in her seat, waiting.

"Avery, last night you told me a lot about yourself, and I am truly grateful."

Avery's eyes narrowed. "That sounds like there is a 'but' coming..."

Craig laughed nervously, his mouth drying out. *Come on man, you can do this.*

"I am not sure what is happening with us and to be honest, I can't figure out what is right and what is wrong. I am so attracted to you BUT you are grieving your husband's death. I don't know what the time protocol is here. I don't want to take advantage of your vulnerability and make you do something we might both regret."

Avery held up her hand. She looked down for a moment, then directly into his eyes.

"Let me understand this. You're saying you think you're taking advantage of ME? And that YOU might make me do something we'll both regret? Is that right?"

Uh-oh. Avery's voice had a dangerous edge, but Craig was already in over his head.

"I grew up in a dysfunctional home," he continued. "I never wanted kids. Or a wife. I wanted to work and to travel. No emotional obligations. In the short time I've known you, all of that has gone out the window." Craig paused.

"My dad was not a nice man. Or a good man. He was a terrible father and absent husband. I might be just like him and I'm not willing to take that chance. I like fun and temporary, not deep and permanent."

Avery's green eyes flashed as she interrupted him.

"No buts. First, NO ONE can make me do something I don't want to do. Second, I never asked you to MARRY ME or give me children. I shared my story with you over wine and appies – now THAT I may regret in the future – and I kissed you. Why? Because maybe I am falling for you too. AND yes,

I am grieving for my dead husband, but who are you to tell me what I can and cannot do while I grieve? Am I vulnerable, yes, maybe? What is grief supposed to look like, anyway?? And for how long? Is it a month, a year, forever? Are you the grief police who decides that, Craig? Are you? AND how does anyone ever know how they will be in a situation until they've actually tried it? You are good and kind with animals – don't you think that shows your inner self? Or are you too busy worrying about something that may never happen?"

Avery was almost standing up, and she was magnificent. Her emerald eyes glinted, and every time she moved her head, her hair swung from side to side. God, she was impressive, and Craig knew in that moment that he was a goner, and no one else would ever come close to instilling that feeling in him. But he had to continue. He couldn't risk his job, his partnership, his sanity by getting involved with her. She was a Heart Creek McCoy, for heaven's sake, and her sister and fiancé were his partners in the practice.

"Avery," Craig kept his voice calm and low. "No, I'm not the grief police and no, I'm not trying to tell you what to do. What I am trying to say, badly as it turns out, is that my respect for you and your family means that I need to step back from any kind of relationship with you. Your future brother-in-law is my partner. Your sister is my other partner. I come from a messy childhood. I can't risk screwing that up by an ill-timed, inappropriate affair with you just because I'm at least halfway in love with you." Oops. As soon as the words left his lips, Craig knew he'd blown it. He'd screwed up big time.

Avery's face was white as she stood and slid out of the booth. Opening her purse, she tossed money on the table.

"Well, I was going to talk to you about us just being friends. And no, not friends with benefits either BUT God forbid we have an AFFAIR. Can't risk that, oh no. Don't want to annoy the MCCOYS! Guess what? You've annoyed THIS McCoy! Thanks for dinner and the outstanding pep talk." And she strode out of the restaurant just as their server brought a platter of nachos to their table.

"Uh, can you make that to go?" Craig asked, sweat pooling down the back of his shirt. He wanted to smack himself on the head. That wasn't how the conversation was supposed to go. Not one iota. Oh boy.

Chapter Eleven

Avery fumed all the way back to her room. What a jerk! And she thought she was in love with this guy. She sat heavily on the bed. Oh yeah, she was in love with this guy. Rightly or wrongly. And now, thanks to her hot temper and his stupid hardheadedness, they couldn't even be friends. Aaargh.

It was over five months since Josh had died, but in reality, their marriage had died a few years before that. The twins weren't planned. In fact, she had been thinking about leaving the ranch that spring. She loved her boys more than herself and she would never be sorry she had them, but to be honest, she had spent a lot of time grieving what she and Josh had somehow lost well before the boys were born. They'd drifted apart, maybe because they'd married relatively young or maybe because he wanted different things than she did. She'd never wish him ill and his death and the guilt for the part their fight had possibly played in his death was something she would never get over or forgive herself for. She was happy for the good times they'd shared and that he'd given her their sons.

As for Craig, well, she did understand what he'd meant about not wanting a fling to ruin his relationship with the other McCoys. His career was important to him, and he was a good man. Too good for her. God, he probably thought she was throwing herself at him the way she'd kissed him the other night. She could see the headline now: *Grieving Widow Latches onto the First Available Man She Sees.* Sheesh.

He had said he was falling in love with her though. Or maybe he was just saying that to let her down easily? Something else to not be sure about.

Avery sighed and stretched her neck. She missed her boys, and she missed home. Heart Creek home. Checking her phone, she noted that her two appointments were in the morning so she could check out early and head back to Heart Creek. A few days alone before the boys got home would give her time to draw up some designs and get her head on straight.

She was a Heart Creek McCoy. Better start acting like one.

Craig watched the hockey game in his room and tried not to think about Avery. *Good luck with that. The picture of her striding away in the restaurant stuck in his mind – she was brilliantly angry, almost throwing sparks as she walked. That hair. And the way her face showed everything she was thinking. She was really something special.*

The third period buzzer signaled the end of the game and Craig realized he'd missed the last half of the period, lost in thought. Probably a good thing he was heading back to Heart Creek in the morning. Plenty to talk about with Finn and Chelsea.

Maybe Heart Creek wasn't the place for him. With his experience, he'd have no problem finding a job somewhere else and maybe even a partnership. Plus, with nothing and no one to tie him down, he was free to go wherever he wanted. Visions of Avery and her sons flitted through his mind, but he hastily forced his mind elsewhere. That door was closed. Shut, finito, done. Of course, he'd stay until the clinic found someone else. That could be a while, but he could live with that. If he knew he wasn't staying, he could keep living in the apartment by the clinic and not worry about buying a place.

Had he just talked himself into leaving the clinic and Heart Creek?

Avery slept through her alarm the next morning and had to hurry to get to the north end of Edmonton in time for her meeting. Fortunately, she'd missed rush hour traffic on the Henday and made it with two minutes to spare. Afterwards, inspired and motivated to create her products, she hit a fast-food drive-through and thoroughly enjoyed her fries and soda on the way to her last meeting. That done, she drove back to the hotel and packed her bags. She couldn't find a luggage cart, so it took two trips with all the bags, which persuaded her to nip to the coffee shop for an iced coffee for the trip south. Twenty minutes later, she was on her way home.

The first person she saw when she pulled up to the ranch house a few hours later was Ryker, back from Houston. Parking, she jumped out of the vehicle and raced onto the deck to give him an enormous hug.

"Whoa there, girlie," he said, adjusting his hat that she had almost knocked off his head. "Lemme look at you." Holding her out in front of him, he kissed her forehead. "Looking mighty good, Avery," he said finally. "I like your hair. Haven't seen it this short since you were sweet on that young fella Wade whatshisname back in eleventh grade. Looks good on you."

Avery blushed. "Wade Armstrong, I think. He was cute." She rolled her eyes.

Ryker laughed, then sobered. "How are you really, mama?" he asked.

Avery's eyes flooded, much to her chagrin. "I'm good, Ryk. I miss Josh, but I'm okay. Really."

"Okay then," Ryker said. "Glad to have you home. Can't wait to see those young varmints of yours."

"Saturday. Tasha and Bernie will bring them up then."

"Excellent. Need a hand?" Ryker looked over at the SUV.

Avery nodded. "Sure do. Follow me."

At the vehicle, she loaded Ryker with bags and parcels.

His eyebrows rose almost to his hairline. "Did ya leave anything for the other folks?" he complained. Avery laughed and patted his shoulder.

"Plenty."

"Highly doubtful, from what I can see." Ryker pretended to limp to the deck. "So heavy, going down..."

"Oh brother," Avery called. "Getting weak in your old age, are you?"

Ryker's only answer was a grunt. Avery closed the truck and headed up the walkway with her luggage. It was good to be home.

Craig pulled up to the clinic, parking as close as possible to his apartment. He'd stopped on the drive home for a long walk along the waterfront in Sylvan Lake, then had an early supper at the local barbecue joint. As a result, it was dark when he pulled in and the clinic lights were off. The parking lot was lit, and his outside light was on, so he had no trouble getting to the stairs leading to his place.

Once inside, he unpacked and started a load of laundry in the washer. It felt empty and uninviting somehow, feelings he hadn't noticed about his home before. Or maybe it was just his mind projecting now that he'd decided to leave Heart Creek. Opening the fridge, he perused the contents, glad he was only away for a few days and almost everything except a head of lettuce was still good. He wasn't really hungry, but he was feeling snacky. Filling a bowl with potato chips and cracking open a beer, he sat down to find something to watch.

As he munched, he contemplated what he might do next. He enjoyed the work with both small and large animals but would be open to something different. He wasn't sure what, but he knew it was out there, just waiting for him to find it.

It was nice to be home, even if it was just temporary.

Chapter Twelve

A very had spent much of the evening thinking. She could go back to teaching. She loved that. The boys were three, and that was a good age to send them to daycare. They were pretty social, having each other for company, but being around other kids and doing different things would be fun for them, too. Her mind drifted, remembering she'd seen listings in Cochrane for teachers. Harder in Heart Creek, of course. She did love making her jewelry and creating holistic and organic pet supplies, but would it be enough to satisfy her craving for more? She wasn't any the wiser by the time she went to bed.

After breakfast, she decided to head to the boutique and see if the ideas she'd had in Edmonton would work. She met Ryker as she was leaving the ranch house.

"Where you off to?" he asked, after saying good morning.

"To see the boutique," she replied. "Wanna come?"

"Sure, I have nothing better to do right now," Ryker said.

"Oh gee, thanks," Avery mumbled. Ryker fell into step with her as they got into the SUV to drive around to the clinic.

After parking, Avery dashed into the clinic to say hi to Chelsea, then patiently waited for Ryker to finish talking to Finn. As they walked around the building to the path to the boutique and rescue facility, Avery stopped short.

Craig was walking from the rescue area towards them.

Uh-oh. She wasn't ready for this yet.

"Um, maybe we can go later," Avery said to Ryker, pulling at his sleeve.

Ryker pushed back his hat and looked at her. "What's going on with you?"

"Good morning!" Craig's voice floated towards them.

Too late. Avery sighed and turned around. Face the music time. "Good morning," she said primly. "Excuse me, I'm in a hurry." She pushed past Craig, leaving Ryker behind. In her mind, she could imagine her brother's expression and knew she'd have to answer later.

She could hear the men's voices as they chatted. She didn't slow down until she got to the boutique, then she drew out her sketchbook and pencil, sat on a bench at the far side of the store, and caught her breath.

"What in the Sam Hill was that all about?" Ryker stood beside her, waiting for her reply.

"Uh, I was in a hurry to get started," she tried.

Ryker scratched his head. "One second before that, you wanted to leave. And you were a bit short with Craig."

Avery bit her lip, thinking of her answer.

"Oh." Ryker's face got a knowing look.

"Where were you these past few days?" he asked.

Avery sighed. "Edmonton."

"And Craig was in Edmonton, did something happen with you two?" Ryker's hands clenched.

Avery stood up. "Oh God, no," she said quickly. "We just don't get on."

"Like hell you don't. I saw how he looked at you." With those words, Ryker turned and strode out of the store.

"Nuts." Avery ran after him. "Nothing happened, Ryker," she yelled.

"Let him tell me that. Your husband isn't even cold in his grave and this guy is making moon eyes at you? Not on my watch."

"Ryker, no, it wasn't like that!"

"Hey, you! Craig," Ryker's voice rang out, hard and deep.

Craig turned and walked toward him, just as Avery got to Ryker on the other side.

"What's up?" Craig said cheerfully.

Avery could hardly catch her breath. She had to stop this before it got ugly. Ryker had it wrong.

"Ryker," she rasped. "Nothing happened. Or well, hardly anything. I kissed him but he said no." Uh-oh, that wasn't what she'd meant to say.

Craig's face flushed as he realized what was happening. Ryker grabbed him by the shoulder and started marching him towards the parking lot.

"Ryker, stop, stop," Avery hollered, running up behind them.

Ryker stopped. "You!" he pointed to Craig. "Talk. Now."

Craig looked at Avery. She threw up her hands. "He thinks you took advantage of me."

"Whhhaat?" Craig floundered. "No, no, not at all."

"Did you kiss?" Ryker demanded.

"Uh, well, yes, but..." Craig obviously didn't know what to say.

Ryker lifted his arm and Avery grabbed onto it with all her strength.

"What the heck is going on?" Finn and Chelsea came around the corner from the clinic.

"This guy," Ryker yelled, "took advantage of Avery's situation."

Both Craig and Avery threw up their arms.

"No, no, he didn't!" They both yelled, then looked at each other and started laughing. Avery couldn't help it, and she couldn't stop. Soon her sides were aching.

"Would somebody please tell me what's going on," Chelsea begged. "I am pretty confused and there's a lot of yelling. Stop laughing." She looked at Avery and Craig pointedly.

Ryker opened his mouth, but Avery cut him off.

"Ryker thinks that Craig took advantage of me, a vulnerable widow, while we were in Edmonton."

Craig jumped in. "I didn't. I kissed her back and maybe a few hugs, but that was it."

Avery closed her eyes. That made it sound bad.

"Yes, I did kiss him. Yes, he kissed back. Is that a crime?"

Ryker fumed. "You are a widow. A recent widow, in fact."

Avery counted to ten. "Yes. Yes. I am a widow. My husband died five months ago. Yes, I am grieving. Does that mean I am dead, too? Can't I be attracted to someone enough to kiss them?"

Ryker roared, "No, you can't. You haven't had time to mourn. To process Josh's death."

Avery exploded.

"Says who? You? What do you know about grief? What do you know about me? Or Josh? Or our marriage? Who are you to say when the time is right?" Her chest heaved with indignation.

Ryker's mouth snapped shut with a click. Chelsea's eyes were round, and Finn was looking at them all as if they were crazy.

Craig moved closer to Avery. "I love her," he said simply.

"And I love him," Avery announced.

Avery looked deeply into Craig's eyes and sighed. "Yes, Craig, I am in love with you. I know that isn't what you want, but..."

"Hang on. I know I did say that, but I was wrong. I do want that. I do want you. I want to be stepdad to your boys, and I want to love you for the rest of my life."

"Really?" Avery's voice quavered. "What about your dad?"

"I love you so much I can't even bear it," Craig said, cradling Avery's face in his hands. "You are all I can think about, and I can't imagine a life without you."

Avery held her breath then felt tears fill her eyes as Craig brought his mouth to hers. When their lips touched, her heart flipped, and she wrapped her arms around his neck and kissed him back. When he lifted his head, she smiled into his eyes and was lost, hook, line, and sinker.

"Whoa!" said Finn.

Ryker came over. "Avery, I owe you an apology," he said. "I overstepped..."

Avery gazed at her big brother with love in her eyes.

"You were only looking out for me," she said softly, patting his arm. "But you know what? I'm okay, and I can look out for myself. Josh will always be part of my family, he's the father of our sons, but my heart has room for more. For Craig. I don't think love picks a time or place. It just happens."

Craig added, "There is always room for Josh. I never thought I would say this, but I am thankful there is also room for me."

Ryker chuckled. "Welcome home, you two."

About Lynn Gale

Lynn Gale has dreamed about writing romance ever since she read *If This Is Love* by Anne Weale in 1972. Years went by and she fell in love with romance all over again watching movies like *Romancing the Stone*, *American Dreamer*, and *Pride and Prejudice.*

Her first sweet romance novella *A Heart Creek Christmas* was published in 2023 as part of *A Cowboy This Christmas: A Sweet Romance Anthology* through the Calgary Association of Romance Writers of America (CaRWA) under the pen name Joanie Wilde. This novella will be released as a stand alone title in February 2025.

Each Heart Creek Book can be read as a stand alone title as well as part of the ongoing series *Return to Heart Creek*.

Acknowledgements

This book would not have been possible without the assistance and support of many people in my life.

My mentor romance author Katie O'Connor, who has been instrumental in guiding me through the process of honing my craft. She is my first reader and I am truly grateful for her direction and support, and for introducing me to my editor and my writing software Atticus.

My editor Terri St. Clair, for her thoughtful comments and excellent editing. My cover designer Laura Heritage of P.S. Cover Design & Author Services for the gorgeous covers for the Return to Heart Creek series.

My family for their love and support. I love you all so much! My sister Anne – remember when we wanted to be authors? It's happening! My super fan and dear friend Anne Marie – yes, there is a fine line between fan and stalker! My amazing island bestie Pat – miss you always.

And especially you, my readers – without you, these are just words on a page. Thank you for your support and for hanging in there with me while I develop my craft.

xxoo Lynn

A Heart Creek Wedding

Book Four - Return to Heart Creek Series

Lynn Gale

WINDSONG PUBLISHING CANADA

A Heart Creek Wedding

A Return to Heart Creek Novel

This book is a work of fiction. Names, characters, places, and incidents are either products of the author's imagination or used fictitiously. Any resemblance to actual events, locales, or persons, living or dead, is entirely coincidental.

Published in April 2025 (e-book and print book)

Digital ISBN: 978-1-0688010-2-0

Print ISBN: 978-1-998643-01-1

Cover design by P.S. Cover Design & Author Services

Copy Edited by Terri St. Clair

To JP, always. xo

Contents

Chapter One

"I now pronounce you husband and wife!"

Applause broke out in the small church at the pastor's pronouncement. Ryker McCoy brushed tears from his eyes. His brother Mac and the love of his life, Carrie, were married! The happy couple turned to face the crowd of family and friends who had gathered for their special day. Mac then wheeled himself down the aisle as Carrie walked at his side. Ryker linked arms with his sister, Chelsea, who was Carrie's bridesmaid, and followed the bride and groom out of the small church.

Outside, the early February sun was shining and although there was snow on the ground, the balmy temperature of 40 degrees held a hint of the promise of spring. The wedding party and guests loaded into waiting vehicles, heading to the reception at Heart Creek Ranch's main house. As best man, Ryker had the privilege of standing up for his brother and acting as his chauffeur. Lowering the ramp on the specialized van, he waited while Mac maneuvered his wheelchair into place. Once Carrie had settled herself and her wedding dress into place, Ryker raised the ramp and stepped into the driver's seat. Chelsea joined him in the passenger seat.

"I'll give those two a bit of privacy and ride up here with you." Chelsea's face was rosy and her eyes bright.

"Thinking about you and Finn? I think it's your turn next." Ryker grinned as he joined the line of vehicles leaving the church.

Chelsea laughed. "Well, Mom beat us all!" To the family's surprise and delight, their widowed mother Elizabeth, and the ranch's foreman Beau Boucher had tied the knot on New Year's Eve and then headed to Los Cabos for a honeymoon in the Mexican sun. "What about you, big brother? Any thoughts of heading down the aisle?"

Ryker frowned. "It would be easier if I had someone in mind," he replied drily. 'Not really on my agenda." Yet jealousy pierced his heart whenever he looked at Mac and Carrie and how in love they were.

"Love gets you when you least expect it," his sister quipped wisely.

Ryker grunted in reply as he turned the van into the long McCoy driveway and inched his way to the parking spot in front of the main door. Finn Buchanan, the local vet and Chelsea's fiancé, was there to open Chelsea's door, making sure her dress didn't get wet, and then assist Carrie and Mac's exit from the back of the van.

Chelsea fussed with Carrie's hair, straightening her veil and dress. Ryker ran a critical eye over Mac, noting with satisfaction the happiness that radiated from his brother. Ryker straightened Mac's collar and adjusted his cowboy hat. "I guess that's as good as you get, Macaroni" he drawled, using his brother's childhood nickname and deftly stepping out of range of Mac's hands. Mac laughed. "You're just jealous of my divine good looks."

Ryker nodded. "Agreed. You two all set for your big entrance?" Watching the newlyweds gaze into each other's eyes, so much in love, his heart twinged. He was jealous. He'd be the last to admit it, but he was lonely and longed for what his siblings – and even his mom – had found in their partners. Companionship, love, and something else he couldn't quite define.

When both Mac and Carrie nodded, he assisted Mac up the ramps and into the foyer inside the main doors. From there, he moved forward into the main room. Using all the dramatic flair he remembered from long-ago high school drama classes, he mimed an imaginary drumroll and announced, "Ladies, Gentlemen, and Cowboys, may I present Mr. and Mrs. Mac and Carrie McCoy!" He stepped aside to let the happy couple through. Once again, he marveled at the aura of happiness and love surrounding them. It had been a tough couple of years since Mac's rodeo accident and Carrie had made a world of difference to Mac's attitude and outlook. For not the first time, Ryker thanked his lucky stars that he'd met Carrie in Houston and invited her to join Heart Creek Ranch as an equine osteopath for their rescued and recovering race and rodeo horses. She had a magical way about her – not only with the horses, but also with his brother Mac. Their journey to the altar had not been without its challenges, but together they had overcome them. They had combined their dreams, and the result was Heart Creek Haven, a rehab center for retired rodeo cowboys, which now took up several acres of land on

Heart Creek Ranch. Part of the building included an accessible apartment for Mac and Carrie to live onsite.

"Excuse me." A sweet voice behind him startled him from his thoughts.

"Sorry?" Turning, he looked at the young woman standing there. Startling blue eyes in a heart-shaped face gazed up at him, surrounded by clouds of long dark hair. His first thought was *holy cats, she's gorgeous,* and his second was *I am so done for*! He shook his head to clear his thoughts.

"May I get past?" Her voice was soft and liquid, slipping over his skin like warm silk. Whoa.

"Uh, of course, sure, sorry." He moved out of her way and watched her walk across the room towards Carrie, giving the bride and groom each a hug. Her flowy midnight blue dress ended above her knees, with petite dark blue cowboy boots on her feet and silver bracelets adorning her wrists. She was a charming blend of down-to-earth cowboy chic and uptown sophistication. Ryker didn't recognize her. Was she new to town? Of course, he realized there were many people in town he didn't know, seeing as he spent most of his time on the ranch. Although she wasn't very tall – maybe five foot four? – she had an air of confidence that made her seem taller. As she moved over to greet other people, he realized who she was. The wedding planner. They HAD met at the wedding rehearsal last night although he couldn't recall their conversation. He'd shown up late to the rehearsal because of problems with a horse. He remembered her frown when he finally appeared, but the rest was blurry.

"Lynsey Adams. You met her last night."

Ryker started. Finn was at his elbow, grinning.

"Her name is Lynsey Adams," Finn repeated. "Wedding planner."

Ryker nodded. "Right, right, I knew that."

Finn laughed out loud. "You don't remember meeting her."

Ryker frowned. "I was pretty beat. Long day with the horses."

"Sure thing. We'll go with that. Hey, looks like you could use a top up, and it's just about time for dinner."

Ryker followed Finn to the dining room, where the head table sat. The room dazzled in blue and silver, Carrie's colors, with a dash of flaming red here and there. The three-tiered wedding cake held a bride with a groom in a wheelchair on top, and icing horseshoes in gleaming silver around the tiers, with forget-me-nots in between.

"Admiring the cake?"

Ryker almost jumped out of his skin.

"Hello." he smiled at the woman. "I'm Ryker, best man and brother to the groom."

"I know who you are. We met last evening, but I guess you've forgotten already. I'm Lynsey Adams, the wedding planner."

The coolness in her voice startled him. "Oh, last night. Right. I was late to the rehearsal. We had a sick horse and I..."

Lynsey shrugged. "No problem. It all worked out despite your rudeness."

Ryker opened his mouth to apologize, but Lynsey had walked away. Oh, nuts. Had he said something last night to tick her off? He'd been so tired that he scarcely remembered the rehearsal itself, let alone any conversation.

At that moment, the guests spilled into the room, finding their names on the beautiful horseshoe place cards. He moved into the kitchen, smiling at the staff and inhaling the delicious smells before stepping into the washroom to cool his burning face and wash his hands. He sighed as he glanced into the mirror, acknowledging that his nearly forty years on the ranch had carved themselves into every line and wrinkle on his face.

Mac and Carrie had taken their seats at the head table when he arrived just before Chelsea breezed up, followed by Finn. A few taps on a wineglass, the traditional kiss, and the dinner began. Ryker scanned the room for Lynsey, seeing her now and again as she slipped in and out. Unclear what a wedding planner did, he imagined it didn't allow time to sit or eat or to be still much at all.

Oh, it was toasts and speeches next. He stood to deliver his speech, hoping he'd remember what he'd planned to say and didn't make a horse's rear end of himself. He hated public speaking!

Lynsey Adams moved around the spacious ranch house, making sure all was in order. So far, it was going according to plan, and she breathed a sigh of relief. She loved her job as a wedding planner, but it could be stressful. Fortunately, Mac and Carrie were easy to work with and didn't have any crazy demands for their wedding. She'd had her share of bridezillas in the past.

Pausing at the back of the room, she watched Ryker McCoy stand for his speech. He was tall and broad-shouldered. With his sun-kissed blond hair and brilliant blue eyes a stunning contrast to his tanned and weathered face, he was breathtakingly handsome. White teeth flashed, his grin appearing now and then to punctuate his words. She knew he managed the ranch, and his capable manner and confidence shone through as he spoke. The McCoys were a tightly knit family and cared for each other a great deal. She'd felt the pull of attraction when she'd met him last evening, but he had pretty much shut her down. Arriving late, he'd brushed off her attempts to catch him up, instead moving to Mac's side and simply standing there while they went through the rehearsal. In retrospect, she realized he was probably exhausted, she'd reacted and immediately categorized him in the 'rude and overbearing' male column. She'd had more than her share of experiences with that in her day job as a firefighter, and it still riled her whenever it happened.

Bringing her focus back to the wedding, she was thrilled to see how beautifully it had come together. Romance was her heart's secret joy, and weddings helped her bring that joy to life. Plus, it paid well and gave her something to do in her spare time. Firefighting was in her blood – her dad and her grampa had both been firefighters, and she loved everything about it, except the occasional prejudice she encountered. She was strong, fit, and more than able to hold her own. One day, though, she knew she would be happy to hang up her gear and focus fully on wedding planning. At thirty-seven, she knew her window for having children was starting to close, and most of the time she was okay with that. Her first marriage had ended because of her insistence on pursuing her chosen career. She still believed that true love meant being yourself and both partners accepting each other as they were, not changing to fit someone else's idea of how the other should be.

"Lynsey?" Sammy, the photographer, approached her. "I think it's time to cut the cake, is that right?"

Lynsey checked her itinerary on her tablet, realizing she'd lost track of time and missed the end of the speeches.

"Yes, then we'll do some photos with different guests with the happy couple." Sammy nodded in agreement and meandered to the head table, camera in hand. Lynsey scanned the rest of the list, noting her presence would soon not be required. As much as she loved this job, her feet were tired, and a cup of cocoa and a book would end her evening nicely.

Waiting for the cake to be cut, she stood to the side. Ryker and Chelsea were helping Carrie hand out the cake; suddenly, a plate was thrust into Lynsey's hand. Gazing up to meet Ryker's gaze, she smiled, despite her less than stellar feelings about him. "Thank you."

"I noticed you haven't sat down this entire evening," Ryker's deep voice rumbled over her. "I thought a coffee and a piece of cake might be just the thing. Everything is under control. You did a great job."

Surprised at his words, Lynsey gratefully sank into a vacant chair. He produced a cup of fragrant coffee which he placed beside her cake plate. He sat beside her with a plate of cake and a cup of coffee. "It's decaf," he noted. "Just in case that's what you prefer."

Lynsey nodded gratefully and took a sip of deliciousness before using her fork to scoop a bite of cake.

"This is so good!" The marble cake was light and fluffy, and the melding of vanilla and chocolate danced over her taste buds.

"Did you even eat dinner?"

"Um, I had a protein bar a while back. I rarely eat when I'm working."

Ryker frowned at her. "Here, please have my piece of cake, too. I ate plenty of dinner."

"Your speech was surprisingly good," Lynsey shared in between bites.

"Thanks. Public speaking isn't my forte," Ryker admitted.

"Really? I never would have known."

Ryker guffawed. "Yeah, well, usually it's just me and the horses."

Lynsey laughed, almost choking on her mouthful of cake. Patting her back, Ryker handed her a glass of water. She drank deeply, marveling at the breadth of his hands. A hands-on rancher if his large, weathered palms were any indication.

"Thanks."

"Um, hey, I think we may have gotten off on the wrong foot. Last night?"

Lynsey swallowed, embarrassed. "Oh, it's okay."

"I was exhausted, and I think I ignored you when I arrived. When you were trying to tell me what to do. Sorry about that. Mac tells me I was a bear."

Lynsey gaped at him. She wasn't used to apologies.

"Uh, thanks, Ryker. It's all good."

He nodded and finished his coffee. "Good. Oh, Carrie is waving me over. First dance time. Must go do my best man duties."

When he had gone, Lynsey shivered. His closeness held a warmth that had encompassed her. What an interesting man Ryker McCoy was turning out to be. Huh.

She watched enviously as the bride and groom danced - Mac in his wheelchair and Carrie holding his hands as they swayed side to side. Ryker and the maid of honor joined them, followed by the rest of the wedding party. Lynsey loved this part of a wedding- when the happiness was real and the love in the air was addicting. Made one believe that happily-ever-afters were still possible. Maybe not for her, but certainly for her brides and grooms.

"Would you care to dance?" Ryker's sudden appearance at her side broke her train of thought, and she gazed up at him with a smile.

"Of course."

He pulled her to her feet, and as the music slowed to a waltz, she felt his warm hand on her back and his other hand holding hers. Rough and callused, as she already knew, but also gentle. So gentle.

"Not bad, cowboy," she whispered. He grinned and drew her closer to his broad chest. She lay her head on his shoulder and let the music fill her, while Ryker's powerful body moved her capably around the dance floor. As the song drew to an end, she lifted her head to thank him and got lost in his eyes. He leaned forward until their foreheads barely touched before he stepped back and, lifting her hand to his lips, kissed the back of it. A jolt ran through her, and by the widening of his pupils, also through him. Wow! Just wow. Breathless, she whispered a barely audible thank you and returned to her table.

What the heck just happened? Her limbs felt like cooked spaghetti, and her heartbeat pounded in her ears. She looked across the room to find Ryker watching her. Wow.

"Lynsey! Thank you so much! It's been amazing!" Carrie slid into the chair beside Lynsey and for the next few minutes, Lynsey lost herself in the happiness of a beautiful bride on her wedding day, grateful to have been part of it. This was what she loved most about her job-the connection with happy people, families, and romance. Vicariously, she shared in their joy, and it brought light and love to her own life. Each wedding brought her closer to her dream, saving money and building her network of wedding professionals. One day, she'd have a wedding boutique. Maybe even here, in Heart Creek. A girl could dream, couldn't she?

Chapter Two

"Penny for your thoughts, son." Elizabeth McCoy Boucher's gentle voice nudged Ryker from his musings. Nursing his second cup of coffee, he smiled at his mother. Elizabeth picked up the carafe, topped up his cup and filled a cup for herself before settling in at the large, scarred oak table.

"You look happy, Mom. Married life suits you."

His mother blushed, which, together with the sparkle in her eyes, took years off her age. "Beau is a good man. I am blessed to spend my future with him."

Ryker reached over and took her warm hand in his. "I'm glad you two finally found each other."

"And what about you, Ryker? It's been a long time since you've had a woman in your life."

Ryker sighed as he drained his cup. Lately, conversations always circled back to him and his lack of a partner.

"No time, Mom. You know the ranch keeps me plenty busy. Besides, who'd want a scruffy old hound dog like me?" He kept his tone light, but deep inside, he worried that maybe he'd missed the love boat and was too past his prime to get back on.

His mom frowned. "Nothing wrong with you that a little attitude adjustment can't fix. You just need to be a bit more open to the possibilities around you."

"Mom? A love lecture? I don't think so..."

"I'm still your mother, young man, and don't you forget it. Beau and I are heading home soon. Such a lovely wedding yesterday. Thanks for letting us stay over. You'll be all by your lonesome in this big house. It's about time you did something about that, don't you think?"

Ryker laughed, despite his growing irritation. "Yes, ma'am," he drawled, bowing his head and tipping an imaginary cowboy hat. Loading his cup and breakfast plate into the dishwasher, he kissed his mother on the top of her head and headed to the back foyer. Donning his rugged rubber boots and ranch coat, cowboy hat firmly in place, he headed for the big barn.

As Ryker tended to the horses and caught up with the ranch hands, his mind whirled. He was thirty-nine years old, and his mother was still trying to give him advice. Of course, he wanted someone to share his life. Be with. Confide in, and talk about things, good and bad. To reminisce about their day over an enjoyable meal. To have a child with...

Whoa! Where did that come from? He had long given up hope of having children and was content with his two nephews. Darn his mother and her ideas. Now he was thinking silly thoughts and getting himself worked up.

"Boss?"

"What's up, Brendan?" Relieved to have his thoughts interrupted, Ryker listened intently to Brendan's concerns about Sadie, a former chuck wagon racer. The horse suffered the stiffness and pain that came with old age. Carrie, now his sister-in-law, spent hours each week with these horses, and as an equine massage therapist, her goal was to help them be as pain free as possible. Lately, though, Sadie had been showing signs of distress and Brendan was concerned. Stopping by her stall, Ryker examined the old mare, noticing definite discomfort and trembling as he perused her body. She even turned away from the apple he offered, a sure sign that something was off.

"Call Finn. Or Craig. Whoever is on today." Finn Buchanan had taken over the local vet clinic when the old doctor had retired, joined by Craig Willmott several months ago.

"I'm on it. I'll keep you posted." Brendan covered Sadie with a blanket and spoke quietly into his cell phone.

Ryker moved on, inspecting the rest of the horses before heading to the barn where the healthy horses lived. Saddling his favorite stallion, Sweet Daddy, he settled himself onto the horse's back. He could use an ATV to get around the ranch, but riding his horse calmed his soul, and he needed that today. The fences needed inspecting and that would keep him occupied until the vet determined what was going on with Sadie. Deep down, Ryker figured it was just her time to go, and if that were the case, at least they had done all they could to give her a comfortable passing. That was the ranch's mission-helping horses recover, rehabilitate, and spend their last years in comfort and peace.

I wonder if Lynsey rides, he mused, then caught himself up short. *Where had that thought come from?* They hadn't started off on the best foot, but something about her piqued his curiosity and interest. Of course, she was gorgeous and appealing. The memory of her warmth against him while they danced, and those bewitching eyes haunted him, but there was something else too. *Whoa. Her confidence maybe?* He wasn't sure, but for the first time in a long time, he wanted to find out. Maybe his mother wasn't so far off the mark after all!

Now that Lynsey had crept to the forefront of his thoughts, Ryker was finding it impossible not to think about her. Like a snippet of a song that annoyingly sticks with you, her brilliant blue eyes and dark silky hair wound in and out of his mind. He hadn't asked if she was married or what she did when she wasn't helping brides plan their weddings. Maybe she had a husband and dozens of little kids running around at home. The thought jolted him, and he pulled back on the reins, bringing Sweet Daddy to a sudden stop. "Sorry, buddy," he soothed, sensing the reprimand in the big horse's body. "Let's go for a ride!" He flicked the reins and let the stallion move into a gallop, the cool air rushing past, blowing errant thoughts of Lynsey and her life right out of Ryker's mind.

"Good morning, Chief." Lynsey smiled as she passed the Fire Chief's office, registering the grin on Fire Chief Rob Montgomery's weathered face.

"Deputy Chief Adams," the Chief acknowledged. "How was your weekend?"

"Weddings and laundry. My usual."

Rob laughed. "I don't know how you do it. Working here all week, then your wedding business on the side."

Lynsey settled into her office, across the hall from the Chief's. "Well, it's not like we are crazy busy here," she said. "At least not all the time."

The Chief nodded. "True, true."

Heart Creek Protective Services consisted of fire, ambulance, and bylaw officers housed in the same building. The Fire Chief, Deputy Chief, and two captains were full-time positions, Monday to Friday, and the other firefighters worked on-call as needed. There was also a full-time fire admin. There were two ambulance paramedics and one driver, plus a bylaw officer on staff. In the event of a big incident, county firefighters and paramedics were available to help.

After ten years of being on the floor then five years as a captain in a career fire department in Regina, Saskatchewan, Lynsey was thrilled to land the position of Deputy Fire Chief in Heart Creek. Years of working shifts made the straight day shifts even more welcome. Long shifts and multiple callouts, coupled with the demanding work, had taken a toll on her marriage to Mitch Adams, her high school boyfriend. She had trained as a paramedic, then firefighter, and they had gotten married when he graduated from university with a degree in business. His job was nine to five, and hers was not. It took a few years for the relationship to dissolve, and by the end, they hardly ever saw each other. Since then, Lynsey was determined to keep relationships casual. She loved what she did, and even though her soft heart longed for her own happily ever after, she was content to experience that feeling through the weddings she planned and the happy couples she met along the way.

Today she was doing one of her favorite things-teaching fire prevention at the local elementary school. Being in the red fire engine always gave her a thrill, and the kids loved seeing the big truck pull up outside the front entrance. The captain on duty, Joe Kline, accompanied her, driving the truck and wearing full bunker gear to demonstrate for the class.

After class, when she and Joe were packing up the equipment, the teacher, Molly Davis, came over to thank them.

"By the way, I heard that Mac and Carrie's wedding was amazing!" Molly raved. Joe chuckled as he carried the heavy bags out to the fire truck. Lynsey picked up the remaining bag and walked out with Molly.

"Carrie has great taste, and it was fun bringing her dreams to life." Lynsey smiled.

"Hoping you can plan my wedding one day," Molly spoke wistfully.

Lynsey nodded her head enthusiastically. "I'd love to!"

"It won't be soon, just dreaming on my part."

Lynsey loaded the bag in the back hatch and climbed into the right-hand seat. "Maybe we can do coffee sometime?"

Molly's red curls bounced as she agreed. "That would be nice. I still don't know very many people here."

"Me either. I'm free next Saturday if you want to meet up at Homegrown for lunch."

They settled on a time, and then Lynsey slammed the door and nodded to Joe. "Let's go, Captain."

The engine pulled away from the school, pausing at the playground to run the flashing lights for the kids, before heading back to the station.

"She seems nice," Joe said as they drove through town.

Lynsey chuckled. "Why don't you come to lunch with us?"

Joe blanched. "No, it's a girls' lunch. Maybe another time."

"I'll put in a good word for you."

Joe shrugged his shoulders as if he didn't care one way or the other, but Lynsey knew he was interested in the sweet young teacher. In his mid-thirties, Joe was single, and although he'd been in Heart Creek for a few years, he had yet to find someone. Maybe Molly would be his someone. And, as a side benefit, it would give Lynsey another wedding to add to her growing list. Even in a small community, weddings were plentiful. It was one reason she hadn't minded leaving the bigger city of Regina for the smaller community of Heart Creek.

That evening, Lynsey curled up on her comfy couch, romance book in hand, popcorn standing by, and pulled a soft blanket over her body as she settled in. The book's title, *A Cowboy This Christmas,* spurred thoughts of Ryker McCoy, the big rancher at Mac and Carrie's wedding. Mac's brother. Rude and somewhat overbearing had been her first thoughts but after speaking with him at the wedding, she realized he'd been busy with the ranch. Such a gorgeous hunk of man-tall, broad-shouldered, with streaky blond hair and denim blue eyes. Solid and capable, with strong hands. Gruff but kind. Probably he gave great hugs if his dancing was anything to go by.

Wait, whoa there, girl. Where are you going with this? You're getting caught up in your fantasies.

Grabbing a handful of popcorn, she shoved the fragrant buttery morsels into her mouth to prevent the drooling that thoughts of Ryker were inducing and opened her book. With nine shorter romance stories, the anthology was perfect and a great way to lose herself in someone else's love story for a time.

The next couple of days were filled with meetings and the completion of reports for the previous month's statistics to the province. The hours flew by and suddenly it was Saturday and time to meet Molly for lunch. Dressed in soft jeans and a pale blue cashmere sweater, she tucked her feet into waterproof boots. The early morning air was warm, and the roads and sidewalks were sloppy with melting snow. As she walked the short block to the restaurant, she inhaled fresh mountain air and the sweetness of baking bread from the bakery around the corner from her condo.

"Lynsey, hi!" Molly's voice sang out in the busy café and Lynsey made her way past full tables, smiling at people as she went to the booth in the back where Molly waited.

"This was a great idea. Umm, what are you having?" Lynsey picked up the menu and cast her eyes over the list before gazing at the chalkboard with the day's special listed.

"Minestrone, yum! And a cinnamon bun." Molly laughed. "I can't resist them."

"Right? I'll have the same, oh, and coffee too."

After giving the young server who approached the table their order, Lynsey settled into her seat. "How are you liking Heart Creek?"

Molly smiled. "I'm loving the kids. Second grade is such fun to teach. And I enjoy being so close to the mountains." The server dropped off their coffees and Molly added cream to hers before taking a deep sip. "The town is beautiful and quaint. My hometown is a similar size, so it feels comfortable to me. The people seem nice. Of course, I've mostly only met parents."

Lynsey nodded in agreement. "Heart Creek rocks the small-town vibe. I love the shops here. There's a bakery near my condo and oh my, it's a wonder I don't gain ten pounds just from breathing the air. It smells divine!"

Molly nodded. "I'm renting a place near the school. It's great because I can walk most of the time. I have a one-year lease. If I decide to stay after this school year, I want to get a place of my own. I'm here on a term contract covering a maternity leave, but it sounds like Mrs. Olsen may not be returning. If that's the case, I hope to continue teaching here. And what about you, Lynsey? Or shall I say, Deputy Chief Adams?"

"Lynsey's fine, thanks. I've only been here five months myself. I was going to rent until I was sure the position would work out, but this condo kind of fell into my lap when I was looking for a rental, and it was too good a deal to pass up. So, I bought it. I figured, why not? I can always rent it if the job doesn't pan out."

"How are you finding the station? I find it fascinating that you work in fire services. I know there are more women in that field all the time."

Lynsey took a big sip of coffee before she answered. "The guys are great, for the most part. There are always a few who find it hard when their officer is a woman, but thankfully, the chain of command is respected no matter what. The chief is planning on retiring next year, so who knows what will happen then?"

"How did you get into that line of work?"

"My grampa was the fire chief in a small town near Regina. Dad joined the RCMP, and we moved fairly often. I trained as a paramedic and did volunteer firefighting, then fell in love with the fire side of things. Fire is fascinating, as well as cruel and unforgiving at times. I signed up for the basic training and took it when I was off shift, then was able to get on full-time. That was fifteen years ago, and I've never regretted it."

"I'll bet your grampa is proud of you."

Lynsey sighed. "Grampa died before I made Captain. But yes, I think he would have been."

Molly started to speak then stopped as the server brought their food. Tucking into their soup, Lynsey realized it had been a long while since she'd had a female friend. Yes, she'd been busy with moving and working, but that wasn't a good excuse. The thought popped into her mind that she'd been avoiding people. Maybe for fear of judgment, or maybe just finding it easier not to get involved. It was high time she changed that.

Chapter Three

Ryker slammed the tailgate closed on the truck and then hopped into the driver's seat. Usually, Tommy or one of the other ranch hands took care of garnering any supplies they needed in between regular shipments, but today, he'd volunteered himself to do the run into town. He had a hankering for the big, gooey cinnamon buns over at Homegrown Café. Ida made the best ones. Even thinking about it tickled his taste buds.

He stopped at the hardware store, then the farm store, before making his way to the south end of town to the café. It took a few minutes to find a parking space. Once inside, he could see why. The place was full. Joining the line for the counter, he gazed around, nodding at people he knew. He caught a glimpse of shiny dark hair – on a woman sitting near the back of the café. She had her back to him, but from the way his breathing increased, he knew it was Lynsey, the wedding planner. He didn't know the red-haired young woman sitting with her. He stared at their table long enough that the redhead lifted her eyes and gazed at him. Belatedly, he realized he was being rude, so he smiled slightly before looking away. Of course, he couldn't help sneaking another peek, and noticed she'd leaned forward and said something to her companion, who then turned to look at him. Yep, it was Lynsey. He could feel the heat of her cobalt blue-eyed glance from across the room.

"Ryker McCoy, as I live and breathe! Haven't seen you in here for, well, I don't know how long." Ida's hearty voice broke into Ryker's trance, and he realized it was his turn.

"Ida Mae, I swear you get younger every time I see you! What are you doing here today? I thought you retired?"

"Oh, tosh, boy. I still help out whenever Rosemary needs a hand. Now, what can I get you? Cinnamon buns, I'm thinking?"

"Two of your finest, please. Hang on...make that six. I can pop them in the freezer."

Ida deftly placed six buns into a cardboard bakery box and fastening the lid, she placed the box on the counter. "Anything else?"

"That's good for me." Ryker paid and placed the change in the tip cup. They chatted for a few more minutes, and then Ryker realized he was holding up the line. With a smile, he bid her farewell.

"Ryker."

He stopped and turned, seeing Lynsey waving him over to her table.

Yikes. His insides were churning suddenly, but he made his way through the tables, dodging hands that were reaching for his box in jest.

"Good morning."

"Good morning to you. Would you care to join us?"

No. Yes. Yikes. They were in a booth for two, and there was no way his big frame was going to fit beside either of them. Fortunately, there was an extra chair at a table near them, so he grabbed that and planted himself at the end of their table.

"Hello, Lynsey. And...?"

Molly reached out her hand to shake his. "I'm Molly Davis, grade two teacher at Heart Creek School."

"Nice to meet you, Molly. I'm Ryker McCoy. I own Heart Creek Ranch."

Molly squealed. "Oh, the horse rescue ranch. And now I think you have something for retired cowboys, too?"

Ryker grinned at her enthusiasm. "Yes, Heart Creek Haven. My brother Mac and his wife run that. Maybe your class would like to do a field trip to the ranch one day?"

Molly nodded enthusiastically. "That would be fantastic. Thank you so much."

Ryker turned to Lynsey. "And how are you? Any more weddings on the horizon to keep you busy?"

"A couple in June and one in September. Oh, and a tentative one for Christmas Eve."

Ryker nodded. "I hope business picks up for you."

"Me too," Lynsey agreed. "And what brings you to town today?" Her blue eyes held his gaze, his breath once again quickening. This woman sure had some kind of effect on him! He held up the bakery box. "These. And a few errands. Usually, one of the hands does our town trips, but it's nice to step away from the ranch for a change."

A loud buzzing sound interrupted the conversation. Lynsey reached into her backpack and pulled out a cell phone, glancing at the screen before frowning.

"Sorry, I must go. Thanks, Molly. Let's touch base soon. Ryker, always nice to see you." She deftly moved through the still crowded café and took off running when she got out the door.

Ryker looked at Molly. "A wedding emergency?" he wondered out loud.

She gave him an odd look. "No, she..." Her words were cut off by a large man clapping a hand on Ryker's shoulder.

"Thought that was you, Ryker McCoy. Don't see you often in town. How's the ranch?" Ryker chatted with the man for a few minutes ,then turned back to Molly, his face apologetic for the interruption.

"Sorry, what was that you were saying?"

"Oh, nothing important. Nice to meet you, Ryker. I have some shopping to do. Enjoy the baking. It's delicious!"

"Don't forget about the field trip. Nice to meet you, Molly." Ryker rose so Molly could vacate the booth, and then he left the café himself.

Odd about Lynsey. Wonder what that was all about.

At the station, Lynsey donned her bunker gear. Normally she and the chief didn't go on calls unless it was a massive structure fire needing all available personnel, but they were down a man this weekend as one captain was on vacation.

Within ten minutes, she was in the right-hand seat, and the fire engine was heading down Main Street, lights flashing and sirens blaring. The ambulance followed a safe distance behind. Fortunately, they could change the traffic lights, and the residents of Heart Creek did a good job of pulling over when the engine went through. It wasn't often, but often enough to build awareness.

The emergency call was for a kitchen fire, with one known injury. As they pulled into the short street where the residence was located, people were gathered in the small front yard, standing over someone lying on the ground. Examining the house, she could see dark smoke billowing out a side door. She flew into action. Calling out commands, she approached the bystanders while the firefighters connected the hose to the hydrant. Two firefighters entered the house, and after ensuring no one was inside, directed the hose where it was needed. Two paramedics tended to the person on the ground, loading them onto a stretcher and into the ambulance. It took off, sirens wailing a short time later.

"DC, the fire appears contained in the kitchen area. Started on the stove but spread to the attached dining room. I would say the patient tried to put out the fire, but it looks like the pan fell, and the fire caught the curtains and other items. Fire, smoke, and water damage present but the fire appears to be out. Will monitor."

Lynsey relayed the information to the crew and control, donned her mask, and then entered the house to view the situation. The house was thick with smoke residue. The kitchen was a dripping mess of burned furniture and water stains. Drywall and wallpaper had burned and were hanging in shreds. Melted wires hung from the walls, and the ceiling was singed. Black, charred remains on the melted linoleum and showed the path of the splatter. The stove was coated in black, and it was obvious there had been additional oil or caked debris under the burners, which had ignited. Despite the mask, the odors clung to her throat, and she once again marveled at the power of fire and how easily it could get out of hand.

Back outside, Lynsey removed her mask and headed over to Joe, her second-in-command.

"How is the patient?" She asked.

"Third-degree burns to the arms and thighs. He's heading to Edmonton now, DC."

"Age?"

"Seventy-six."

Oh dear. Burns were horrible at any age, but seniors had less resilience, and healing would be a tough battle. "Thanks." Although she kept her face neutral, inside she wept for the poor man and his suffering. It was the part of her job that broke her heart the most.

"Thanks, Joe. Everything out here under control?"

"Yes DC. We will maintain surveillance for 24 hours to ensure no hidden sparks or further ignition. The back-up crew brought over the smaller engine so you can take Engine 1 back to the station."

"Ten-four. Keep me posted."

She climbed into Engine 1 and waited for the departing crew to join her. As they pulled away, she drew a deep breath and addressed them. "Great job, as always. Thank you."

Back at the station, the crew changed and showered. She was currently the only woman on the crew but there was a full washroom attached to the Chief's office, which she had access to. "See you in half an hour for debriefing."

After the debrief, she entered her office, sinking into the chair. She was grateful that the fire wasn't worse. She couldn't stop thinking about the burn patient and his future journey to healing. Fire calls were exciting but exhausting. Adrenaline ran high, then once it depleted, the resulting low was a shock. She reached into her drawer for a protein bar, which she ate slowly, willing away the smell of smoke that lingered in her nostrils.

Wonder what Ryker would think of me now? She found it sweet that he was concerned about her wedding planning schedule, but had she told him about her day job? She wracked her brain but couldn't recall. Huh. Oh well, he'd find out soon enough, she was sure. In the meantime, she had work to do.

Chapter Four

B ack at the ranch, Ryker unloaded the supplies at the storage building and then headed to the house. Leaving his boots at the back door, he padded to the kitchen in his sock feet. Pouring himself a large glass of milk, he tucked into one of the cinnamon buns, moaning when the sweet flavors hit his taste buds. The house was eerily quiet. He hadn't noticed that before. The housekeeper who had been with them since he was a kid had retired after almost thirty-five years, and Mac hadn't had time to even think about replacing her. She had become part of the family. Now that the rest of the family had moved, Ryker was left to ramble about the big house all by his lonesome.

Sweet tooth sated, he made a half pot of coffee, poured a big mug, and settled into a comfy big armchair near the huge west-facing windows in the front room. Gazing thoughtfully at the snow-capped mountains, he sipped his hot brew and contemplated what was next for him now that his siblings and mother were following their own paths.

The ranch, of course. Horses were in his blood, and he couldn't imagine not living at Heart Creek Ranch and working with the animals. The dream of rescuing retired and injured former rodeo horses had come to fruition, and the ranch was never short of horse owners looking for a comfortable and safe next stage for their former champions. With the addition of Heart Creek Haven and the rehab center for cowboys, the circle completed itself. His brother and sisters were in solid relationships and even his mom had found happiness with Beau after years of waiting and putting the ranch and her children first.

Ryker sighed deeply. In May, he would turn forty. After a lifetime of putting the ranch and his family's well-being first, he was realizing what that had cost him. His mother, his sisters, and even his brother had life partners to share the future with. Not him. He had dated off and on, but the women soon became frustrated by his long hours and frenetic schedule.

What about Lynsey? Yeah, what about Lynsey? He knew he was attracted to her, and she ticked all his boxes. Did he even know how to have a relationship anymore? It had been years since his last girlfriend, and she'd gotten tired of the constant demands of the ranch on his time. Now he realized that she may have had a point, but back then, he couldn't see it.

In the meantime, he needed to find a new ranch foreman, a housekeeper slash cook, and a dog. Their last family dog, Piper, had passed in her sleep a few years prior, and Ryker just couldn't find it in his heart to replace her. Now, he craved the companionship a dog would offer. Maybe a mutt like Carrie's Winnie, or even a puppy. He could check out the Rescue Center next time he was over at Finn's vet clinic as well as ask around. Farmers and ranchers usually knew someone who had puppies looking for homes.

The general foreman part might be as easy – he could approach his two lead foremen and see if one of them was interested. He had meant to start that before Beau retired but with the frantic business of his mom and Beau's wedding then Mac and Carrie's, the time got away from him. The housekeeper might be harder to find. He gave himself a mental head smack. He could have asked Ida while he was in town. She was a great community resource and might even help with the puppy situation.

Those problems of his world still unresolved, he drained his cup and headed for his boots. A visit to Mac and Carrie was in order, and on the way, he could check out the fence repairs they'd made last week on the north field.

The day had warmed considerably, and he took the ATV to save time. As he approached the new buildings of the rehab center, he was once again amazed to see how perfectly it blended with its surroundings and the peaceful, welcoming vibe it held. Mac and Carrie were sitting on the patio in the sunshine, and as he approached, they lifted their hands in a welcoming wave.

"Good day, newlyweds!"

Carrie came over to hug him. "Hey, Ryker, nice to see you."

"And you, Mrs. McCoy. Married life agrees with you. Mac. Looking good, brother."

Mac laughed. "Living the dream, bro. Literally." As Carrie sat back down, Mac reached for her hand. She leaned over and kissed him.

A deep and resounding pang of envy coursed through Ryker's body. They were head over heels in love, and he wanted that too. For the first time he could recall, he wanted someone in his life. To love. To share with. "I thought I'd pop by and see how you two were faring. Quiet at the house.""I'll bet it is!" They sat and chatted for a while, then Ryker rose and, with a farewell wave, headed out to check on the newly repaired fence. He was happy to see his brother and Carrie enjoying their time together, and he breathed a sigh of relief that they had each other. One more thing he could mark off the ranch's never-ending to-do list. Or at least, off the list he carried around in his head: Mac. OK. Check. Chelsea. OK. Check. Mom. OK. Check. Avery. OK. Check. Ryker. Uh, oh. No check here.

He'd have to do something about that last one. He just wasn't sure where to start.

***

The local paper *Heart Creek This Week* came out every Friday and it was one of the many things Lynsey loved about this town. Usually there were more flyer inserts than actual paper, but the articles were always interesting. She loved reading about what was happening in council, and trying the recipe of the week, or catching up on the livestock reports. This particular Friday, she was surprised to see her face splashed on the front page at the fire scene from earlier that week. Her face was dirty with soot, and she looked tired but the headline **First Major Fire of the Year – No Deaths** made her happy. It wasn't always about stopping the fire. More, it was about controlling its spread, saving lives, and minimizing damage. Still, her vanity wished it were a more flattering photo, even though looks don't matter at an emergency scene. Or anywhere else, for that matter. At least, that was what she believed. Until she met Ryker, and her vanity kicked back in. For some reason, he made her want to present the best version of herself outwardly.

If he saw that photo, what would he think? She shuddered, then let the thought go. *You can't control what he thinks. Just be yourself, girl.*

Tying her hair into a ponytail, then wrapping that into a bun, she glanced in the mirror. In her uniform, she looked capable and put together, which was her goal. As Deputy Chief, she needed to convey confidence and authority. As a woman in her protective services role, she needed that to be tenfold. She made a face at herself, then picked up her travel mug and jacket. Time to head to work.

Ryker parked in front of Homegrown Café on his way to the vet clinic/animal rescue. As he breathed in the fragrant bakery aromas, his stomach growled, and visions of tasty baked goods again beckoned, making his mouth water. He could take something for the staff and keep one or two for himself, he decided. He remembered that there were still four cinnamon buns in the freezer at home, but what the heck? He could live on the edge.

"Ryker McCoy, twice in one week? I'm not sure my old heart can handle this!" Ida clasped her hands to her ample bosom as her familiar grin lit up her face.

"Two dozen of your finest cinnamon buns, please. And a tall coffee to go."

Ida laughed. "Going visiting, are you?"

"Heading to the rescue and vet clinic. Hey, you wouldn't know of anyone with pups, would you? Or a housekeeper looking for work?"

Ida paused as she thought. "Not offhand, but if I hear of anyone, I'll let you know." She handed Ryker his coffee and two large boxes. Rosemary, Ida's daughter, and the owner of the café came out from the back.

"Look what the cat dragged in! Things must be darn quiet at the ranch now with Mac and Carrie married and Elizabeth and Beau moved out."

Ryker nodded as he paid for the food. "Just me now. That's why I'm looking for a pet. A dog, actually. It's quiet there with just me. And I'm looking for a permanent housekeeper." They chatted for a few more minutes, and then he bid them goodbye and turned. At that moment, the door opened, and Lynsey entered. He almost didn't recognize her. Her hair was wound in a bun, and under her light jacket, she wore a uniform. A dozen thoughts went through his mind, the main one being, why would a wedding planner wear a uniform? A fire services uniform...

"Awesome picture in the paper!" Rosemary's voice rang out over the murmur of the café crowd, and Lynsey's face turned rosy with a blush. "Great job, Deputy Chief!"

Deputy Chief? What the heck?

Rosemary came around the counter and swept Lynsey in a hug. Turning, she held the paper up so that Ryker could see the front page showing the photo of Lynsey at the fire earlier in the week.

"But I thought you were a wedding planner," he mumbled, somewhat stupidly, as it was obvious she was much more than that.

"I am. I'm also the Deputy Fire Chief."

Ryker could have been knocked over with a feather. *Firefighter? Deputy Chief?* He felt his grasp on the bakery boxes sliding and it was all he could do to keep his composure and not spill his coffee all over himself. Setting the boxes safely on the counter, he paused.

"That's a very dangerous job." He frowned. She could get hurt, burned, or killed. What was she thinking doing a job like that? Every protective instinct in his body leaped to the forefront, his muscles tightening.

"They both can be, in their way," Lynsey grinned. She pointed at the boxes in his arms. "Hungry much, Ryker?"

He'd forgotten about his cinnamon buns. Tightening his grip, he forced a smile and left the cafe without responding, his head buzzing. The last thing he wanted was to be involved with someone who took such risks with their life. His heart couldn't take it.

Lynsey watched Ryker walk away, confused by his sudden coolness towards her. Was he one of those men who believed women shouldn't be in careers like firefighting? Even as a paramedic, she'd run into that. But Ryker?

Rosemary patted her arm. "Ryker is an old-fashioned type of man. Cowboys usually are. But give him time. He'll be fine."

"Really? That surprises me."

Rosemary shrugged. "Ranchers are typically traditional folks. He'll come round."

Lynsey frowned as she ordered her coffee. Nodding her head in thanks, she picked up her full travel mug and went to the fire hall. At least there she was respected for what she did.

Later that morning, as she drained the last of her coffee, a knock on her door raised her head from the budget reports she was compiling for the town council.

"DC? Do you have time to talk?"

"Of course, Bruce, come in. Shut the door behind you." Bruce Cassidy was one of the fire captains. By the time she'd met with him and discussed scheduling - his wife was just days shy of delivering their second baby – it was lunchtime. She'd brought lunch from home and once she'd eaten that, she headed to the exercise room to lift a few weights in the hopes of lifting her spirits. In fairness, she realized that it probably was a bit of a shock to Ryker to learn she was deputy fire chief, especially if he'd somehow thought that she was a full-time wedding planner. Forty-five minutes later, sweaty, but good mood revived, she had a quick shower and returned to her desk. Firefighting wasn't glamourous the way it was depicted in movies or television, and paperwork was a huge part of the job.

Ryker walked into the vet clinic lifting the Homegrown bakery boxes high so as not to entice any animals in the waiting room. After depositing them in the staff room, he had a few words with Finn, then left through the side door to visit the rescue shelter. As he walked along the path, thoughts of Lynsey drifted in and out of his mind. It wasn't that he didn't think she was a capable woman; he just didn't like women in general doing anything dangerous. Well aware that line of thinking made him chauvinistic, he shook his head; that wasn't who he was. He knew too, that what Chelsea encountered as a vet tech and Carrie as an equine osteopath weren't without inherent dangers. But fire and emergency job situations seemed rife with them. He didn't want to worry about Lynsey at her job – and then it struck him that he was already in big trouble. Somehow Lynsey *mattered* to him. Her well-being mattered to him. *Well, crud. How had that happened?*

"Ryker!" Chelsea's cheerful voice pierced his thoughts. "What brings you here, big brother?" She hugged him enthusiastically.

As he disentangled himself, he grinned. "Need a pup. And a housekeeper."

Chelsea hooted. "Come on in. I can help with the pup but not the housekeeper." They spent the next several minutes visiting the residents of the rescue area while his sister updated him on their progress from a temporary structure to a permanent one.

A medium-sized mixed breed pup caught his eye, huddled in the back of the pen. "What's this one's story?"

"About ten months old. Lab cross. Female. Neutered. Found out by Sylvan Lake and brought here two weeks ago. No chips or tags. Healthy but shy. We call her Trixie."

Trixie. Ryker knelt outside the pen and shooed Chelsea away. Opening the gate a little, he sat down and leaned his head back against the side. Quietly he waited, watching the pup but not too intently, letting her get used to him being there. Lost in his thoughts, he was almost startled to feel a warm, wet nose on his hand. He waited while she settled beside him, then very gently and slowly raised his hand to pet her. Oh yeah, this one would do just fine.

Scooping her into his arms, he stood up.

"Found yourself a friend, I see."

Chelsea had the paperwork ready, and Ryker signed it and then headed to the pet boutique to get the necessary supplies he'd need for Trixie at home.

His other sister, Avery, already had a pile of goodies on the counter when he walked into the geodesic dome that housed her boutique. She aahed and cooed over Trixie, then took his credit card happily, handing him two large bags full of toys and necessities, as well as a pet carrier to get the pup home.

Another female to worry about, he reckoned as he stowed the bags and coaxed Trixie into her carrier. Somehow, though, his heart felt light and happy to have the little dog in the back seat of the truck. If only he could reconcile his feelings about Lynsey this easily. Lynsey fascinated him, but he couldn't risk his heart on a woman whom he might lose in an unfortunate accident.

Chapter Five

March blew in on a chain of snowstorms that left the region covered in snow, and most people Ryker knew hunkering inside. Temperatures dropped dramatically and trips into town became the exception for several days rather than the norm. Ryker kept busy at the ranch, making sure the livestock and horses were taken care of. He had plenty of more than capable staff to make that happen, but he liked to lend a hand and do what he could.

At the main ranch house, Trixie had already made herself quite at home. In the past, ranch dogs slept by the back door, where a cozy nook had been set up for them, but Ryker caved almost instantly and let Trixie sleep on the bed with him. She pretty much had the run of the house. Her sweet personality was coming out, and she was growing gangbusters. Her short black fur glistened with good health, and her brown eyes followed Ryker adoringly. She loved riding in the truck or running alongside him while he walked or rode.

After long hours on the ranch, without family backup, he was fast learning how much his mother had done for him and was sorely wishing he'd continued his search for a housekeeper.

What he couldn't do was make the house less empty or lonely. Sure, it helped immensely having Trixie around, but there was still a gap. The house needed a family again. And that was up to him.

He had a lot of time in the evenings to think and stew about his life. He'd always known he would inherit the ranch, and he loved every inch of it. He just hadn't expected it to be so early in his life. Now the family was gone, and it was just him. Almost forty. His life was full in all ways but one. He wanted a companion to share his life.

Lynsey frowned at the snow outside her window. She couldn't believe how cold it had gotten or the amount of snow they'd received. Fortunately, fire calls were almost non-existent, and medical calls had been limited in severity. She was down one firefighter because Captain Bruce's wife had delivered a healthy baby boy just before the storms hit, so they were safe and cozy at home. The school had closed for a week and was set to reopen the following Monday, weather permitting.

Being close to the fire hall, she'd walked over every day, as had most of the others. The chief had chosen to stay home. She knew he was eagerly awaiting retirement, but there was something she couldn't quite put her finger on going on with him. His enthusiasm for the job was still there ,but there was an underlying *something* that was bothering him. Or maybe she was reading too much into his actions, based on her perceptions and feelings. Still, you never knew.

She thought about Ryker a lot. Like her ex-husband, Ryker wasn't happy about her choice of career. With Mitch, it had affected their relationship. Unlike her ex, she wasn't married to Ryker, and they weren't in a relationship. So why did it matter so much to her what he thought?

Because she *wanted* a relationship with him! Oh, good grief. She was drawn to him in ways she couldn't understand. She got that he wanted to protect her. In fact, that was something she craved, but she wanted him to accept that she was strong and capable at her job. Could that happen? Wondering if that was possible made her crazy.

Sunday afternoon brought in unexpected high winds and snow squalls. The temperature plummeted again, and the world became a whirling dervish of winter.

Lynsey had just dropped off to sleep when the alarms went off. Industrial fire. Fully engulfed. The lumber yard on South Avenue. All Call. Everyone on deck. *Oh, heavens no, no.* She hurriedly dressed and headed to the station. Once there, she clicked over into deputy chief mode and soon the two fire engines were on their way, with one ambulance following. Dispatch was requesting assistance from the county for their aerial truck and neighboring towns for additional engines, but that would take a while with the weather and the poor road conditions.

As they sped along the icy roads in town towards the address of the fire, Lynsey said a silent prayer for all involved. The industrial area ran for three blocks, and as they turned onto South Avenue, the huge flames soared through the blowing snow and ice pellets. The first engine stopped at the gate to cut the locks to allow access, then the engines pulled up near the town fire hydrant. As First-in-Command, Lynsey put on her air pack and directed crew members to different areas while she set up the perimeter. A truck came sliding in after them, and a man wearing only a T-shirt and sweats, despite the weather, ran across the snow to the crew.

"It's my building," the man choked. "Oh, my God!"

Lynsey took his arm and removed her mask. "Is there anyone working in there?"

He shook his head. "No, no, the last shift ended at five."

Thank God. Lynsey replaced her mask and assigned one of the ambulance attendants to assist the man, mostly to keep him from running inside. The crews had the hoses secured and were aiming water at the roof of the extensive building. A second hose was aimed at the huge lumber pile adjacent to the structure. Lynsey sped around the building, stopping abruptly when falling debris blocked her way.

The county's aerial ladder truck arrived with lights flashing, and within minutes, a firefighter was up the ladder aiming more water at a different spot on the burning roof. The wind didn't aid them, but the snow and ice pellets provided welcome dampness. Soon the equipment was covered in ice, and fresh firefighters replaced the ones at the front. The ambulance was set up in a secluded spot, with water and aid for the crews as they switched over.

As Lynsey waited her turn on the ladder, she studied the site. The fire was out of control, but it wasn't spreading beyond the lumber piles. The nearest business was several hundred feet away, so that wouldn't be an issue. Thank goodness for that.

Lynsey strapped herself in, and the platform lifted her into position, then she aimed the hose expertly at the flames.

Ryker woke from an uneasy sleep to the insistent ringing of his cell phone.

"Bart, hey, what's going on?"

"Big fire, boss, at William's Lumber Yard. Some of the hands have headed in to help. It's a big one. Thought you'd want to know."

As he hung up from his new general foreman's call, Ryker sat up in bed. Crud. A fire at a lumber yard was never good – that place was nothing but tinder. His jaw clenched. Well, dang it, Lynsey! She would be there! His chest clenched. He patted Trixie's head and ran downstairs. He wouldn't take the pup and expose her to the frozen temperatures if he didn't have to.

Following the tracks of the other vehicles into town, he switched into four-wheel drive, swearing only once when the visibility dropped to near blackness. As he approached town from the west side, an eerie glow hung over South Avenue.

Parking outside the gate, he leaped from the truck and ran towards the emergency vehicles, sliding along the way on the ice runoff from the hoses. It was like a scene from an action movie. The area was cordoned off, the aerial truck lifted ,and the ladder raised. Hoses seemed to be everywhere, spraying the flames, and smoke and ash were everywhere. Where was Lynsey? He paused to catch his breath.

"Can I help you? No one is allowed through."

"Lynsey?" Ryker managed to croak out the words. "Deputy Chief..."

The firefighter pointed to the area around the ladder truck. "She's over there at Incident Command."

The breath left Ryker's body. "Thanks."

He stood behind the barricade and watched as Lynsey directed the crews. When she signaled, the hose stopped spraying and the platform lowered, and another firefighter strapped in and took over. It was like watching a well-choreographed dance, and Ryker marveled at how smoothly the firefighters moved despite their heavy gear and the fact they were lugging water-filled, ice-crusted hoses. Teamwork in action. He didn't know how long he'd been watching until he heard his name.

"Ryker?" Lynsey moved toward him. Her face was hidden behind the mask. She was covered in ice and ash. Raising her visor, she took him in. "What in the name of God are you doing here?"

"I was worried about you," Ryker answered. Her face was streaked with soot, and she looked exhausted. Annoyed. Ticked right off.

"I am perfectly capable of.... Oooh, Ryker, be careful!"

As he moved along the fence, Ryker hit a patch of ice. His feet slid out from under him, throwing him backwards and cracking his elbow and head on the frozen ground. His vision went in and out of focus, then slowly righted itself.

He was dimly aware of powerful arms lifting and moving him. The noise of the fire and running water pounded through his veins, and the next thing he knew, he was wrapped in a blanket with a young paramedic examining him.

"Nice to have you back with us," the paramedic grinned. He helped Ryker sit up. "You'll have quite the goose egg on your head, and your elbow will bruise. Your vitals are good, so I expect there's no permanent damage."

"Good thing you have a hard head." Lynsey's voice wove its way through Ryker's consciousness.

"How did I get in here? I remember someone carrying me?"

Lynsey shrugged. "That was me. And Bob." She nodded, indicating the firefighter he'd spoken to earlier.

Wait, what? *She* carried him. Even with help, that was amazing. He was a fully grown man, for heaven's sake. He was beginning to feel like a real jerk for underestimating her, which only added to the agonizing throb in his head and the deep ache in his elbow.

"I told you I was strong and capable." Lynsey's voice had an edge to it.

"Yes, I seem to recall that."

Lynsey grunted. "Well, I'm here for a while yet. I'll get someone to drive you home."

Ryker's face flamed. "No, I'm okay, I can drive myself."

Lynsey sighed. "Ryker, you hit your head. Hard. We need to have you on concussion watch."

Ryker nodded, then regretted the movement when instant pain pulsed across the back of his head. "I'll be fine. I'll sit here for a while out of the way then I'll call someone to come and get me. I've already disrupted you enough."

Lynsey contemplated him for a long moment, then shrugged. "Yes, you have. FINE. Take care of those bumps. Stay awake for a few hours. I gotta get back to work. IF that's okay with you?"

Ryker watched her stride across the parking lot to the engines. The fire blazed in the background. The flashing lights of the vehicles, the roar of the blaze, and the crackle of the frozen pellets created a cacophony of lights and sounds that he knew he wouldn't soon forget. The look on Lynsey's face as she walked away from him in utter disgust and disappointment chilled his heart even more than the ice shards pelting his face.

Lynsey was magnificent when she was angry.

He, on the other hand, was the worst kind of idiot.

Chapter Six

Lynsey couldn't believe it! Ryker had driven to the fire in the middle of the night to check on her! Did she drive out to the ranch when things were happening there to check on him? *No!* She automatically trusted that he knew his stuff well enough to do it properly and take care of the job at hand.

Maybe he was worried about you.

Pshaw.

She shook off that thought. Yes, he likely was, *but* was it because he didn't think she could do her job? *Was that why? Or was he falling for you and worried about you in that way?*

Bah, she scoffed, not willing to let the annoyance at Ryker disappear just yet.

Fire crews stayed on site overnight and then monitored the property for a couple of days before finally pronouncing the fire extinguished. The support from volunteer firefighters from neighboring towns was spectacular, and even though it was a tragedy that brought them together, the sense of community was overwhelming. The losses to the business were great but thankfully no one had been hurt. Oh, except, of course, Ryker McCoy.

Ryker. The name curled around her mouth and made her teeth clench. Nails on a chalkboard! That man annoyed her! *You care about him, or he wouldn't annoy you.* Pshaw. She shook her head to quiet the inside voice. She didn't want to care about him! Caring led to hurt and disappointment, *especially* after the little stunt he'd pulled by coming out to the lumberyard fire. He could have endangered himself, and potentially her firefighters if he had distracted them. Plus, he didn't trust her to do her job capably and safely. *Just like her ex, Mitch hadn't trusted her. ...*

WHOA! Now where did THAT thought come from? She thought she was over feeling bad about her marriage to Mitch. Obviously, the old hurt was still there. Well, that was just great, just ducky.

I wonder how Ryker's head is feeling.... Hang on there, girl. None of that thinking about the hard-headed, chauvinistic cowboy. And yet, deep in her memory, she could see his worried face at the fire scene. Worried for her. *Why would he bother coming to the fire unless he cared?* The more she thought about it, the more sense it made that maybe she'd been too hard on him. Maybe her feelings of being judged and found lacking in the past were coloring her feelings now. If that was true, she mused, she was blaming Ryker for something that wasn't about him at all. Food for thought.

The rest of the week passed in a blur of mixed emotions, in-cident reporting, and expressions of gratitude from the towns-people. Heart Creek residents were amazing, and she and the protective services staff had enough baking and meals to last for several days. She hadn't paid for anything at Homegrown

Café all week and she knew the other firefighters were receiving the same treatment.

On Saturday, her veneer cracked. She had to see Ryker and find out how he was.

Her plan was simple. She'd call Carrie and invite herself for coffee, then just happen to run into Ryker somewhere on the ranch. Carrie was thrilled to get her call and instantly invited Lynsey for lunch at Heart's Haven. "We can show you what we've done since we moved in," Carrie insisted when Lynsey said lunch wasn't necessary.

"I'll bring dessert then," Lynsey promised. She'd pick up one of those yummy fruit pies that Rosemary made at the café. Any kind would do; she loved pie! She dressed in slim jeans and a soft pink sweater, leaving her long hair free and unconfined. Pink lip gloss was the only makeup she added. In her job, makeup wasn't a requirement and felt like more work than it was worth. Usually, she wore her hair braided and pinned, and it felt great to have it loose for a change. Glancing in the mirror as she added her parka and scarf, she was surprised to see the sparkle in her eyes. Her skin glowed, and she looked happier than she had in a long time. Not that she'd been UN-happy, just not as happy as she felt right now. Was that because she was going to see Ryker? Before she could get too much inside her head, she pulled on her boots and left the condo. Pie was calling her name!

The two days after the fire were the most humiliating days Ryker had ever known. He'd called Chelsea to come and get him from the fire scene, which brought both her and Finn to his aid. Chelsea insisted on staying overnight at the ranch, to make sure he wasn't concussed. She fussed over him constantly, and he had barely a moment to breathe without her asking if he was all right. Then she wouldn't leave him alone and ended up staying over a second night. By Tuesday morning, Ryker was exhausted and exasperated, albeit grudgingly appreciative that she cared for his well-being.

When Finn showed up Tuesday morning on his way to the vet clinic, Ryker all but begged him to take Chelsea with him. Finn hemmed and hawed, his expression showing way too much enjoyment of Ryker's discomfort, but eventually, he gave in.

"Chels, he's fine, honey. Let's go to the clinic. You missed yesterday, and I need you there today. Ryker will live."

Chelsea's eyes narrowed as she gazed at the two men. "Okay. Call me if you need me, Ryker. And take it easy. Oh, and ..."

"I'm okay, honestly. Thank you for looking after me. I appreciate it more than you know. Now go play with the cats and dogs, or whatever it is you do."

Chelsea huffed at his words, then realized he was teasing.

"You need a keeper, brother dear, so you don't go bumping your poor head again."

Ryker smiled. "Just some better decision-making skills, Chels." He rubbed his head, which was still a little tender.

Chelsea grinned, and she and Finn finally left. Thank goodness! Ryker was ready to climb the walls! He wanted a shower and a nap, in that order, with no one bugging him. Thoughts of Lynsey drifted through his mind, but he determinedly ignored them. She'd made her point at the fire. She was perfectly capable of managing herself and didn't need or want anyone.

Message received. Full stop. Besides, he didn't want to face her. He felt foolish and, worse, he'd pulled her away from the emergency at hand and wasted her time. Giving himself a mental head shake, he moved towards the stairs and the hottest shower he could manage. Then blessed, uninterrupted sleep.

By the weekend, he felt more like himself. His elbow and head were doing well, and the ranch and outside world beckoned. He could stop at Heart's Haven later in the day to check in with Mac and Carrie. The day was sunny, and the snow was melting once again. They'd had huge accumulation over the past two weeks, but today was warmer, and the sky was clear. He whistled a tune as he went about his work, surprising himself. He hadn't whistled for many years. His dad used to whistle, and, as a kid, Ryker had loved the sound of familiar songs when they did the farm rounds together.

It was going to be a good day.

Lynsey gently cradled the lemon meringue pie while eying the apple one. Which one to choose?

"You can always take both," Rosemary teased, expertly wiping the counter while watching Lynsey ogle the baking. Lynsey sighed.

"It's hard to choose. Okay, I'll take both, please." Rosemary grinned as she rang up the sale.

"Two for one for you today." Lynsey was about to protest, then snapped her mouth closed.

"Thank you, Rosemary, that is kind of you. See you Monday!" With a wave, Lynsey balanced the pies and left the café. Breathing in the fresh air, she marveled at the change in the weather. From the recent winter storms to this beautiful, warm day. Rolling down her window, she welcomed the slight breeze moving through her hair as she drove towards Heart Creek Ranch. Despite the snow-covered fields, the roads were clear, and the ranch seemed to stretch forever as she drove by the main house.

She planned to stop in to see Ryker on her way home from visiting Carrie. Oh, she could take him the leftover pie. That would give her a viable reason for stopping by, since she was in the neighborhood anyway and would have to drive past his house on her way home. The thought of seeing him warmed her cheeks and her heart. *Goodness me, girl, you are a living contradiction. You want him to care, but you don't want him to care. What do you want? I want him to.... I don't know what I want him to do. I sure don't.*

Later that afternoon, after an enjoyable visit with Carrie where they each demolished two pieces of decadent pie, Lynsey said goodbye to her friend. Sitting in her vehicle, she debated whether she still wanted to stop and see Ryker or not. She did have some leftover pie to share, but doubts niggled her. What if he didn't want to see her? Lost in thought, a movement caught her eye.

Someone was riding across the field towards her. A large black horse moving at a good speed. The rider was silhouetted against the sky, and the sight took her breath away. As the horse drew closer and slowed, she recognized the rider. Ryker. His black cowboy hat and duster coat emphasized the breadth of his shoulders. His wind-kissed cheeks glowed as they came to a stop near her. She stepped out of the car, amazed at the horse's height and the sheer presence of the cowboy on his back.

Ryker dismounted and wound the reins around one of the posts that was located around the parking area. As Ryker started walking towards her, she breathed in fresh cold air and a hint of his personal masculine scent. It was exhilarating. He stopped in front of her and removed his hat.

"This is a surprise. Wasn't expecting to see you here."

Well, I sure hoped to see you. Lynsey brushed the thought away. "Hello Ryker. Nice day for a ride."

He chuckled, the deep sound resonating. "Sweet Daddy here needed a run and I, well, I needed a breath of fresh air."

"How's your elbow? Did it interfere with your riding?"

Ryker grimaced and had the grace to look sheepish. "A bit tender but much improved. Hey, Lynsey, I owe you a big apology. I was an ..."

Before he could elaborate on exactly what he was, Lynsey held up her hand. "Ryker, no need. I overreacted. Although I *was* surprised to see you at my incident scene."

"Yeah, about that. I kind of lost my mind. Won't happen again."

Lynsey smiled. "Okay then. I have pie. Want me to drop it off at the main house when I drive by?"

Ryker grinned. "I have a better idea. Why don't you and the pie come to dinner?"

Lynsey stared at him for a long moment. "I'd love that. And, let me check...um, the pie says yes as well."

"I just have to talk to Mac about something then I can meet you there. The house is open. Make yourself comfortable."

Lynsey nodded. "See you there."

She got back into her car and sat there. *What in the blazes had just happened? She was having dinner with Ryker! At the ranch. Oh boy.*

Chapter Seven

Ryker's heart was pounding. Did he just invite Lynsey to dinner? At the ranch? What was he thinking? *You were thinking with your heart, buddy. It's just dinner. You might enjoy it.* Of course he would enjoy it! But was he ready for it?

A short time later, Ryker took his time stabling Sweet Daddy, then cleaned himself up in the washroom at the stable office. Wouldn't be right to turn up smelling to high heaven of goodness knows what. On the drive to the ranch house, he questioned his rashness in inviting Lynsey for dinner. Did he even have anything he could make for her? Egad.

Her vehicle was parked outside the front door, and he found her curled up in a chair in the spacious but cozy front room.

"I put the pie in the fridge," Lynsey smiled as she spoke. He sank into the chair across from her.

"How's your head?"

Ryker sighed. "It's fine. A bit tender, but it would take a whole lot worse to crack this hard noggin. I wanted to talk to you about that..."

"Your hard noggin? Or something else that's hard to crack?" Lynsey's voice was soft, but her eyes locked onto Ryker's, and he felt the heat spiral right down to his toes.

He lost his train of thought for a moment. "Um, yeah, about that..." He settled himself more fully on the seat and paused, trying to find the right words. Or better yet, not the wrong words. He had a bad habit of putting his foot in his mouth – and banging his head on the ground with this woman.

"Lynsey, I was way out of line."

"Yes, you were. And..."

Ryker swallowed, his mouth tight and dry. "And I am sorry I doubted your capability to perform your job."

Lynsey sank back into the chair. He could see the smile in her eyes, but her face didn't change expression.

"I was wrong?" he added, unsure where to go next.

"Is that a question? And, yes, you were."

He blinked at her tone. She didn't sound too accepting of his apology. Hoh, boy.

"So why did you do it, Ryker?"

He sighed. "I don't honestly know. I guess I care about you and when I heard about the fire, all I could think about was making sure you were safe."

"And how were you going to do that, exactly? Pull me away from the scene and lock me in your truck for safekeeping?" Lynsey's tone lightened, but her blue eyes were dark and held no trace of a smile now as she waited for his reply.

Tread carefully, big guy. Think, then speak. "Yeah, hadn't thought that far ahead, to be honest." He ran his hand through his streaky blond hair.

Lynsey leaned forward. "Ryker. I didn't get this far in my career through not being able to take care of myself or, indeed, not being there to take care of a fellow firefighter."

Ryker nodded slightly, listening and watching her beautiful face as different emotions flitted across it.

"Yes, Lynsey, I get that. Now. But at the time..."

"At the time, you thought you and your white stallion would race in and save the maiden in distress."

Ryker grinned. "Sweet Daddy is black, but I get your point."

"Do you? Because it's vital to our relationship that you understand where I'm coming from."

"Yes, ma'am," he gave her a sheepish look.

"It's 'Yes, SIR'."

"Yes, sir."

Their eyes locked once again, and Ryker marveled at how her blue eyes changed depending on her mood. A man could get lost in those deep eyes.

"Thank you for caring about me," Lynsey whispered, as she moved closer to the front edge of her chair.

"You're welcome." Ryker moved forward until their knees touched, never breaking eye contact. They stood at the same time, and Ryker's hands moved of their own accord to cup Lynsey's face and his lips found hers. She smelled like fresh air and cinnamon, and he wanted to crush her against his chest and hold her forever.

"I care for you too," Lynsey mumbled against his mouth.

"I know."

Lynsey stepped back and, grabbing a pillow from the chair, she whacked him playfully with it.

"What? What do you mean, you know?"

Ryker laughed, a deep throated chuckle that rumbled through the room.

"I don't think you are the type of girl who shares their left-over pie with just *anybody,*" he joked. "So, I guess that means you're sweet on this old cowboy."

"Yes, I might be a little sweet on you. Despite your recent behavior."

Ryker stopped stock still. "Am I forgiven?"

Lynsey paused long enough for sweat to start beading down his back before she relented.

"Yes, Ryker, you are forgiven. However, I do have one very crucial question to ask."

"Yes?" Ryker's mind ran through different scenarios, fearing the worst.

"Ryker."

"Yes, Lynsey?"

"What are you going to make me for supper?"

Ryker exhaled with a big whoosh. *Oh, holy cats and dogs. What was he going to make for their meal?*

"Um, I know we have cereal. Hot oatmeal, maybe?"

Lynsey nodded. "I can work with that." She stepped towards him and kissed him firmly, then placed her arms around his broad chest and hugged him.

"Thanks, Ryker."

He hugged her back, his mind racing. "Let's go meet Trixie. I left her in my room when I went out."

Trixie pressed a wet nose into her hand, making Lynsey squeal. The pup was gorgeous and still growing if the size of her feet compared to her body was any indication. Every bit of the dog quivered with joy as Lynsey petted her.

"She's gorgeous! When did you get her?"

"A while back. House was too darn quiet. So, about that meal..."

They headed to the kitchen, Trixie weaving in and out of their feet. Ryker scrounged around in the fridge and came up with leftover lasagna and fixings for a salad. Lynsey found a loaf of French bread in the freezer and peeled off two slices for garlic toast. The smell of fresh tomatoes and cucumber filled the air, soon joined by the pungent scent of the garlic Lynsey was mashing into a small bowl of butter. The lasagna was heating, and the garlic toast was ready to go in the oven. Lynsey tucked the finished salads into the fridge and joined Ryker at the table to wait for the food to heat through.

"This is a beautiful kitchen." The south-facing kitchen had white cabinetry, granite countertops, and a massive island. The gleaming stainless steel double fridge and freezer held scads of food, and the polished oak flooring and spring green backsplash provided a beautiful garden effect, helped by the natural lighting from the windows. Ryker nodded. "My mom had an open-door policy, and all were welcome at our table. She wanted a kitchen big enough for that to happen efficiently. A few years after Dad died, she upgraded the cabinets, then about five years ago, we replaced all the appliances."

Lynsey looked around the large yet welcoming space and imagined herself baking cookies while looking out the windows at the yard behind the house. An area was fenced and would provide safety for little ones. *Wait, what? Hold on there, girl. You are getting WAY ahead of yourself again. Didn't you already decide you were okay with not having kids?*

Lynsey looked over at Ryker, catching him staring at her. She flushed but didn't lower her gaze. She liked this man. He was kind, caring, and loyal to his family. The fact that he was drop-dead gorgeous didn't hurt one iota, either.

"Lynsey..." Ryker leaned toward her so close she could feel his breath on her cheek. At that moment, the stove timer went off, and they both fell back in their seats.

"Dear lord, my heart stopped there for a minute." Ryker grinned as he got up to turn off the timer and check the lasagna. "Done," he pronounced.

Lynsey was still feeling the nearness of Ryker's mouth to hers, and it took a minute for her composure to return. "Ok, turn the heat to broil and we'll toast up the garlic bread." Ryker placed the lasagna dish on a wooden board and covered it with a towel to keep it warm.

"I'll set the table." Lynsey stepped toward the counter. Ryker turned at the same moment, and they collided mid-step. Lynsey's pulse quickened as she heard Ryker groan softly in his throat. Then his arms were around her, and all she could think about was how wonderful it was to be held by him. Her mouth softened and her hands crept behind his neck, grabbing onto tufts of his hair. When he finally raised his head, breaking contact, they stood forehead to forehead, breathing deeply.

No words were spoken. They merely stood quietly, holding each other.

Finally, Lynsey stepped back. "Where is the silverware kept?"

Ryker lifted his head, his eyes still liquid from their kiss. "Far drawer, on the left." His voice was husky, and it was all Lynsey could do to stay focused on her task and not run back to him right then and there. *Baby steps, sweet girl.*

Ryker put the garlic bread in the oven, then uncovered the lasagna and brought it over to the table. Lynsey retrieved the salad bowl from the fridge, and they sat to wait for the garlic toast. Once it was ready, Ryker cut the lasagna into squares and placed one on Lynsey's plate and two on his own. They helped themselves to salad and garlic toast. Glasses of cold water rounded out the meal.

The lasagna was cheesy and heavy enough to stop your heart. Lynsey sighed in bliss after her first bite. Ryker's laugh filled the sunny room.

"Sorry," Lynsey muttered in between mouthfuls. "What can I say? I love good food!"

Ryker reached across the table and took her free hand, holding it gently. Lynsey's heart leaped when he gazed into her eyes. She was falling for this guy, big time. Her emotions were all over the place. First she was mad at him for treating her like a fragile blossom, then she was sinking into his arms craving his touch. Love was a lot like fire, and it could be volatile and sometimes unpredictable. Fire she could handle – but this sweet bear of a cowboy was quickly becoming her undoing.

Chapter Eight

Over the next several days, Ryker kept humming as he completed his rounds and chores. He blamed it on the approaching spring. Warmer weather always brought out his lighter side. Deep down, he knew the real reason for his joy was Lynsey. He had fallen, hook, line, and sinker. He had no idea the future would hold but for right now, he was enjoying the giddy sensations that came with being in love.

Love. He hadn't been in love for years, maybe never. Of course, he loved his mom and his family, his work, and now his sweet dog, Trixie, but that was different. This had edges that were sometimes soft and sometimes hard but always exhilarating.

"Earth to Ryker, come in please," came an exasperated voice behind him. Blinking his thoughts away, he turned to see Chelsea eyeing him across the stall he was mucking out.

"Sorry, didn't hear you there," he grinned at his sister.

"No wonder, with all that humming...what the heck, Ryk? Ohhhhh, wait, I know..." Chelsea's eyes gleamed and she snapped her fingers. "You're in love!"

Ryker flushed but before he could deny it, Chelsea bounded across the stall and grappled him into a huge hug. Her squeals brought a couple of the guys running over but Ryker waved them away with a laugh.

"Chelsea, I am not in..."

"Yes, you are! I'd recognize those signs anywhere! Happy, humming, lost in your own little love bubble world!"

Ryker sighed. She had him there. He grimaced before grinding out his answer. "Fine, have it your way. But keep it to yourself, okay?"

"Can I tell Finn? I *have* to tell him, Ryker. We had a bet, and I won!"

"You were betting on my love life? Nothing better to do with your time, eh?" He should probably be annoyed, but strangely, he wasn't.

Chelsea smacked his arm. "Plenty to do, thanks very much, brother dear. But your love life has always been, shall we say, mysterious?"

"I'm a private man," Ryker argued. "Don't need my feelings and stuff broadcast over half the county."

"Then you shouldn't hum love songs while you work," Chelsea retorted. "And how does Lynsey feel about all this?"

Ryker stopped cold. "How did you know it was her?"

Chelsea let out a loud whoop. "Oh, Ryker, you've had it bad for her since the wedding reception. Anyone with half an eye could see that. Except maybe *you*."

Reluctantly, Ryker nodded. "Hey, why are you here? Everything okay at the clinic?"

Chelsea's head bounced up and down, her smile still stretching across her face. "I've got news..."

Ryker finished the last of the mucking, taking the broom, mop, and bucket with him as he left the stall. "Talk, girl, I don't have all day to be lollygagging."

"We've set the date! Finn and I are getting married in October! Thanksgiving Saturday."

"Congratulations! I knew he'd make an honest woman out of you yet." This time, it was Ryker who hugged his little sister first, happy for her. She and Finn hadn't made things easy for themselves and it was a blessing to have them together.

"Oh Ryker, you are so old-fashioned. *I'm* making an honest man out of *him*! Oh, and Lynsey will be the wedding planner, she did such a great job with Mac and Carrie's wedding."

"Well, at least this time, I don't have to be in the wedding party." Ryker chuckled. He hated having to give a speech, so not being the best man this time around would be a relief.

"Well, about that," Chelsea wrung her hands together. "I was wondering if, well, would you walk me down the aisle? Since you practically raised us with Mom after Dad died."

Ryker's heart clenched, and his throat unexpectedly filled with tears. This being in love was wreaking havoc on his emotions.

Touched beyond words, he struggled to express his feelings. "Chels, I would be honored to," he managed to keep his voice steady,

"Thanks, big bro! Off to tell Mac and Carrie. Talk later! Finn says hi."

Ryker watched her run out of the barn, her happiness spilling everywhere like liquid gold. For the first time, he understood how you could love someone so much that you wanted them to be part of your family and in your life for always.

He whistled as he headed to the outbuildings behind the barn, thoughts of Lynsey lingering in his mind.

Lynsey squealed when she got off the phone from Chelsea's call. Another wedding to plan! And a McCoy wedding, to boot. *Maybe one day, you can plan your wedding to Ryker. That would be the ultimate McCoy celebration. Whoa, girl, let's bring that back a step or two.* She hugged herself as she imagined the possibilities. Not only for Chelsea, but for herself.

The day had dawned clear and warm, with enough breeze to carry the smells of late spring. There was a wind warning for the evening but no rain in the forecast. High winds were common at this time of year.

Finishing her lunch, she headed to her desk. The station was quiet, and lately, the incidents had been few and far between. Just the way she liked it, although there was always a sense of unease that accompanied such times. It was almost like waiting for the other shoe to drop or when things pivot on a dime.

"Lynsey, do you have a moment?" Chief Rob poked his head around the corner into her office.

"Sure. Here or in your office?"

"Mine please." She followed him to his office and waited while he closed the door and settled into his chair.

"I am moving up my retirement," Rob said. "My health hasn't been too good, and I want to leave while I'm semi-healthy. We are going to need an Acting Chief."

Lynsey nodded. "I'm so sorry to see you go, sir."I've recommended you for the position, Lynsey. Council has agreed. How do you feel about that?"

Lynsey gaped at her superior officer. "Um, well, I don't know what to say. I haven't been here that long..."

"True, true. But you've done a remarkable job and the town supports you. Even some of the doubters here in the station don't have any complaints about working with you. That's high praise in a fire station." His eyes twinkled, but Lynsey knew exactly what he meant. She'd had more than her fair share of trouble fitting in during the early years of her career.

"I am honored, Chief. Yours are big shoes to fill, both literally and figuratively." She gazed pointedly at his size fourteen boots, and he smiled as he stood up.

"Yes, I accept. Thank you for believing in me." She rose to shake the Chief's hand. "Thank you so much! I won't let you or the town down."

"I know you won't, Lynsey. Or Acting Fire Chief Adams, I should say. The announcement about my early retirement and your new role will come out later today. Once the permanent job is posted, I highly encourage you to apply. This town needs you."

Oh my. What will Ryker say? What if he thinks it's a bad idea? You've wanted this your whole career, Lynsey. If Ryker loves you, he will support you. But would he? He was already worried about her safety on the job.

She could only hope that he would understand why this step was so important to her.

Ryker was just contemplating finishing up for the day when he smelled it. Smoke. The past few weeks had been unusually dry for this time of year, and he'd heard about the pending wind warning on the morning news.

Someone was burning brush. That was odd. He hadn't pulled a permit. But someone was burning something on McCoy land. It was late March and typically they only burned from November to February.

At that moment, the wind direction changed, and the breeze lifted into a gust. The smoke changed from a lazy curl into a wall of gray, and flames rose from the base, visible even from a distance. Ryker's gut clenched. That fire was going to be a problem! Running towards the main barn, he dug out his cell phone and barked orders after hitting speed dial. As the ranch hands spilled from the different areas on the ranch, heading for the ATVs and the water hauler, he dialed 9-1-1.

When the fire station tones pealed for the outdoor grass fire call, Lynsey was on her way home. Turning around, she sped back to the station and donned her fire gear.

As she jumped into the right-hand seat of the fire engine, her blood ran cold as more information was transmitted. *Holy cats, it was the McCoy ranch!* She quickly dispatched a water hauler unit as she knew that fire hydrant access would be non-existent. As the truck approached the approximate area, the flames were high and moving with the wind. Contacting dispatch, she upgraded the call to All-Call.

·♥·♥·♥·♥·♥·

It took almost two hours to contain the fire. Between the ranch's water haulers and the one from town, they had barely enough water to extinguish the blaze and hose down the surrounding yard and outbuildings while crews created firewalls and moved combustibles away from the area. Everyone pitched in, working for the common goal of suppressing the fire before it spread further. The gusting winds didn't help. Thankfully, they didn't reach the speeds previously forecast, but they were enough to create a few anxious moments. Ryker watched Lynsey in action and could see how good she was at her job and how well she worked, not only leading the team but delegating and stepping in wherever needed.

When she walked over to Ryker, a wave of love washed over him for this incredible woman.

"Ryker, I think we got it. I'll leave a crew here overnight to make sure it doesn't flare up. Who was in charge of the site?"

Ryker shrugged. "At this time, I'm not sure. I will find out, though."

"Yes, please do. Not a good day to be burning brush and, as far as I know, no fire permits have been issued."

"Lynsey, you were fab…" The words were ripped out of Ryker's mouth by someone calling from the site.

"Acting Chief?"

Acting Chief? When did that happen? Ryker's mouth went dry, and his previous words crumbled.

"I thought you were Deputy Chief?"

Lynsey grinned, her dirty face at odds with her gleaming smile. "Rob Montgomery is taking early retirement. I'm Acting for now."

"But..."

Lynsey's smile faded. "But what, Ryker? You know I'm a firefighter. It's not just my job, it's my career, my life."

Ryker swallowed hard. "If we got married, would you still be a firefighter? Still be Acting Chief, or Chief, for that matter?"

Lynsey drew in a hoarse breath. "Yes, Ryker, I would. I am and always will be."

"But then I will always worry about you. *Always*."

"You were just telling me what a good job I did. So, let me get this straight. As long as I'm not your *wife* or *girlfriend*, I can do my job well?"

Ryker balked. "No, you were amazing. You command well, and you know what you are doing. You're a complete professional."

"And you, Ryker McCoy are a complete moron. I can't believe I was ever considering having a life with you. I should never have fallen for you." Lynsey turned on her heel and left Ryker standing there with his mouth hanging open like the idiot he was.

The love of his life was walking away, and he couldn't – or wouldn't – do a darn thing to stop her. What kind of fool was he?

Chapter Nine

Two Months Later

"Okay, is everyone here?" Lynsey's voice rang out across the McCoy ranch living room. Everyone stopped talking and looked around, taking stock of who was there.

"Just Ryker's missing," Chelsea pointed out. "As usual. Can't that man ever be on time?"

"I'm here. Sorry, I'm late." Ryker's neatly combed wet hair revealed his recent shower and his clean jeans and spotless chambray shirt clung to his damp skin. He smiled and sank into a chair.

"Chelsea has invited us here today to talk about the wedding plans to date," Lynsey said. "Chelsea, over to you."

Chelsea rose and faced her family. "This isn't about my wedding. Ryker asked me to call you all together, as he had something he'd like to share." She smiled at Lynsey's startled expression, then made herself comfortable in a big chair.

Ryker cleared his throat as he stood to face the room. He snuck a glance at Lynsey then wished he hadn't. Her expression was unreadable. His heart sank, but he knew he had to carry on with his plan.

"As you all know, I am an ol- school, simple cowboy from way back. While I have been able to travel the past few years and meet new folks like Carrie, I've come to realize that the best place for me is right here on this ranch doing what I do best. Horses and the ranch."

His mom nodded from her seat beside Beau.

"What I don't tend to do well is people. I'm kind of stuck in my ways, and relationships have never come easily to me."

Lynsey shuffled in her chair. Ryker realized he'd better get to the point before he lost all sense.

"Over the past year and a bit, I've been privileged to be here and watch my family fall in love and move on. Carrie and Mac, Chelsea and Finn, Avery, and Craig. And even Mom and Beau managed to figure it out. For myself, well, I'm just a little hardheaded and a whole lot of slow. Not to mention stubborn."

He paused and looked at Lynsey.

"I met an amazing woman, and from the get-go, I wrong stepped. I thought I'd figured it out, but that's where I went sideways. It was never up to *me* to figure it out. It was up to *us*. But I never gave *us* a fair chance."

He knelt in front of Lynsey. "I am in love with you, Lynsey. This may be too little, too late, but I have come to realize over the past two months – the longest blasted two months of my whole life, I might add – that I need you in my life, and I want you to be my wife." He paused.

"I told you that I didn't like you being a firefighter because I would be worried about you all the time. Well, hello. I've realized that I'm going to worry about you all the time no matter what you do. Because I've fallen for you. They say you always worry most about those you love, and that is true."

Reaching forward, Ryker took Lynsey's hand. "I don't care if you are the fire chief or the mayor, or anything else, for that matter. I ruined something beautiful that was happening, and I want to ask you to forgive me. And if you can forgive me, will you do me the honor of giving this old cowboy a second chance? Dating first so you can see I trust you with everything I've got. Then before too much longer marrying me? I don't have a ring. If you say yes then when the time is right, I want us to pick it out together – the first step in a life together. Not you. Not me. Us."

Lynsey looked at him for a long moment before speaking. Her breath caught as she whispered, "You know I've applied to be the new Fire Chief, right?"

Ryker nodded. "Yes, sir, ma'am."

Lynsey's strangled laugh ended with a sob. "Ryker, you are the most frustrating man I have ever met. And that's saying *a lot*! I can't believe it. Yes, yes, a thousand times, yes, I will date you. And yes, I will marry you. I've fallen in love with you too, despite my best efforts not to. I will even consider withdrawing my application for the new chief position. I want a life with you, and it's not just about you accepting me as I am. It goes both ways."

Ryker's heart almost jumped out of his chest as he reached over to hug his bride-to-be.

"I don't want you to withdraw your application. What I do want is a ride in the fire truck."

"You can ride in the truck whenever you want, Ryker McCoy! As long as you don't intrude on my fire scene ever again."

Ryker wrinkled his nose. "Yeah, that was pretty bad, wasn't it?"

Lynsey grinned. "Yes, it was. But it was also very sweet. I think I fell for you that day, and goodness knows, you fell for me in a big way, too!"

"I did. And I have the bruises and bumps to prove it!"

Lynsey's tight hug told him more than any words could. He kissed her gently.

Ryker held her hand as they accepted the best wishes of his family. His eyes caught his mother's, and she nodded, a look of complete contentment on her face. Another McCoy generation to live at the ranch and possibly grandchildren.

"Oh, and Ryker?"

Ryker turned to look at his future fiancée.

"Yes, Lynsey?"

"You still need to find a housekeeper."

The End

About Lynn Gale

Lynn Gale has dreamed about writing romance ever since she read *If This is Love* by Anne Weale in 1972. Years went by and she fell in love with romance all over again watching movies like *Pride and Prejudice*, *Romancing the Stone*, and *American Dreamer*.

Her first sweet romance novella *A Heart Creek Christmas* was published in 2023 as part of *A Cowboy This Christmas: A Sweet Romance Anthology* through the Calgary Association of Romance Writers of America (CaRWA) under the pen name Joanie Wilde. This novella will be released as *Book One in the Return to Heart Creek Series* in November 2025 under Lynn's real name.

Each Heart Creek book can be read as a stand alone title as well as part of the ongoing series **Return to Heart Creek.**

Acknowledgements

This book and series would not have been possible without the assistance and support of many people in my life.

My mentor, romance author Katie O'Connor, who has stuck by my side through the bumps and challenges of writing this novella series. Our coffee Zoom meetings always leave me with a new sense of direction and quell my constant new author doubts. She is still my first reader and I appreciate her insights.

My editor, Terri St. Clair, for her prompt and thoughtful edits. My cover designer, Laura Heritage of P.S. Cover Design & Author Services for the gorgeous covers for the Return to Heart Creek Series.

My family for their love and support. My husband for his patience and long-suffering support as I learn the craft of writing.

My sister Anne Carey and my lovely friend Jessica Schultz for being my beta readers.

My dear friends who buy my books without fail and show up at book signings to support me.

And especially you, my readers. Thank you for reading and reviewing my stories. You make me want to write!

xxoo Lynn

Where to Find Me

Find me at:
Email: lynngalewriter@gmail.com
Website: https://www.lynngalewriter.com
Facebook: http://www.facebook.com/lynngalewriter
Instagram: http://www.instagram.com/lynngalewriter
Bookbub: https://www.bookbub.com/profile/lynn-gale